THE OTHER SIDE
OF PARADISE

It is 1941, and while Britain is in the grip of war, ex-pat life in the Far East remains one of wealth and privilege. In Singapore, Susan Roper spends her time dancing, playing tennis and flirting with visiting naval officers – her life is devoted solely to pleasure. When she meets an Australian doctor who warns her of the danger they all face she dismisses him as an ignorant colonial. Singapore carries on partying, but when Japan invades, Susan finds herself in grave danger. As she becomes closer to the tough, arrogant doctor, she has to face many hardships before she can acknowledge the truth.

THE OTHER SIDE OF PARADISE

THE OTHER SIDE OF PARADISE

by

Margaret Mayhew

Magna Large Print Books
Long Preston, North Yorkshire,
BD23 4ND, England.

British Library Cataloguing in Publication Data.

Mayhew, Margaret
    The other side of paradise.

    A catalogue record of this book is
    available from the British Library

    ISBN   978-0-7505-3127-6

First published in Great Britain in 2009 by Corgi

Copyright © Margaret Mayhew 2009

Cover illustration © Rod Ashford

Published in Large Print 2009 by arrangement with
Transworld Publishers

Magna Large Print is an imprint of Library Magna Books Ltd.

Printed and bound in Great Britain by
T.J. (International) Ltd., Cornwall, PL28 8RW

To Memories

Acknowledgements

I have received a great deal of help in researching the background to this novel, and I should like to thank the following kind people.

In England: Geoffrey Howe who personally put me in touch with the British High Commission in Singapore. Daphne Barcroft, Anne Scott, Frances Francis, Joyce Townend and Ros Henry who were all living in Singapore before it fell to the Japanese and who lent me private photographs, letters and accounts of those times. 'Lofty' Tolhurst who let me drive his immaculate Austin K2Y ambulance and Richard Brotherton of the British Motor Industry Heritage Trust.

In Singapore: Carole Johnson and the staff at the British High Commission. Geraldine Lowe-Ismail, an exceptional tour guide who showed me the hidden Old Singapore and translated into Malay for me. Dr Perry Travers of the Alexandra Hospital. Ray

Perry, general manager of the Singapore Cricket Club. Stefan Voogel, general manager of the Tanglin Club and Mary Shotam and Nan Sandford also of the club. Leslie Danker at Raffles Hotel. Nancy Cheng and her mother Joon Eng. Pat Monkman at the Eurasian Association.

The following books have been of particular interest and help to me. *The Fall of Singapore* by Frank Owen, *Out in the Midday Sun* by Margaret Shennan, *White Coolies* by Betty Jeffrey, *Sinister Twilight* by Noel Barber, *Malayan Postscript* by Ian Morrison, *You'll Die in Singapore* by Charles McCormac, *Shenton of Singapore* by Brian Montgomery, *Journey by Candlelight* by Anne Kennaway.

As always, I thank my editor at Transworld, Linda Evans, and last of all, but never least, my husband, Philip.

Pride goeth before destruction, and an haughty spirit before a fall.

Proverbs

*O! What a fall was there, my countrymen;
Then I, and you, and all of us fell down.*

Julius Caesar

Prologue

We lived in Cavenagh Road, Singapore. On the opposite side of the road stood Government House – the palatial white residence of the Governor, positioned on a hill with the Union Jack flying from a flagpole high on the roof. Its hundred immaculate acres were tended by a small army of gardeners, the residence staffed, so rumour had it, by more than seventy household servants.

Our house, owned by my father's company, was two-storeyed and rather more modest, standing in a mere three acres. It was also whitewashed, with broad eaves and wide colonnaded verandahs fitted with black and white striped rattan roller blinds known as chicks. The chicks were lowered against the burning daytime sun or the torrential monsoon rains and raised in the evening to admit any cooling breezes. The east verandah, furnished with a teak table and chairs, was used for breakfast; the west, with a rattan divan and armchairs cushioned in

15

chintz, was for relaxing with sundowner drinks in the magical hour before nightfall: whisky and soda *stengahs* for my father, iced lime juice for my mother and myself. After dinner the houseboy served coffee and my father drank more *stengahs* and smoked a cigar while insects fluttered and flapped around the lamps. Palms and ferns and flowering tropical plants grew in giant pots – in the rooms, on the verandahs, lining the steps that led down to the lawn where my mother took afternoon tea in the shade of a jacaranda tree.

The house had been built at the turn of the century in a style faithfully echoing Edwardian England, but it had been constructed with the steam heat of Singapore in mind. Louvred shutters and latticework walls ventilated the rooms. The floors were tiled, the sweeping staircase made of cool marble, archways allowed the constant passage of air and the lofty ceilings were equipped with electric fans that revolved night and day. My mother had brought furniture from England – family heirlooms of fine English woods that coped poorly with the heat and humidity and succumbed to the ravages of voracious insects that tried to devour us too. At night we slept under mosquito nets in rooms sprayed by Flit guns.

We had eleven servants – Malay, Chinese and Indian. Our Chinese cook, known as Cookie, had a Chinese assistant and our number one Indian houseboy who served at table and cleaned the downstairs rooms was helped by another Indian boy, number two. Three Chinese *amahs* cleaned and tidied the bedrooms and bathrooms upstairs, a wash-*amah* did the personal washing and ironing, a Malay *syce* drove the Buick, and two Tamil gardeners – *kebuns* – took care of the grounds. Once a week a *dhobi* came to take the household linen away to be laundered, together with the white drill trousers and shorts that my father wore.

The Indian houseboys wore white trousers and white jackets buttoned to the neck; the Chinese *amahs* silky black trousers and short-sleeved white cotton blouses with high collars, soft and silent slippers on their feet indoors and clog-like *trompahs* outside; the *syce* a sarong, a white *badjhu* and a brown velvet *songkok* on his head; the Tamil gardeners wound brightly coloured gar- ments round their bodies and turbans round their heads and their gums were stained blood red from chewing betel nut. The

17

kitchen and storerooms were in a separate building connected to the back of the house by a tin-roofed walkway and the servants lived behind the house in huts built from attap palms. Some had families and children who lived there too, and my father turned a blind eye to any poor relations who arrived. They were all housed and fed and, if necessary, the doctor was sent to attend them and the bill paid. My mother had never learned more than a few phrases of kitchen Malay and communicated with the servants mainly in pidgin English, whereas my father was fluent in Malay, Cantonese and Tamil. I could speak Malay and some Cantonese.

As a child I was cared for by Nana, a Eurasian *amah* who was the illegitimate offspring of an English *tuan* – the respectful Malay term for sir or mister – and a Chinese girl. Her proper name was Nancy and she had come with impeccable references as nurse, first to my brother and then to me. Her features, hair and skin tone were Chinese and she dressed in Chinese clothes – black trousers and white tunic – but she spoke very good English, which is why my mother had employed her. Her father had died young. He had been a rubber planter, a kind and gentle man who had sat her on his knee and taught her English nursery rhymes, English nursery sayings and English poems learned in his own childhood. I was brought up on them, in turn, just like any child ten thousand miles away in England. I knew *A Child's Garden of Verses* and all the A.A. Milne books. I knew all about Squirrel Nutkin, Peter Rabbit, Jeremy Fisher and the rest, and about The Owl and the Pussycat going to sea in their beautiful pea-green boat. I knew all the flowers in *A Flower Fairy Alphabet.* I read *Little Black Sambo* and *Alice in Wonderland* and *Through the Looking-Glass,* and *Peter Pan* and *The Secret Garden.* I ate up bread crusts to make my hair curl, stopped pulling hideous faces in case the wind changed, jumped over lines so the bears wouldn't get me.

Mixed in with English superstitions were some Chinese ones, learned also from Nana. For instance, I knew never to pick up a flower fallen to the ground in case it put a spell on me. Flowers cut from the garden were safe and Nana and I offered those to the fat green glass Buddha who sat on the table at the foot of the staircase, facing the front door. He had been given to my father by a rich Chinese businessman to protect our house from evil spirits, and I loved his smiling face and his fat tummy. We would

19

place fresh flowers in his hand or behind his ear as a mark of respect, and I would, dis-respectfully, rub his tummy for luck when I passed by. The Chinese loved colour. Their paper lanterns and silks and paints were always in vivid colours. Black and white signified death and mourning.

It was Nana who taught me Cantonese, but since my mother did not approve of my speaking native languages, we kept it a secret between us. She stayed until I was ten and then left to look after an English baby in another family. She had meant far more to me than my mother and I missed her deeply.

My father had been born in Penang island, on the north-west coast of the Malay peninsula where his father worked for an international bank. In the early days the island was rented from the Sultan of Kedah for one dollar a year and was famous for its beautiful tropical vegetation, for its nutmeg trees and for the cable car that took you up to the top of Penang Hill to admire spectacular views of islands, the silver ocean and distant peaks on the mainland.

Like most English boys in Malaya in those days, my father had been sent away to boarding school in England and it was expected that he would eventually join the bank where my grandfather worked. Instead, he had chosen a career in rubber and at the age of nineteen had started work as assistant to the manager of a remote estate upcountry, surrounded by jungle and many miles from civilization. He had learned everything about the rubber trees, planting them and tending them and tapping them, and how to oversee the native workers and how to speak their languages. At the end of three years he had been taken on by a rubber company with offices in Kuala Lumpur.

In those days, single young men employed by such companies were not allowed to marry for several years. In any case, marriageable white girls were in very short supply in Malaya, and when the time came to find a wife my father took his long leave in England. He met my mother at a dinner party in London, fell in love with her, became engaged and, very sensibly, married her before the end of his leave so that he could take her back with him to Malaya. Fiancées left to follow on their own were liable to encounter someone else on the long sea voyage.

My brother, Richard, had been born a

year afterwards but he had lived only three months before he had died from a snake bite when a cobra had slithered into his pram. I had been born in September of the following year, 1923, but I never replaced my brother in my mother's heart.

My mother had hated Malaya from the moment she stepped off the P&O liner from England. She detested the stifling wet heat, the violent thunderstorms, the monsoon downpours, the dirt, the smells, the food, the animals and reptiles and insects, the black, brown and yellow faces gabbling away in strange tongues ... almost every single thing about a country that she blamed ever after for the death of her son. And she was bored and homesick for London. In Kuala Lumpur she met the same few people over and over again. Letters took weeks to arrive from Europe, magazines were months out of date, films shown at the cinema even more so. Clothes were out of fashion and the dance tunes played at the Selangor Club were many years old.

However, my father continued to climb steadily up the promotion ladder and was eventually offered a senior post with Malayan Latex, a flourishing rubber export business based in Singapore. I was ten years old when we moved to the house in Cavenagh Road.

Unlike my mother, I loved Malaya and, especially, Singapore. Its very name was magical to me: *Singapura* ... Lion City. There is a Malay legend that a Sumatran prince visiting the island spotted a lion while he was sheltering from a storm and took it as a good omen to found a city. There may have been lions on the island once upon a time – there were certainly tigers in the jungle upcountry on the peninsula, as well as elephants and all kinds of exotic wildlife. The only tiger seen in Singapore within living memory, however, was one that escaped from a circus and hid under a billiard table in Raffles Hotel before the poor creature was flushed out and shot.

When I was eight years old, I made a trip to England with my mother and Nana to visit my grandparents in London and was sadly disappointed by what I saw as un-relieved drabness. By contrast, Singapore was a bubbling cauldron of races, languages, creeds, customs, dress, colours, stirred up into an exotic and potent brew. Chinks, Stinks and Drinks, as people termed it crudely, but with affection. I loved the heat and the noise and the particular smell of

Singapore – its special and very distinctive aroma of dried fish and spices, swamps and drains. I loved the dazzling shimmer of the sun on the sea, rickshaws jamming the narrow streets, the little yellow Ford taxis scooting about, the ponderously slow-moving bullock carts.

I loved the labyrinth of Chinatown in the North Bridge Road, the gaudily painted shop-houses selling porcelain and jade and silk and ivory, and the washing draped on poles sticking out like flags from upstairs windows. I loved the glittering temples, the junks and the sampans packed tightly together along the stew of a river, the satay stalls, the hawkers with their wares swinging from bamboo sticks bent across bony shoulders, the natives cooking meals at the roadside, crouched over smoky wood fires.

I loved Little India and Buffalo Road with the snake charmers, the jugglers, the fortune-tellers, the street traders with their trays of cheap trinkets, the Moorish mosques, the flower-garland shops and their sweet scent of jasmine, marigolds and roses, the pepper and curry aroma of the Indian market and the mounds of ripe tropical fruit spilling over into the street – mangoes, lichees, papayas, pomelos, mangosteens.

The sight of plucked, dead chickens hanging by their feet, heads still attached, never bothered me because I was used to it, as I was used to seeing strips of dried crocodile meat, bottled black sea slugs and skinned snakes. I loved the life and colour and noise that contrasted so dramatically with the imperial dignity of British Colonial Singapore, north of the river

East met West at the City Hall, the Supreme Court, Parliament House, St Andrew's cathedral, the Victoria Memorial Hall, the government offices, the banks and big companies – the buildings all set off by wide boulevards with trim grass verges lined with scarlet flame trees and pink and white frangipanis. The Singapore Cricket Club – white European members only – lay close by, its fine pavilion and verandahs overlooking the immaculate green *Padang* with the sea on one side, a line of flame trees on the other. Not far from this orderly oasis, there were the English shops – Robinson's department store in Raffles Place, and Whiteaways and John Littles. The Cold Storage in Orchard Road sold English ice cream, tins of English foods, French bread and pastries. Its refrigerators kept meat and fish fresh and its glass shelves displayed strawberries flown in from Australia and roses trucked daily from upcountry. In Battery Road round the corner, the latest English books could be bought or ordered at Kelly and Walsh and all kinds of pills and potions found at Maynards the chemist. The thirteen-storey Cathay Building was the tallest in Singapore and the only one to be air-conditioned. It housed the Malayan Broadcasting Corporation and Government offices, as well as a cinema, a restaurant and apartments.

There was dancing six nights a week in hotels and clubs and restaurants, and till dawn in the Coconut Grove. The Coq d'Or was swanky but Raffles Hotel was the most elegant. A tall and turbaned Sikh greeted you at the door, Chinese waiters glided with trays between the tables, a Filipino orchestra played Mozart or selections from light operettas and musical shows, and heads were bent close in delightful gossip behind the potted palms.

You could swim at the Singapore Swimming Club near the seashore or at the small and exclusive Tanglin Club in the suburbs which, besides its swimming pool, also offered grass tennis courts, squash courts, billiards and bridge, and a ballroom for

Saturday night dances to its own band. Nobody carried cash. Chits were signed for everything – dinners, drinks, tins of cigarettes, lunches, clothes, cars, church collection ... everything.

On the sea voyage returning from England, my mother had stayed unhappily in her cabin while I, watched by Nana, played energetic deck games, ate my way through the long menus and counted the days left until I saw Singapore again. My father felt the same. After all, we had both been born in Malaya – born and bred to it. England wasn't Home to us, as it was to so many expatriates who dreamed of ending their days there. I think my father knew and understood the native people better than almost any white man in the city. He treated them well and they respected him.

The island of Singapore, only about a hundred miles from the equator and separated from the southern tip of the Malay peninsula by the narrow Johore Straits, is about the same size and shape as the Isle of Wight. The man-made causeway linking the two by road and rail is not much more than a mile long. When Thomas Stamford Raffles sailed there in 1819 to set up a trading post, he would have seen a

27

long, low expanse of green with gently rolling hills at its centre. With great foresight, he also saw and understood its worth. He snatched the island from under the noses of the Dutch, staking a claim for Britain to the maritime superiority of the eastern seas. The island was swamp and dense tropical rainforest, inhabited only by fishermen and pirates, but the pirates soon fled, the fishermen stayed, the swamps were drained, the jungle hacked back.

The grounds of our house were still bordered by a dense and dripping jungle foliage of huge banana leaves, palm fronds, creepers and vines, mosses and ferns. Yellow-beaked mynah birds chattered among the trees and monkeys swung in great flying leaps from branch to branch. From the upstairs verandahs we could see the roofs of attap huts in native *kampongs,* and the orderly lines of rubber trees planted on cleared land. The cicadas provided their incessant background chorus and at night the bullfrogs croaked loudly in the mangrove swamps.

Our garden bore little resemblance to an English one, except for the lawns of neatly scythed grass – not the fine grass of England but a coarse, bright-green kind called lallang that could withstand the climate and the sun-baked soil. There were mango trees, flame trees, papaya trees, butterfruit trees, cinnamon trees, rambutans and bananas, the yellow-flowered cassia, the big jacaranda, the monkey-cup with red flowers shaped like little cups, the feathery casuarina trees that whispered in the wind, the tall tembusu with creamy-white flowers that smelled wonderful after rain, as well as the sweet-scented frangipanis that grew all over Singapore. I remember, too, the yellow and red canna flowers, the golden jackfruit, the tall clumps of feathery bamboo, ripe black figs hanging from vines, a hedge of bright-pink hibiscus, purple bougainvillea scrambling over trellises, the smell of the curry leaf and of the lemon grass that Nana used for an infusion to relieve my mother's frequent migraines.

We had a grass tennis court, and a pond full of goldfish, and we kept a big aviary with canaries and budgerigars, merboks and sharmas singing their hearts out. More singing birds – canaries and budgerigars – were housed in cages hanging from the eaves of the upstairs verandahs and white fan-tailed doves lived in a dovecote and fluttered down every morning and evening to be fed, sitting on my shoulder and cooing in my ear. Geckos and little transparent lizards, called chee chows, skittered up and down walls and across ceilings. It was said that if you could grab a chee chow by its tail, the tail would drop off, but I never managed to catch one: they were too quick. I had a succession of all the usual English pets: white mice, guinea pigs, tortoises, rabbits, puppies and kittens and, for my tenth birthday, a pony. As the pets died off they were buried with ceremony in a shady corner under the frangipani trees, each grave dug by one of the *kebuns* and carefully marked by me with a bamboo cross.

I was horribly spoiled, of course. Waited on by gentle servants, cared for devotedly by Nana – bathed, dressed, fed, taken for walks by her and to paddle at the beach holding her hand. I went to children's birthday parties arrayed in fancy dress or in frilly organdie frocks that she had made specially for me. I was given expensive toys: a big doll's house, a coach-built doll's pram, a swing and a see-saw in the garden, a Wendy house, a shiny red tricycle, a Dunlop tennis racquet, a three-speed bicycle that made a satisfying click-click-click sound when I pushed it along … everything I asked for.

And I was lucky in another way. The hot Singapore climate was thought unsuitable for an English girl's development and, like the boys, many girls were packed off to boarding school in England. Passenger air travel was in its infancy and the sea voyage took at least four weeks, which meant being away for several years. Various English schools were discussed for me and the London grandparents had agreed to have me for the holidays, but, in the end, and to my huge relief, I was allowed to stay in Singapore and went daily to the convent school of St Nicholas on Victoria Street. I was never sure why I had been spared the fate of going to an English boarding school. Perhaps it was because my education wasn't considered as important as a boy's, or because I was an only child. I suspect, though, that my father was afraid that if my mother accompanied me on the long voyage to England she would make it an excuse to stay there.

The convent's religious motto, in French, and written large across a wall above a painting of Christ, translated roughly as *Walk in My Presence and be Perfect*. I was far from perfect but my life was – especially in the holidays. A never-ending round of picnics at the pure-white sand beaches along the east coast of Malaya, the fun of swimming at night in phosphorescent seas, weekends up in the Cameron Highlands – at a hill station near Ipoh – playing tennis and swimming at the Tanglin Club or in the bigger pool at the Singapore Swimming Club, watching matches from the Cricket Club pavilion, sailing at the Yacht Club, horse riding – the fat pony replaced by a pretty dappled grey mare who was sold when I eventually tired of horses at around sixteen.

When the war broke out in Europe, ten thousand miles away, Singapore went on dancing. There were no shortages, no rationing, no blackouts or restrictions such as people were suffering in England and which were all very hard to imagine in the warmth and plenty of Malaya. The demand for Malayan rubber and tin increased, shiploads left from Keppel Harbour for Europe and America and the economy boomed. The good life was even better in the duty-free port where whisky and gin and cigarettes were cheap. The Germans might be invading other countries, which was appalling, of course, but there was no reason whatever for us to fear the same fate. We were living in an island fortress under the protection of the British flag. The RAF and the Royal Australian Air Force warplanes flew constantly over our heads, we could hear the big boom of the Royal Navy's fifteen-inch guns at firing practice, and the naval base on the north-east shore of the island was said to be the finest and best equipped in the world. British soldiers from famous regiments strode about the city streets, as did Australian and New Zealand servicemen. And so did tall, bearded Sikh soldiers, tough little Gurkhas and the Malays of the Malay Regiment. At the theatre and cinema or dancing after dinner at Raffles, three-quarters of the men were in uniform, the dance halls packed with them. The fortress was impregnable; the island a garrison.

I left the convent after taking School Certificate and loafed around for a while, doing nothing but enjoy myself. The European war had been going on for two years by the time I eventually started a secretarial course in the mornings at Pitman's College in River Valley Road – more because I was getting rather bored than with any serious intention of working as a secretary, or as anything else for that matter The course would fill in the time conveniently until I got married. I received my first grown-up invitation to a ball at Government House where I wore my first long evening gown – white satin with a bodice decorated with pink silk roses, a single row of pearls round my neck and elbow-length white kid gloves. The Governor and his Lady descended the grand staircase to greet their guests with all the majesty of the King and Queen whom they represented. Other formal invitations soon followed – cocktail parties, dinners, dances in the Officers' Mess at Changi, at the Royal Air Force bases and at the Royal Navy base. In between, I spent a great deal of time studying my reflection in the triple looking glass on my dressing table, experimenting with new hairstyles, new make-up, different-coloured lipsticks and nail polish, different perfumes, and I spent hours shopping in the stores, signing for whatever took my fancy. As a child, my frocks had been hand-sewn by my beloved Nana – pretty shantung or lawn dresses with bands of intricate embroidery and smocking across the bodice. When she had left they had been bought from Robinsons or John Littles, but now the Indian *dersey* who made clothes for my mother came to the house bearing bundles of fashion magazines and swatches of material, and I was acquiring a whole new and grown-up wardrobe.

There was no shortage of unattached young European men in Singapore. They worked in the Colonial service, or in the banks, or for the big commercial companies, and there was a constant supply of young army, navy and air force officers. The men easily outnumbered the girls and stood around like male wallflowers at dances. Even the plainest girl danced every dance. We bright young things led a gilded life. We swept through the tennis club, tangoed at Raffles, frolicked on the beaches, clapped our hands for servants to do our bidding.

I barely listened to the occasional chatter about the Japanese. We knew that they had been at war with the Chinese, had taken over Indo-China in July that year, 1941, and were generally throwing their weight about a bit in the Far East, but it was unthinkable that they would ever dare to take on the mighty British Empire. They were comical little yellow men in wire spectacles with slitty eyes, bandy legs and tombstone grins – vastly inferior to white Europeans. There were quite a number of them living in Singapore – photographers, dentists, masseurs, hairdressers, dressmakers, small shopkeepers selling cheap and shoddy goods. A lot of people couldn't tell them apart from the Chinese; nobody believed them to be any sort of threat. It was said that they couldn't see to shoot straight, that they didn't know how to sail ships and that they were no good at flying aircraft, especially not in the dark.

And so the leisured life and the giddy social round went on. The cocktails and the dinners and the dances. The swimming and the sailing and the picnics and the moonlight beach parties. The curry tiffins, the morning coffees, the ladies' luncheons, the afternoon teas, the theatre visits, the shopping, the bridge, the mah-jong, the tennis, the squash, the billiards, the rounds of golf, the gentlemanly cricket matches, the unhurried games of bowls, the rugger, the hockey, the polo. An idyllic life with servants and sunshine. A paradise. We were like passengers on the *Titanic* – in First Class, of course – having a perfectly lovely time and blissfully unaware of the iceberg lying in wait.

I can see myself now, just the way I was then. Eighteen years old. Spoiled, lazy, self-centred and vain.

I am lying by the swimming pool at the

Tanglin Club on a hot Sunday afternoon in late October 1941, the Year of the Snake. Eyes shut, thinking of nothing in particular, and without a care in the world.

Part One

BEFORE THE FALL

One

'I say, it's Susan, isn't it? Susan Roper?'

She opened her eyes slowly, shielding them with her hand. Some chap was standing there in swimming trunks with a towel draped round his neck; she couldn't see him properly against the glare of the sun.

He said, 'I'm Roger Clark. We met at the Chambers' party a couple of weeks ago. I don't expect you remember me, though.'

She sat up to get a better look at him. He did seem vaguely familiar. A nice face with an eager, hopeful sort of expression, like a dog waiting for you to throw its ball. At any moment he might wag his tail.

'Of course, I was in uniform,' he went on. 'We look a bit different out of it.'

That was very true. Uniform – especially the Royal Navy's – improved most men. It made even the duds look good.

He squatted down on his haunches beside her. 'I must say this is a jolly nice club. Very decent of them to let us army chaps in here. Do you come here often?'

Now that she'd mentally dressed him in uniform she did remember meeting him at the Chambers' cocktail do. Mrs Chambers had brought him over and introduced him but then some other chap she knew had come up, and then somebody else, and after a bit she'd moved on. The trick at that sort of party was to avoid getting stuck in a corner with anybody boring. To keep circulating.

'Quite often,' she said. 'It's very popular at the weekends.'

He glanced over his shoulder at the pool and the swimmers splashing merrily about. 'I can see that. And they have dances here, don't they? With a band. There was a notice on the board.'

'Every Saturday.'

'That sounds wizard. Our regiment only got here last month so we're still finding our way around. Learning the ropes, so to speak. Singapore's an amazing place, isn't it? Terribly exotic. I've spent most of my life in Esher ... not counting school, of course, and the army.

'Esher?'

'In Surrey. The parents live there. Very quiet. Nothing like Singapore. Actually, this is my first time abroad. I missed the whole show in Belgium and France. Just as well, really. I'd probably be a POW now, or dead.'

He smiled, as though it was all rather a joke. She felt a bit sorry for him; he was a long way from home and Esher. His face was pink from the sun and the white skin on his body was turning red like part-cooked meat. If he wasn't careful, he'd burn.

'And you've come all the way out from England to help protect us from the Japs? How frightfully brave!'

He went even pinker. 'Actually, it doesn't seem as though you need much help. The island's absolutely stiff with troops. Safe as houses. The Japs would never get anywhere *near* here.' He wiped the back of his hand across his damp brow. 'I say, it's most awfully hot, isn't it?'

'Why don't you go in for a swim?'

'Jolly good idea. I think I'll do that. Cool off a bit.' He looked at her hopefully. 'Any chance of you coming in as well?'

'Not just now. I'm going home in a minute.'

'Oh ... what a shame. Another time, then?'

She said kindly, 'We're bound to run into each other. Go and have your swim.' If she'd had a ball, she'd have thrown it in the water for him to go fetch.

She watched him run and dive into the deep end. Rather a good dive – he'd probably been in the school team – and he was rather sweet, but he could become a bit of a nuisance. It was amusing to have so many of them fighting over you, but it could get quite boring at times. Some were really hard to shake off and she'd had three marriage proposals in the last two weeks. She watched him swimming the length of the pool – a fast crawl that she knew, like the dive, was being done for her benefit. Men always showed off, even the sweet ones. They couldn't help it. As he reached the shallow end and flip-turned to come back, she gathered up her things and made her way to the changing rooms. When she was dressed, she stopped by the card room. Her father was still playing bridge and it looked like it was going to be ages before he was ready to leave. At the front entrance, the Indian *jaga* who knew every member's car and number plate sent a boy off on his bike to fetch Ghani. The *syce* brought the Buick round to the club steps.

'*Tuan* not come, *missee?*'

She answered in Malay. 'Not yet. You can take me home and come back for him.'

On the way she told him to stop the car.

44

'I'll drive now, Ghani. I need to practise.'

He slowed the car reluctantly. 'The *tuan* not pleased if he knows. The *tuan* very cross with me.'

'He won't know, I promise.'

She got out of the back and took over the wheel. The *syce* sat beside her on the bench seat, his brown moon-face creased with anxiety. At sixteen she'd bullied him into teaching her to drive and practising whenever there was the chance – another secret, like the Cantonese lessons from Nana. She'd been asking for a car of her own for months – something fun to whizz about in, not a great heavy thing like the Buick – but for once her father had refused her.

She drove around the back roads for a bit, taking some of the corners quite fast.

'*Missee* go too fast. Not safe.'

'Nonsense, Ghani. I'm only doing forty miles an hour.'

She put her foot down still further and the needle crept round to forty-five, forty-six, forty-seven, forty-eight, forty-nine, fifty.

Ghani clutched at the velvet *songkok* on his head. 'Slower, please, *missee*. Very dangerous. *Berenti! Berenti!*'

She took pity on him and braked to a stop. 'You can drive now, Ghani. If you like.'

She climbed into the back again and the *syce* drove on sedately, his neck stiff with disapproval. They turned down Cavenagh Road and into the driveway of the house and, as the Buick drew up under the front porch, the Indian houseboy, Soojal, came out on to the steps.

He opened the car door smiling, his white teeth showing glints of gold. '*Missee* good swim?'

'Yes, thanks, Soojal. Is the *mem* at home?'

'Up in bedroom. Very bad headache. Li-Ann look after her. You want to feed the doves? I fetch food for them.'

She couldn't be bothered; it was too hot. 'You do it, will you, Soojal. I'm going to lie down.'

Rex, the latest in a long line of Sealyhams, appeared and she patted the dog's head and then rubbed the tummy of the smiling glass Buddha as she passed by the table at the foot of the stairs. On the upper verandah she met Li-Ann creeping out of her mother's room, a finger to her lips.

'*Mem* very bad head, *missee*. Not to disturb.'

'I wasn't going to.'

She walked along the verandah to her own room, pulled off her frock and dropped it on

46

the floor for one of the *amahs* to take away and wash. Nana had always cleared up after her: picked up her clothes and her toys, made her bed, tidied her room, looked after everything. At night Nana had slept on a truckle bed on the verandah outside the room, ready to fetch drinks of water, to rearrange pillows, to bring comfort after bad dreams. Always been there.

The shutters were closed, the room dim and cool, the fan humming overhead sent little draughts of air across her bare skin as she lay on the bed. She could hear the flutter-flutter of the doves flying down from the dovecote and the lovely cooing sound they made. Soojal would be throwing food for them and they would be pecking about his sandalled feet. When she fed them, she sat on the verandah steps and sometimes they sat on her shoulders and cooed sweetly in her ear.

Her mother had been having migraines for years. Whenever they came on, she would go to lie down in her room – sometimes for several days. In fact, she spent a great deal of time there, with or without a migraine. She always had breakfast in bed on a tray instead of coming downstairs to the east verandah, and she stayed there until midmorning when she discussed the menus with Cookie in the dining room. After lunch there was a siesta during the hottest part of the day, and then tea served on the lawn in the shade of the jacaranda. When that was finished it was soon time to dress for dinner. Her father, who got up very early and stayed up very late, slept in another room. There had been rows – bad ones. Susan had eavesdropped and heard her mother threatening many times to go back to England. When the war had begun in Europe there had been even bigger rows about returning to be with the London grandparents, but the German U-boats had started to sink liners and the Luftwaffe to bomb England and it had been thought too dangerous to travel.

She stared up at the ceiling, watching the fan and wondering what to wear that evening at the Bensons. Not a full-scale party, just supper and a bit of dancing afterwards to gramophone records. It would be mostly the same old crowd, Milly had said, so no need to dress up or make much of an effort. The blue and white cotton would do and now that she'd grown her hair longer she could sweep it up at the sides with combs. The new Elizabeth Arden lipstick would go rather well and she could paint her fingernails with the matching polish. What about shoes? The white peep-toe platforms, or the navy courts? The peep-toes were much more fun but they were tricky to walk in and they hurt.

She slept for about an hour and then got up and took a cool shower. In the end, she decided on the peep-toes and found some big ear clips like outsize white buttons to match. The hair combs looked rather good and so did the scarlet lipstick. She painted her nails the same colour and dabbed her favourite scent, *Je Reviens*, behind her ears and on her wrists.

Soft-footed, genie-like Soojal appeared as she went down the stairs.

'The *tuan* send message, *missee*. He stay at Tanglin for dinner. Not home till late.'

'Is Ghani here?'

'Yes, *missee*. He stay after the *tuan* telephone. Later he go to the club to fetch the *tuan*'.

'Tell him I'd like him to drive me over to Colonel and Mrs Benson's house.'

'Yes, *missee*. You want at once?'

'At once.'

'I tell him. Looks like rain is coming. Sky very black.'

As she waited on the front steps for Ghani

to bring the car round, the first drops were splashing heavily on to the ground.

The Bensons lived on Winchester Road, Alexandra Park, in one of the black and white, red-roofed houses built for senior army officers. Susan liked Colonel Benson – he wasn't pompous like some of the other older servicemen – and Mrs Benson was nice too. The two sons had been packed off to school in England, but Milly Benson had gone to St Nicholas's convent and was one of her best friends.

Ghani stopped the car under the portico outside the front door.

'What time you leave, *missee?*'

'I don't know. I'll probably get a lift back with somebody.'

'The *tuan* does not like this. Please telephone when you are ready, *missee.*'

What a silly old fusspot he was! 'I'll see.'

The Bensons' Chinese houseboy opened the door and they had a little chat in Cantonese.

'How are you today, Meng?'

'Very good, thank you, *missee*. I hope you are well too.'

'I'm fine. Is it going to be a good party?'

He grinned. 'Always a good party in this house, *missee*. Everybody has a good time.'

'Anybody new?'

'Some Australian officers, *missee.*'

She pulled a face. 'Oh, God.'

Aussie soldiers were an uncouth lot. They rolled up their shorts, turned up the brim of their awful bush hats and saluted as though they were flapping away flies. And they spoke with a sort of horrible cockney twang.

She said hallo to Colonel and Mrs Benson and several army chaps immediately clustered round, offering cigarette cases, flicking lighters under her nose. She could see with one glance that she was easily the prettiest girl in the room. Milly came up. Poor Milly, she'd put on even more weight but she never seemed to care a row of beans what she looked like.

'Come and meet some Australians, Susie.'

'Must I?'

'They're very nice. They're army doctors at the Alexandra. I met them when I was working on one of the wards and they were doing the rounds.'

'Doing what?'

'The rounds. You know, looking at the patients. I was trailing along behind.'

Milly was always vague about her voluntary duties at the Alexandra Hospital. She helped with this and that, she said.

Carried things, held things, fetched things, tidied things, made herself useful to the real nurses.

'Then I ran across them again in the canteen. We got talking and I asked them along this evening. Come and say hallo.'

She was dragged over to three men standing together on the other side of the room. They were in khaki uniform and she would have known from the steak-fed, sun-bronzed, outback look of them that they were Aussies – even before they opened their mouths. One was called Geoff, the next Vincent, the last, Ray. The first two seemed all right but she wasn't so sure about the third one. He didn't smile admiringly at her like the other two.

She made gracious conversation, as one did to colonials. How long had they been in Singapore? The answer was one week. Where did they come from in Australia? Geoff and Vincent both came from Brisbane, Ray came from Sydney.

'How nice,' she said, thinking how absolutely ghastly ... the ends of the earth. 'And I gather you're doctors at the Alexandra. How long will you be staying?'

Ray answered. 'As long as we're needed.'

She looked at him, noticing the captain's

pips on his shoulder for the first time. Australian ranks probably weren't quite the equivalent of English ones. 'Well, I hope you enjoy yourselves while you're here. Singapore's the most wonderful fun.'

He said, 'Yeah, I've noticed how busy everyone is, having fun. They're not too worried about the war.'

'The war's thousands of miles away in Europe.'

'It's not the war with the Germans that I'm talking about, Miss Roper. It's the one with the Japs.'

'The Japs? We're not at war with them.'

'We soon will be.'

'That's nonsense. What can they do?'

'Take Singapore.'

'Singapore belongs to the British Empire.'

'The Nips might not think so.'

'We don't actually care *what* they think.'

'I've noticed that too.'

Milly stepped between them. She said brightly, 'I hear there's a marvellous new film on at the Capitol. Has anyone seen it?'

Supper was served. The Bensons' Indian cook had made a wonderful *biryani*, served with *sambar* and big rounds of *roti prata*. Susan steered well clear of the Australian doctors – there were plenty of other people to talk to. A sunburned rubber planter down for a few days' jolly in Singapore introduced himself. He was from the north of the peninsula, he told her – about thirty miles east of Betong. He'd come out from England two years ago and gone straight there. He liked the work but it was good to get back to civilization for a break. His aunt was an old schoolfriend of Mrs Benson, so he'd wangled an invitation.

He took a swig from his glass. 'I'm a bit out of touch, to tell the truth, but Singapore looks much the same. A lot more troops around, of course, but that's not a bad thing. Good idea to wave the flag, just in case the Japs get any silly ideas.'

She said impatiently, tired of the subject, 'What do you mean, silly ideas?'

'Well, Singapore's pretty important, isn't it? Commanding position, gateway to the East, jewel of the Empire, and all that. The Japs would give their eye teeth for it. But of course, the Royal Navy's got the sea approaches well covered. If the Nips try anything they won't get very far with those big guns pointing straight at them.'

'Can we talk about something else? It's awfully boring.'

'Sorry. Would you care to take a spin?'

Milly had put a record on the gramophone and people were dancing to 'Faithful Forever'. 'With a Smile and a Song' was probably on the other side; Milly had the whole *Snow White* set. Personally, she thought all the tunes were rather sickly.

The rubber planter had two left feet and both of them kept landing on her peep-toes. Afterwards she danced with some of the army chaps, who were better, and then a man who had something to do with building bridges and droned on about tensile strength and soil resistance and pressure tables. 'Really?' she kept saying, looking over his shoulder at Milly capering about happily with Geoff. *'Really?* How fascinating!'

Her feet were killing her, thanks to the rubber planter and the uncomfortable shoes. She hobbled out on to the verandah, sat down, undid the ankle straps and rubbed her toes. The rain was coming down in torrents, cascading like a waterfall off the eaves and drowning out 'When You Wish Upon a Star' playing in the other room. Something to be grateful for.

'Having trouble?'

She turned her head. It was the Australian: the one called Ray. He was leaning against the doorpost, arms folded – very outback.

'No.'

'I reckon it's the shoes. You could come to grief in those.'

'You're an expert on ladies' shoes?'

'Not shoes, but I know all about broken ankles and blisters.'

'Well, I don't need any medical advice, thank you.'

'Fair enough. Have a cigarette instead.' He held out a case that looked as if it was made out of an old tin; the cigarettes inside were squashed flat.

'No, thanks.'

'Mind if I do?'

'Carry on.'

She watched him produce a box of matches and fire up one with his thumbnail. Not even a lighter, let alone a decent cigarette case.

'Sorry if I spoke out of turn before.'

'You certainly did.'

He drew on the squashed cigarette. 'The trouble is I can't understand the way things are here. It's weird. Nobody seems to see the danger this island's in. Everyone believes Singapore's an impregnable fortress.'

'It is.'

'So you all keep saying. But it strikes me that's not true. It's a myth. The truth is the island's nothing like a fortress. It's a re-claimed mangrove swamp with no natural defences.'

She stopped massaging her feet and stared at him.

'The Royal Navy's the most powerful in the world and our naval base here is the biggest and best there is. And we've got *thousands* of troops here and plenty of air force planes. They can easily take care of those silly little yellow men – if they were ever stupid enough to try anything.'

'The Japs aren't stupid, Miss Roper. They're very bright.'

'Oh, so you're an expert on Japs as well, are you?'

'I spent three months in Japan and I learned something about the way their minds tick. They don't take kindly to being looked down on or having their economy sabotaged. The whites think the Japs are inferior but the Japs reckon it's the other way round. They believe they're descended from a sun goddess.'

'Which shows that they must be *very* stupid.'

'Underestimating them is what's stupid. They've spent more than four years practis-ing war on the Chinese. And there are eighty million of them.'

What a hideous accent it was! Far worse than American. 'Really? Have you counted?'

'Maybe your Government ought to start doing some counting. Since the Japs marched into Indo-China they're a thousand miles nearer to Malaya. Doesn't anybody realize that?'

She hadn't. But so what? They were still a long way away. 'Do we *have* to talk about them? It's all so tedious.'

He shrugged. 'Suit yourself. What'll we talk about instead?'

'Personally, I can't think of a single thing.'

'How about the weather? That's nice and safe and English. Does it often rain like this here?'

'This is nothing. When the monsoon gets going properly, in a few weeks' time, it'll pour for three months.'

'My word! Still, you must have been used to bad weather in England.'

'I've never lived in England. I was born in Malaya and I've lived here all my life. I've only been to England once.'

He said, surprised, 'I'd never have guessed it. You're very English, same as all the expatriates here. They've brought the Old Country out with them, haven't they?

Transported it lock, stock and barrel – except for the weather. They had the sense to leave that behind.' He drew on the cigarette again. 'What do you do, Miss Roper – when you're not having fun at parties like this?'

'A secretarial course.'

'Somehow, I can't see you as a secretary.'

She said sarcastically, 'Really? What else do you suggest I should do?'

'Well, if you've got any spare time, they need more volunteers at the Alexandra.'

'You mean rolling bandages and running errands? Like Milly?'

'No, not like Milly. You'd be no good on the wards.'

'Why not, pray?'

'You're not the type. Can you drive?'

'As it happens, I can.'

'Could you drive an ambulance?'

'I've no idea. I should think so.'

'You could have a go.'

The rubber planter appeared in the doorway, swaying and plainly the worse for gin slings. 'Found you at last.' He twirled his fingers. 'How about another spin?'

She put the shoes back on, fastened the ankle straps and stood up. 'I'd *love* to.'

Milly said later, 'I saw you on the verandah with Ray. Rather dishy, isn't he?'

'Dishy? *Him?*'

'Don't you think so?'

'No, I don't. He's awful. Look, Milly, I think I'll head off now, if you don't mind. I'm a bit tired. Could you tell Meng to send for Ghani?'

'No need. Osman will take you back.'

She sat in the back of the Bensons' Ford while their *syce* drove her home. The rain was drumming on the car roof, the windscreen wipers swishing to and fro. She undid her shoes again and kicked them off, wiggling her toes. What utter piffle that Australian had talked! Singapore *was a* fortress – everybody said so. Impassable jungle on one side and the huge Royal Navy guns guarding the other. Safe as houses, as the nice Roger had put it, and the left-footed planter had agreed. And what did Australians know about anything – descended from convicts and living upside down at the bottom of the world?

Soojal was waiting. '*Missee* had nice evening?'

'Not really. It was rather dull. Is the *tuan* back?'

'No, *missee*. Not yet. *Missee* need anything?'

'No, thank you, Soojal. I'm going to bed.'

A bow. A smile. 'Goodnight, *missee*.'

'Goodnight.'

She walked barefoot across the tiles, swinging the peep-toes by their ankle straps. As she passed the green glass Buddha, she rubbed his tummy – for luck, and to ward off any evil spirits that might be lurking in the shadows.

Two

Early morning was the best time of day, especially after rain when everything looked washed and clean. The air was cool and fresh, the lallang emerald green, the flowers smelled honey-sweet, and a golden mist still held the heat of the sun at bay. It was also the time when she and her father had breakfast alone together.

He was sitting at the table on the verandah, eating his boiled egg and toast while he read the *Straits Times*. Rex was stationed patiently under the table, hoping for crumbs to fall. She kissed the top of her father's head and took her place next to him. The number two houseboy, Amith, fetched her papaya fruit and orange juice and poured out her coffee.

'How did your bridge go, Daddy?'

He smiled at her over the newspaper. 'Badly. Too many good players at the club these days. Did you have a nice evening with the Bensons, poppet?'

It was always poppet, never Susan – unless he was angry with her, which was very rare.

'Not particularly.'

'Meet anyone interesting?'

'They'd invited some Australian army doctors from the Alexandra but I wouldn't call them interesting. One of them was extremely rude. According to him, we're all having far too much fun when we ought to be worrying about the Japs attacking us. I told him they'd never dare.'

'Oh, I think the Japs would dare anything, but it doesn't seem likely that they could succeed.'

'Mr Know-All thought they could. According to him, they're very clever and we underestimate them.'

'He might have a point there.

'He also said that the English have transported England to Singapore. Lock, stock and barrel, were the words he used. Except for the weather.'

Her father smiled. 'Well, it's true, I'm

afraid. It wasn't like that in the early days but with more and more white *memsahibs* coming out here, Singapore's getting rather like Surbiton. We're losing touch with the native Singapore and that's a great pity.'

'Surbiton?'

'A suburban district on the edge of London. I used to stay there with an aged aunt in the school holidays sometimes. You'd think it was a very boring place, poppet. I did.'

'Is it anywhere near Esher?'

'Yes, very near. Why?'

'I just wondered. I met someone who came from there.' She started on the papaya. 'Anything in the newspaper?'

'Nothing good. Moscow's still under siege. I hope to God the Russians manage to hold out against the Germans. It's bitterly cold there and deep snow. Poor wretches, fighting in those conditions. It must be hell for any soldier, whichever side he's on.'

Amith was moving softly about with dishes, the birds were twittering and tweeting in their cages, the mynahs chattering in the trees, cicadas in full chorus, Arjun, the *kebun*, rhythmically scything the lallang and the sun beginning to break through the mist to heat the day. The snows of Russia were a million miles away. Unimaginable.

Her father folded the newspaper and tossed the last piece of toast to Rex, who caught and devoured it with one snap of his jaws.

'I must go. I've got an early meeting. Ghani will be back to take you to the college.'

'If I had my own car, I could take myself.'

'It's not a good time to be buying cars. I've told you that before, poppet.'

She pouted. 'I don't see why.'

'Things are too unsettled at the moment. Wait a while and we'll see. Besides, you can't drive yet.'

'Actually, I can. Someone's been teaching me.'

He frowned. 'Who?'

She hesitated. 'Some chap in the army.'

'Well, I'd sooner you waited to have proper lessons. Much safer, and there's no rush.' He laid his hand on her shoulder as he passed her chair. 'Look in on Mummy before you go, will you, poppet? She's still not feeling well.'

Amith came forward, jug in hand.

'You like more orange juice, *missee?*'

She sipped the juice slowly, watching Sweep, the black cat, stalking something near the pond. Maybe she wouldn't bother to go to the college this morning. Learning to type had to be one of the most boring things in the world. Sitting in a stuffy room, bashing away at the keys. Shorthand was even worse. Light strokes, dark strokes, hooks to the left, hooks to the right, words joined on to other words ... she could never read it all back. And what for? So that she could work in an office where some dreary man would dictate dreary business letters for her to type out so he could sign them with an important flourish. She had no intention of ever doing any such thing.

Rex padded over to sit beside her and she gave him another piece of toast. Now, if she accepted the next marriage proposal she wouldn't have to do any kind of job at all. Hey presto! She'd be a married woman with her own home and servants, meeting friends for coffee, going to lunches, shopping, taking tea at Raffles, swimming and playing tennis at Tanglin, giving amusing parties, having a lovely time.

Sweep pounced suddenly and she saw that the quarry had been a frog. Jeremy Fisher took several giant leaps and plopped into pond and safety. The cat braked hard at the water's edge and saved face by pretending to examine a flower.

She gave the last bit of toast to Rex and went upstairs to fetch her swimming and tennis things. Afterwards, she stopped at her mother's room and opened the door. The shutters were closed and the room smelled of the lemony citronella lotion that her mother always rubbed on her temples and wrists when she had one of her heads.

'Li-Ann? Is that you?'

'No, it's Susan.'

'Oh.'

She went over to the bed. Her mother was lying under the mosquito netting with her eyes closed. 'Are you feeling any better, Mummy?'

'Not really. I shan't get up today. Cookie will have to manage without me.'

Cookie had learned to manage years ago. He would bicycle off to the market and the Cold Storage to buy whatever was wanted without needing to be told.

She said, 'I probably won't be in for dinner, anyway. I'm playing tennis at the club this evening.'

'Who with?'

'Clive Godwin, and John and Alison Campbell. I expect we'll have dinner after.'

'Well, don't be late back.'

'I won't be.' She moved towards the

windows. 'It's a lovely morning after all the rain. Not too hot. Wouldn't it be better with the shutters open? You'd get some air.'

'Don't touch them, for heaven's sake! The light would make my head even worse. Just leave me in peace, Susan.'

'Do you want Li-Ann to bring you anything?'

'Tell her to bring some more barley water. And a cold towel.'

She went down and spoke to Li-Ann and Cookie and, by the time she'd done that, Ghani had returned. He drove her to Pitman's College. She was late but her mother's migraine served as a good excuse. When the classes finished at one o'clock she took a rickshaw over to the Tanglin Club. The coolie pulling it was a broken-winded, wheezy old man, his seamed face like chamois leather under his conical hat, sweat rag knotted round his neck, jogtrotting through the dirt on filthy bare feet. But he set her down at the entrance steps to the club with as much ceremony as if she had been Cinderella arriving with her bewigged coachman for the ball. She rewarded him with fifty cents and a dazzling smile. Some people always argued over the fare and treated the poor things badly; her father had taught her never to do that.

There were only a few people at the pool – mostly wives lolling about and gossiping, and a couple of girls she'd known at the convent. She changed into her costume, pulled on her rubber bathing cap and did a few fast lengths of crawl. Swimming was one thing she did very well, though she didn't often demonstrate the fact. It was better to leave the showing off to the men.

The tennis four had been arranged for five o'clock when it was cooler – John and his sister, Alison, against Clive and herself. It was evenly matched but, in the end, she and Clive won. Clive, who minded a great deal about winning, clapped her on the back.

'Well played, partner.'

'Well played yourself. You did some brilliant shots.' He'd also poached like mad though she didn't mention that.

'Bit of a fluke, most of them.'

They had drinks in the clubhouse and then went in Clive's car to see the film that Milly had been talking about. The Capitol was full of men in uniform – British regiments, Gurkhas and Malays and Australians.

Over dinner at the Coq d'Or, she watched Clive and wondered what it would be like to be married to him: to live with him, eat with him, sleep with him. If he proposed – as he well might – would she accept him? He was something up-and-coming in the Hong Kong Shanghai Bank, good at tennis, swimming, cricket, rugger, a fairly good dancer and not bad-looking at all. She didn't love him but that was probably asking too much.

On the following Sunday he took her to the Sea View for pre-lunch drinks. The hotel was at Tanjong Katong, about five miles out of the city on the East Coast road – a Victorian building of faded grandeur with a domed roof, white marble floors and a colonnaded terrace that looked out over its private sandy beach towards the coastal islands. A snake charmer sat on the entrance steps, basket beside him, bulbous pipe in hand. As a child she had always been fascinated to watch the snake emerge and sway to the music.

The terrace was already crowded, the palm court orchestra playing 'I'll Follow My Secret Heart' and the Chinese boys balancing trays loaded with *stengahs*, gimlets, Tiger beers, gin slings. The heat from the midday sun penetrated deep into the corners of the terrace and it was stickily humid, the way it always was just before the monsoon. As they hunted for a free table, a couple waved at them, the man getting to his feet and beckoning insistently.

'That's Paul Fawcett and his wife. He's a colleague of mine at the bank,' Clive said. 'We may as well join them.'

They sat down and Clive called to one of the boys and ordered a round of drinks. The orchestra had moved on to another Noel Coward: 'I'll See You Again'. The wife, whose name was Marjorie, was fanning herself desperately with a card. She leaned forward, baring front teeth like a rabbit's.

'Have you been here before, Susan?'

'Yes, but not for ages.'

'We come every Sunday, don't we, Paul? It's become quite a ritual – ever since the war started. It makes us feel better.'

'Better?'

'About not being at home. Being so far away from England – when they're having such an *awful* time there. Don't you feel like that? Terribly guilty?'

'No, I'm afraid I don't.'

The smile faded, the buck teeth disappeared. 'Oh. Well, Paul and I do. So do a lot of people here.'

The drinks arrived and Clive signed the chit with a flourish. He was never stingy – another point in his favour. Pencil-shy men were not popular in Malaya. The husband, Paul, was overweight and kept mopping his sweaty red face with a handkerchief. He looked as though he was about to melt into a puddle of ghi, like the tigers in *Little Black Samba*.

He eyed her shorts and sleeveless blouse. 'You look marvellously cool, Susan. Don't know how you manage it.'

'I don't feel the heat so much. I'm used to it.'

'You're damned lucky. Marjorie can't stand it – nor can I, to tell the truth. Give me a nice chilly English day, any time.'

'I'll See You Again' had ground to a halt and the orchestra were starting on 'A Room with a View'. Susan looked around the terrace, seeing mostly older married couples, but she spotted one or two young people she knew and waved to them, mouthing greetings.

'We're hoping to go home next year when our leave comes up,' the red-faced Paul was saying. 'Marjorie wants to take the children back and put them in school there. She thinks this climate's very unhealthy for them.'

'Wouldn't it be safer to stay in Singapore?'

He did some more mopping. 'As a matter

of fact, I think they'd probably be a lot safer in England, now the invasion scare's over. The Germans aren't likely to try anything since Hitler missed the boat in 1940. And he's got his hands full with the Russians on the Eastern Front. The only snag is that we've let our house back home, but the lease will be up fairly soon and they could stay with Marjorie's parents until then.'

'Where do you live?'

'Surbiton. Nice part of the world. Near London, but not too near – and we're very close to the river. Do you know it?'

She remembered her father's remark about Surbiton. 'I hardly know England at all.'

He seemed quite shocked, as though such a thing was unthinkable. 'Really? Do you come from somewhere else, then?'

'From Malaya. I was born in Kuala Lumpur.'

'Oh, I see.'

She said firmly, 'I love it here. I'd never want to leave.'

The orchestra rounded off the Noel Coward selection and stopped playing. Everybody suddenly stopped talking, too. The wife, Marjorie, leaned across the table, baring her rabbit teeth again and holding out the card that she'd used as a fan.

'Would you like to have this, Susan? Paul and I don't need it. We know all the words by heart.'

There were more cards on the other tables and people were picking them up, clearing throats, obviously getting ready to sing. After a thumping chord and a roll of drums from the orchestra, they began. By the time they reached the chorus, the singing had swelled to a roar that carried far beyond the terrace, across the beach below and out over the sea.

There'll always be an England
And England shall be free,
If England means as much to you
As England means to me.

Some people were crying. Susan could see tears trickling down faces – of men as well as women – as they sang the sentimental words. Faces shining with patriotic pride and absolute faith. Paul was dashing a hand across his eyes, Marjorie dabbing away with a little lace-edged hanky. She thought, I'm the odd one out. I'm the only one here that England doesn't really mean much to at all.

Three

The monsoon broke in early November, when winds from the north-east swept across the South China Sea bringing torrential rainstorms. With the rains came scaremongering rumours: the Japanese photographers living in Singapore were sending pictures of the island to Japan, thousands of Canadian troops had been sent to defend Hong Kong against attack, Japanese warships had been sighted off Cambodia Point, steaming towards the coast of Malaya, a prospector upcountry had reported news of Japanese activities on the northern frontier. Nobody took the stories very seriously. The naval guns kept hurling their shells miles out to sea. At night powerful searchlights probed the dark waters and the skies. There were occasional blackout practices, and on Saturday mornings the air raid sirens were tested and wailed out over the city. Susan's father joined the Civil Defence while younger men joined the Volunteers. Their initial training and drill took place on the racecourse, interrupted for several days so that a race meeting could be held.

Clive Godwin proposed and when Susan turned him down he was angry and resentful.

'May I know the reason why – or is that too much to ask?'

'I'm not in love with you, Clive.'

'I had the distinct impression that you were.'

'Then you were wrong.'

'But you seemed to enjoy coming out with me.'

'That's not quite the same as marrying you, is it?'

'I believe I'm considered quite a catch.'

'Then you'll easily find another girl.'

'Well, if you change your mind, you can let me know.'

'I won't change it.'

The invitations kept coming – a reception at Government House for several hundred newly arrived servicemen, private parties, a big dance at the Officers' Mess out at the naval base at Krangi. The *dersey* had made Susan an evening gown of pale-blue taffeta and her hair had been washed and set in a new style. A good-looking sub lieutenant commandeered her for several dances. They quickstepped and foxtrotted and tangoed to lovely tunes played by a wonderful band.

'Mind if we take some air?' he said, running a finger round the inside of his collar. 'This kit's most frightfully hot.'

They walked away from the Mess, the dance music fading. It had been raining hard earlier but there were no puddles or mud to spoil her silver shoes or dirty the hem of her taffeta gown. Everything was shipshape: His Majesty's Royal Navy all present and correct, which gave a nice, safe feeling.

She said, 'We can hear the big guns when you're practising firing them.'

'Hell of a racket, isn't it? Any Jap ships would be blown clean out of the water, and the base would be out of range of *their* shells – which is why we built it here, of course. Smart thinking. We've got everything, you know. Floating docks, deep-sea anchorage, harbour room for a whole fleet, if necessary. The Japs wouldn't stand a chance.'

The naval base was on the northern shore of the island and the narrow strip of the Johore Straits lay ahead, bridged by the Causeway to mainland Malaya on the other side. Four hundred miles from there to the borders of Siam and, beyond Siam, Burma. A mountain range like a backbone down the centre. Dense jungle where trees strained upwards a hundred feet or more towards the light. Bamboo thickets and palm groves. A hidden network of sluggish rivers, creeks and fetid swamps. All of it inhabited by crocodiles, tigers, leopards, deadly snakes, malarial mosquitoes, leeches, giant red ants – to name a few of the less friendly residents.

Beyond the twinkling lights of the Causeway, a thunderstorm was brewing up over the peninsula: glimmers of sheet lightning and the rumble of thunder sounding like distant guns.

She said idly, 'But what if the Japs didn't come from the sea? Supposing they came from the peninsula instead?'

'Oh, they'd never try that. The jungle's virtually impassable. A snake couldn't get through.' He grinned at her. 'Leave it to the Royal Navy. We'll take care of you.'

'Britannia rules the waves?'

'Definitely.'

'There'll always be an England?'

'Oh, absolutely. And that's a very beautiful dress that you're wearing, by the way.'

'Thank you.'

'And you're a very beautiful girl.'

She let him kiss her before they went back to the Mess. He was rather good at it – just as he'd been good at dancing.

The restaurant on the fourth floor of Robinson's department store was one of the most popular places in Singapore to meet for morning coffee. Milly was waving frantically from a table.

'I thought you weren't coming, Susie. I've been here ages.'

'Sorry. I got delayed.'

In fact, she'd been having a Saturday morning lie-in after a party the night before.

They ordered coffee and biscuits from the waitress.

Milly said, 'Look, there's that smug cow, Phyllis, showing off her engagement ring. Who on earth would want to marry *her?*'

'Some chap in the Gordons, apparently.'

'I pity him. He couldn't know how awful she is. Do you remember how she used to sneak on us to the nuns?'

She remembered it very well, and the punishments that followed: the wooden ruler six times across the back of the hand, the hundred lines, the extra prep – all thanks to Phyllis. They'd got their own back once by shoving her head down the lavatory and pulling the chain.

Milly took a chocolate biscuit, waved it around casually. 'I've been out with Geoff a couple of times lately.'

'Geoff?'

'You know – the Aussie doctor at the Alexandra. You met him at our house, remember? He took me to Raffles for dinner one evening and to the cinema. I've invited him to play tennis at Tanglin next weekend. Would you like to come too? We could see if Vin could partner you.'

'Just so long as you don't ask that other one. Ray whatever-he's-called.'

'Why are you so against him?'

'I'm not against him, I just didn't like him.'

She'd spotted several of the ladies who came to her mother's fortnightly luncheons. Lady Battersby was only three tables away – poker-straight in her chair, navy crêpe dress, leghorn straw hat on her head, pearl choker round her plucked-chicken's neck. You didn't wave to someone like Lady B.; if you were in favour, she would incline her head in your direction. If you weren't, she simply wouldn't see you.

'His name's Ray Harvey,' Milly said. 'Geoff told me that he's a very good doctor.'

'I still don't like him.'

'He's tall, dark and handsome.'

'He may be tall but he's not particularly dark and he's not at all handsome.'

'*I* think he is. Haven't you noticed his eyes?'

'No.'

'They're a gorgeous colour. I think he's jolly attractive.'

'You've no taste in men, Milly. That's your trouble.'

'Well, anyway, Geoff's super.'

'He's a colonial. He speaks with that ghastly twang.'

'I don't care.'

'I bet your parents do.'

'Actually, they don't. They like him a lot. And I think you're being rather beastly, Susie.'

'Sorry. I didn't really mean it. I'm sure Geoff's very nice.'

'So you'll come over for tennis?'

'If you want.'

'Thanks. Have a biscuit.'

She took a digestive, nibbled round the edge. 'How's it been at the hospital lately?'

'Rather good fun, actually. There's not much to do. Mostly malaria cases, or snake bites, or appendicitis, or cuts gone septic ...

that sort of thing. We had one soldier who'd shot his foot off by mistake – that was gruesome.'

'Where do they all come from?'

'Some from Singapore, but most of them from the peninsula. The one without the foot was stationed at Kota Bahru and we've had a few from Kuantan and Johore and several from Kuala Lumpur. They bring them down to Singapore by train and then ambulances pick them up from the station.'

'Who drives the ambulances?'

'Army chaps mostly. Sometimes it's volunteers – you know, do-good *mems*. Why do you want to know?'

'Just curious.' She nibbled a bit more. 'Milly, does your father ever talk about the Japs?'

'How do you mean?'

'Well, does he think they'd ever attack Malaya?'

'Oh no. He says it's much too well defended. And the Jap soldiers aren't any good at fighting. About as good as the Italians, he says. In other words, useless. Have another biscuit.'

'I'm still eating this one. And you oughtn't to have any more – you'll put on even more weight.'

'I don't care. Geoff doesn't like skinny women. He likes them with some fat on them. Did you know that Aussies call girls sheilas?'

'They would.'

'They've got different words for lots of things.'

'I'm sure they have. It must be like a foreign language.'

'But I'd love to go there one day. It sounds a wonderful country. Geoff says the outback's amazing. You can drive for days and not see a single soul.'

'How incredibly boring.'

'You're being beastly again, Susie.'

'Well, it sounds awful.'

'It isn't. Not according to Geoff.'

'He's used to it.'

Lady B. had turned her head and the leghorn straw in their direction and was inclining it graciously. Susan smiled back very politely at the old trout. 'Are you going to the Tanglin dance tonight, Milly?'

'No. We've got people coming to dinner, worse luck. Friends of my parents. Are you?'

'If my mother hasn't got one of her heads.'

'What are you going to wear?'

'Haven't decided yet. I've got a new dress I quite like. I might wear that.'

'You're so lucky, having so many lovely clothes.'

It was true her wardrobe was crammed with them. The only problem was choosing.

Ghani stopped the Buick at the entrance in Stevens Road and the *jaga* opened the door, bowing. Susan was proud of the way her parents looked as they walked up the steps into the club. Her father, tall and handsome in his white dinner jacket, her mother elegant in a long grey georgette gown — all smiles and in one of her good moods.

Nick's Tanglin Six were playing in the ballroom, people already dancing. It wasn't long before some chap asked her. He was in mess kit and his face rang a bell, though she couldn't remember his name.

'Roger Clark,' he said. 'We met at the Chambers' and then ran into each other by the pool here.'

The penny dropped. This was the eager puppy dog. 'Yes, of course. How are you getting on?'

'Rather well, actually.'

He'd lost his just-out-from-England pallor and he looked very hot. Men always suffered badly in evening dress if they weren't used to the heat.

'You come from Esher, don't you?'

He seemed very pleased that she'd remembered. 'That's right. Though I must say it seems absolutely miles away.'

'Ten thousand miles, more or less.'

'It's not the distance so much. It's another world out here, isn't it? Absolutely fascinating. I do think Singapore's the most marvellous place.'

'Have you been across to the peninsula yet?'

'No. What's it like?'

It was eight years since they had left the Malay mainland for Singapore but the memories were still vivid to her. The sprawling bungalow built on pillars; rooms leading out of rooms to more rooms. Shady verandahs, creaky fans, stone bathroom floors with a drain hole in the middle, washing water kept in big Shanghai jars, beer and soda kept cool down the well, the night cries of wild animals in the jungle beyond the garden, the slow-moving, muddy rivers, the distant view of mountains like castle ramparts against the sky.

She could remember her father taking her on visits to rubber plantations: acres upon acres of glossy-leaved rubber trees, planted in endless rows. Watching the Tamil tappers working the trees and cutting into the bark to harvest the sticky liquid. Attap native huts built on stilts, brown-skinned women squatting over open cooking fires, their children playing in the dust, their babies slung up in saris from beams. Goats, chickens, pariah dogs and the soft-eyed cattle. The scorching sun and hard-baked earth. Hot air pressing down like a blanket. The curry spice aroma of the cooking, the stench from the smoke-houses of latex being turned into sheets of brown rubber. Swimming in a jungle pool beneath a waterfall and being shown tiger pawprints in the dirt close by. None of it very easily described to an Englishman from Esher.

She said, 'Well, it's different from Singapore. Mostly rainforest – except where it's been cleared for the plantations and along the coasts. Lots of rivers, not many towns, and lots of *kampongs*.'

'*Kampongs?*'

'Native villages.'

'Yes, of course. I hope they don't mind us being around.'

'The Malays are very gentle, peace-loving people. Very friendly.'

'Well, I expect they know we're here to defend them. I say, this is a jolly good band, isn't it?'

'Yes, it's very good.'

After a bit more dancing, he said, 'I hope it's not too much of a cheek but is there any chance of you coming out with me one evening?'

She felt rather sorry for him, so far away from England and Esher. And he was easy to deal with, unlike some men.

'All right. If you like.'

He beamed at her. 'That's most awfully good of you.'

Another man came up and clapped a hand on his shoulder.

'Excuse me.'

'Sorry?'

'This is an excuse-me dance, old boy. If you don't mind.'

'Gosh ... is it? Sorry, I didn't realize.' Roger let go of her reluctantly. 'See you later, then.'

She foxtrotted away with her new partner.

'This isn't an excuse-me at all, Denys, as you very well know.'

'Desperate measures are required when there are so many of us chaps and so few of you lovely girls.'

She had first met Denys Vaughan at Raffles. She'd been dancing with an RAF pilot when he'd barged in with exactly the same lie. Gingery hair, toothbrush moustache and a lot of nerve. He was an officer in the Straits Settlement Police and one of the hordes of young bachelors who hung about hopefully at dances. At Raffles they congregated in a corridor off the ballroom known as Cads' Alley, trying to grab a dance partner. He practically lived at Raffles, he'd told her, and had a splendid arrangement with the maitre d'hôtel for any food leftovers to be wrapped up and handed discreetly to him at the end of an evening. Otherwise he survived from dinner party to dinner party. He had no private allowance and making ends meet was always a problem. Terrible pay, he complained, and a grim little house in the compound of Divisional Police Headquarters.

She said, 'I haven't seen you at a Tanglin dance before. Isn't Raffles more your stamping ground?'

'I came with the Governor's ADC. He's an old chum of mine from schooldays. There's a party of us but none of the girls is a patch on you, so as soon as I spotted you here I made a beeline.'

If he had had long moustaches instead of the toothbrush, he would probably have twirled them. 'Won't the other girls be offended?'

'Can't help that.'

They danced a rhumba after the foxtrot. He danced energetically, regardless of the heat, and with a lot of complicated footwork. There were better dancers but they weren't as amusing.

Towards the end of the evening everyone joined in a conga, led by the band round and round the ballroom in a long, snaking line, down the stairway, round the swimming pool and back up to the ballroom again for the last dance – 'Goodnight Ladies'. It was followed by the roll of drums heralding God Save the King, when everybody stood to rigid attention.

Denys reappeared at her side. 'We're all going on to Government House. How about coming too?'

'Government House? Are you serious?'

'The ADC's quarters there. I told you, he's a chum of mine. Free drinks. Free fags. Midnight dip in the pool. Jolly good fun.'

'What about the Governor?'

'On an official visit upcountry.' He winked. 'The cats away, so the mice can play.'

'I'm supposed to be going home with my parents.'

'Tell them you've been invited to Government House. That'll do the trick. And I'll take you home later.'

'In a rickshaw?'

'Certainly not. A chap I know has lent me his car while he's away.'

He went with her to find her parents and gave a faultless performance of a responsible, reliable young man.

'I'll see her safely home, sir. You can count on me.'

Her father frowned. 'I think I'll send Ghani.'

But her mother was on her side – Denys had made sure of that.

'He's promised he'll escort her back, Tom. I'm sure we can trust him.'

In the borrowed MG, Denys said, 'It's the magic words Government House. Mothers love to hear them.'

'You mean you often take daughters there?'

'Whenever the occasion arises.'

'When the cat's away?'

'Usually. But not always. The old boy's rather decent about it, actually. So's his missus. They turn a bit of a blind eye to us when they're in residence. I even get invited to the odd dinner party there as well – to make up the numbers, so to speak, thanks to my old school chum. He sticks my name on the end of the list and I'm in. Free grub and booze. I make myself agreeable to the ladies and I know which knife and fork to use.'

They roared through the entrance gates, Denys waving cheerily at the guard, and followed the other cars up the carriageway towards the great white palace on the hill. Pediments, porticoes and colonnades, surmounted by a rooftop flagpole flying a huge Union Jack. They went in through a side door to the ADC's sitting-room-cum-office on the ground floor, making quite a din.

'Have a drink.' Denys pressed a tall glass of something greenish into her hand.

'What is it?'

'Speciality of the house. One of those made-up things. You'll love it.'

They stood about drinking the free green drink and smoking the free gold-tipped cigarettes, until somebody started up the gramophone for dancing. Denys's cheek was pressed against hers as they shuffled slowly round to 'Time On My Hands'. His moustache brushed her ear.

'You're an incredibly beautiful girl, Susan.'

'So I've been told.'

'There are lots of pretty girls around, but

not many beautiful ones. Trust me.'

'But I don't trust you, Denys. What was in that drink?'

'Lime juice, lemonade, a dash of gin.'

'More than a dash, I'd say.'

'Very refreshing, though, don't you think?'

'No. I don't feel at all refreshed. I feel rather squiffy.'

'Must be the heat.'

After more drinks and more dancing there seemed to be a general move towards the door.

Denys said, 'The others are going for a dip in the pool. Are you game?'

'I haven't got a swimming costume with me.' She had difficulty speaking the words properly.

'No need to worry about that.'

'Why not?'

'Well it's fairly dark, if you see what I mean.'

'I do see what you mean ... and I'm not game.'

'Tell you what, then,' he said. 'I'll give you a private and personal conducted tour of Government House instead.'

'I've been here before.'

'Ah, but I'm talking about the parts you won't have seen. It's quite a place. Come with me, fair maiden.'

He took her hand and towed her after him down a marble-floored corridor. There was nobody about – no officials or servants, nobody to stop them. Silence except for the humming of ceiling fans. Another corridor, wider and even grander. Then another. Her heart was pounding, but from excitement, not fear: the sort of feeling she'd had when she had deliberately broken some silly rule at the convent.

'I thought you were supposed to be a policeman, upholding the law, Denys.'

'Policemen are the worst.'

He opened a door, switching on lights.

'His Excellency's study. Snug little den, isn't it?'

She wandered round the room, inspecting the silver-framed photographs on the desk – including one of the King and Queen – the papers, the books, a leather-bound diary for 1941 left conveniently open for her to read all about the Governor's engagements: meetings, receptions, luncheons, a dinner held for fifty Australian officers, troop inspections.

'He's a very busy man.'

'Rather.'

'What happens if someone catches us here?'

'They cut our heads off.'

They tiptoed on, Denys opening more doors on to more private rooms. They passed display cases filled with silver trophies, jewel-encrusted swords and sabres; official portraits stared down on them with disapproving eyes. Upstairs, they crept along a long dark colonnade.

Denys squeezed her hand. 'Now for the *pièce de résistance*. The grand finale.'

'What is it?'

'You'll see.'

He opened yet another door, switched on another light.

'The Gubernatorial Chamber. In other words, Their Excellencies' bedroom.'

'Golly... We really *will* get our heads cut off, Denys.'

It was a sumptuous room fit for a king or, in this case, for the King's representative and his Lady. She wondered what it was like to be the Governor's wife. To live in such splendour with a hundred servants at her beck and call. To be bowed to and curtseyed to and saluted, just like the real Queen. To give grand balls and dinners and receptions and drive around in open limousines with a flag fluttering regally on the bonnet.

Behind her, Denys whispered, 'Why don't

you try the bed. See what it's like.'

She perched on the edge, bounced up and down.

'That's no good,' he said. 'You have to lie on it properly.'

She kicked off her silver shoes and swung her legs up. 'Like this?'

'That's better How is it, Goldilocks? Too hard? Or too soft?'

She giggled. 'Just right.'

'Let me try...' He sat down. 'So it is. Very comfy.' He leaned over her. 'You make a gorgeous Goldilocks and I feel like Father Bear.'

'Whatever would His Excellency say?'

'He'd think you were gorgeous too.'

When he kissed her his moustache tickled rather pleasantly and they rolled around on the bed. Before long, his hand was sliding under her skirts and wandering up her right leg.

'What happens if someone comes in, Denys?'

'They won't. Trust me.'

'I've already told you – I don't.'

His hand was over her knee now and moving higher. She thought hazily, I ought to stop him before things go too far but I can't be bothered. The room seemed to be going round and round and see-sawing up and down. She closed her eyes, which only made it worse. Suddenly, *much* worse. Oh God!

She pushed him off and sat up, hand clapped over her mouth.

'Get me out of here, Denys.'

'What's all the rush?'

'I'm going to be sick. *Quick!*'

She made it as far as the colonnade and vomited over the balustrade into a flower bed below. Denys mopped her down with his handkerchief.

'I'm terribly sorry, old thing. I'll take you home at once.'

Later, in the MG, she said, 'You're a louse, Denys. It was that revolting drink you kept giving me. You're lucky I wasn't sick all over their Excellencies' bed.'

'A thousand pardons, Princess. I humbly crave your forgiveness.'

'Well, I don't give it. I still feel dreadful and I expect I'll have a shocking hangover. You're an absolute cad. It wasn't the first time you've taken a girl to their bedroom, was it?'

'I cannot tell a lie.'

'How many girls?'

'A few. They seem to get quite a kick out

of it.' He glanced at her wryly. 'I thought you would, too.'

She might have done: might easily have gone the whole way, like he'd planned, if she hadn't felt so sick. Denys was nice – a lot nicer than Clive – and she wouldn't have minded losing her virginity to him. The whole escapade had been a bit of a hoot, except for the being sick part. Next time she saw the Governor passing by with his Lady, it would give her a good laugh to remember rolling around on their bed.

He drove round the corner into Cavenagh Road and pecked her cheek discreetly as Soojal appeared at the front door.

'Goodnight, Goldilocks. Sleep tight.'

'Goodnight, Father Bear.'

She stumbled a little over the doorstep.

Soojal said, 'Everything is all right, *missee?*'

'Yes, thank you. Perfectly all right.'

'I fetch something for you?'

'No, thanks.'

She could feel him watching her anxiously as she steered a careful course for the stairs. For once, she forgot to rub the glass Buddha's tummy as she passed him by.

Lady Battersby said in frigid tones, 'Are you criticizing the Governor, Mrs Cotton?'

96

'Not exactly. He's very charming, of course, only I just feel it would be an advantage to have someone a bit more dynamic at the helm in these difficult times.'

'Difficult times? What is difficult about them?'

'Well, with the war in Europe and the Japs being such a threat to us.'

'The European war is being dealt with very competently by our military experts at home. As for Malaya, our troops are standing to arms across the length and breadth of the peninsula and Singapore Island is a fortress. The Japanese are inferior beings, quite incapable of presenting any serious threat to us.'

'But my husband thinks there's a danger of them bombing Singapore. He says we should be building air raid shelters and digging trenches. Just in case.

'Really? May I ask how long you and your husband have been in the Far East, Mrs Cotton?'

'About three years.'

'Most of us have been here for a great deal longer than that. My husband and I have lived in Malaya for nearly thirty and I consider that we are in a rather better position to judge the situation. I might add that the Governor and his wife are personal friends of ours. We find him excellent in every respect.'

Mrs Cotton, flushed with embarrassment, mumbled her apologies.

Susan had enjoyed the exchange. Usually her mother's ladies' luncheons were ditch-water dull and she avoided them whenever possible. Lady B. had livened things up.

She listened to Mrs Jennings whose hus-band was something to do with surveying, grumbling about her cook who had, apparently, walked out on her without a moment's notice.

'Mind you,' Mrs Jennings went on, 'he was thoroughly lazy and dishonest, so I'm glad to be rid of him. You can never really trust any of the natives, can you?'

Amith was removing her plate as she spoke, his face expressionless.

Lady Battersby stared across the table. 'We have never had the slightest trouble with any of our servants, Mrs Jennings. It all depends on how one treats them. Ours have been in our employ for many years.'

Three cheers for Lady B. for that put-down, Susan thought. The new *mems* like Mrs Jennings – probably from Surbiton – were always finding fault with their servants.

The lunch dragged on. At the pudding stage she excused herself with a headache and escaped. Her mother would be furious with her, but she didn't care. Anyway, the headache was real after the evening with Denys.

She slept until nearly dinnertime, missing tea on the lawn, showered, dressed and went downstairs. There had been another monsoon downpour while she'd been asleep and the air felt beautifully fresh and cool. Her parents were having drinks out on the west verandah and her father had brought two men back for dinner. She had already met fat Mr Forster many times. He was also in the rubber business. His wife had gone to England, taking their son to school, and he was one of Singapore's grass widowers – the *tuans* left alone consoling themselves with drink and native mistresses. The other man was unknown to her.

'Lawrence Trent,' he said, shaking her hand. 'Your father and I met in England many years ago.' He was a thin man with a beaky nose and sharp eyes.

Her father said, 'Mr Trent arrived in Singapore recently. He's a correspondent for a London newspaper.'

She gave him an arch smile. 'Have you

come to report on us?'

He smiled in return. 'Something like that.'

Her mother said, 'Do tell us all about London, Mr Trent. How are things there?'

'I'm sorry to disappoint you, Mrs Roper, but I'm afraid I haven't been in London for a long time. I've spent the past three years in China. In Shanghai and, lately, Chunking – being bombed by the Japanese.'

'Goodness! You must find Singapore rather dull.'

'On the contrary, I'm finding it fascinating.'

'Really? In what way exactly?'

'Well, it's remarkable how calm and confident everyone appears. How completely certain of Singapore's military strength. I've been very struck by that. It's very different in China where nobody feels safe at all, and quite unique in the Far East as things are today.'

Mr Forster growled, 'Of course we're confident. The island's like a fortress. Nobody's going to get near us.' His face was flushed as he drained the remains of what was probably his second or third four-finger *stengah*. 'Damned Nips! I'd like to get my bare hands on them if they ever had the cheek to try anything on. Why the hell we let any of the bastards go on living in Singapore, I'll never know. They ought to be rounded up and thrown out on their ears. Put in an open boat and sent back where they belong.'

Her father said soothingly, 'Another drink, Bill?' He signed to Soojal. 'Tell me, how did that cricket match go today?'

'We lost, dammit. By one wicket.'

'Bad luck. Still, there's always the next time.'

During dinner, the Japs weren't mentioned again. Afterwards her mother went to bed early and her father took Mr Forster and Mr Trent out on to the verandah again where they would drink more *stengahs* or brandies and smoke and talk about politics and the economy and other equally boring subjects. Susan trailed upstairs. It was very hot in her room and she felt too wide awake to sleep, so she went out on the upper verandah and listened to the bullfrogs croaking and watched the fireflies flickering in the dark like Tinker Bell. *Clap your hands if you believe in fairies.* She'd always clapped loudly when Nana had read the story. Fairies, though, belonged to England – to English woods and English glades, not to tropical jungles. One thing in England's favour.

After the rain, the scent of flowers was

heavy and honey-sweet. Cigar smoke drifted up from the west verandah below and pipe smoke, which must belong to the newspaper man. She moved further along the rail and leaned over so that she could eavesdrop. Mr Forster was sounding off again about the Japs.

'They don't know the first thing about fighting. Weedy little types with rotten eyesight. Can't see in the dark. Wouldn't stand a chance against our chaps.'

Lawrence Trent's voice said mildly, 'That's the general opinion, I know, but I'm afraid it's rather a misconception. The Japs know how to fight very well – I've been on the receiving end myself – and I'd be very surprised if they weren't being given special training for jungle warfare. Whereas our troops have received practically none.'

'Rubbish! Our men are trained for anything.'

'Not specifically for fighting in a jungle. The Japs have already learned how to exploit difficult terrain and climate extremes. And they're infinitely adaptable. Their soldiers dress simply and can subsist on small rations they carry with them – not much more than a ball of rice and a canister of water. Supplying and deploying *our* troops is a much more complicated affair altogether ... traditional uniform, large quantities of tinned food, and so on.'

'Well, of course it is. Dammit, we're not bloody orientals. Our men dress properly, eat proper rations and fight the better for it. And we've proper guns, too – we don't just brandish knives.'

'That's another misconception. The Japanese are very well armed – with tommy guns and two-inch mortars. Light, mobile and very accurate. The British in Malaya have rifles and not many automatic weapons.'

'Rifles are damned accurate too, I'll have you know.'

'True. But they're chiefly a long-range weapon and there are not many extended fields of fire in somewhere like Malaya. In warfare the key to success is attack, and the jungle is far more conducive to attack than defence. An enemy can infiltrate unseen, especially if well camouflaged. It's very hard to stop him.'

'Sounds as though you're on their bloody side, Trent.'

'I'm not, I assure you. Anything but.'

Her father said, 'I take it you've been on the peninsula, Lawrence?'

'I've been everywhere they'll let me go.

103

Had a good snoop around and asked a lot of questions that nobody wants to answer. I've picked up some pretty shocking information in the process. Do you know that we haven't one single tank in Malaya? Not one.'

'Surely tanks wouldn't be much good in this sort of country?'

'Why not? They're designed to go anywhere. I'm pretty sure the Japs will use them and we've no defences against them. If you think about it, there's plenty of room for a tank to go between rows of rubber trees.'

Mr Forster was off again. 'I'm telling you, Trent, the Nips aren't going to get near Singapore. The navy has five fifteen-inch guns covering the sea approaches. Nothing and nobody's going to get past those.'

'I agree – so long as the Japs only try an attack by sea. But the guns are fixed in concrete, pointing seawards, and can't be turned. If the enemy should come from another direction, they'd be quite useless. Just like the French Maginot Line against the Germans in 1940.'

'What other direction? There isn't another one.'

'Unfortunately, there is. People refer to Singapore as an island but, strictly speaking, it isn't an island at all.'

'There's water all the bloody way round it. I call that an island.' Mr Forster's face must be puce by now, his eyes bulging like the bullfrogs in the swamps.

'In fact, it's really just a continuation of the mainland, connected by a causeway across a very narrow strip of water. It's by no means the impregnable fortress it's cracked up to be. What if the Japs got ashore somewhere on the north of the peninsula, from Siam?'

'What if they did? Our chaps would soon mop 'em up. Chuck 'em back in the sea.'

'But supposing they managed to get a foothold and started to make their way down towards Singapore?'

'Most of it's jungle. They'd never get through. It's bloody impassable.'

'So everyone says, but, as I said, the Japs will learn how to deal with jungle and use it to their advantage. Nobody seems to understand the terrible danger Singapore is in – least of all our military. Officers put on their finery in the evenings and dance the night away with ladies in ballgowns, as though there were nothing whatever to worry about. It's quite extraordinary to an outside observer like myself.'

There was a snort of rage. 'You sound like

that damned Yank on the wireless who keeps saying we've got it coming to us. I suppose you'll be spinning the same story back in England – except they won't put up with that sort of bloody defeatist talk. I can't stand listening to this rubbish another minute, Tom. I'm off.'

'I'll see you out, Bill.'

She heard Mr Forster blundering off and the sound of his car starting up, engine roaring, tyres spinning. After a moment, her father came back.

'Sorry about that, Lawrence. Poor old Bill can get rather steamed up about things, especially when he's had a few.'

'I'm sorry if I upset him. My apologies. Do you want me to leave too?'

'Not at all. I'd like to talk some more. Were you serious about what you were saying?'

'Deadly serious, Tom. The Japs aren't fools. When they look at their maps they can see how strategically important Singapore Island is. Whoever holds it controls the main shipping route between Europe and Asia – the main link between the Indian and Pacific oceans: between East and West. It's the pivot at the junction of trade routes. There *are* other routes but they're either much longer or more difficult. And whoever holds Singapore also enjoys all the rich resources of Malaya and the Indies. Oil, tin, rubber, tea, coal, iron … with cheap labour thrown in for good measure. The Japs are desperate for raw materials, especially oil. Added to that, the Johore Straits form one of the best natural harbours in the south-west Pacific. They *have* to take Singapore away from us if they want to realize their dreams of expansion in Asia. Their aim and ambition is to be rid of white colonial races in South East Asia. To wipe them out.'

'Not quite so simple for them, surely. We're well defended here.'

'You only *think* you are. There are endless official propaganda bulletins put out about army manoeuvres, naval exercises, troops arriving – all to make everyone feel nice and secure. Yes, there are some fixed defences on the mainland east-coast beaches where the Japanese army might be expected to attempt a landing – Kota Bahru, Kuantan and Mersing – and the big naval-base guns are covering the sea approaches to Singapore, but there are no fixed defences along the Malayan *west* coast, and Penang has precisely two six-inch guns. Incidentally, Singapore Island's north shore has nothing at all to fend off any attack coming from across the Straits. No barricades, barbed wire, ditches, pillboxes, gun emplacements. Nothing. A contact of mine on General Percival's staff tells me the general's view is that to construct anything like that might have a bad effect on public morale.'

'But that's ridiculous.'

'It's more than ridiculous, it's utter folly. Do you realize that the Royal Navy hasn't a single battleship in this area, not one aircraft carrier and no heavy cruisers or submarines? All we have is a handful of destroyers and about a hundred RAF planes that are mostly obsolete – old Wildebeestes and Buffaloes and the like. Our army and the navy need good air cover and they simply haven't got it. We're dangerously vulnerable to attack. The Japs will know all this, of course. Their intelligence is bound to be excellent – after all, there are plenty of them living and working in Singapore. They'll know all about the poor defences. They'll know that there are almost no public shelters in the city, that practising air raid drills or blackouts or local defence isn't taken very seriously, that most civilians are only thinking about the next party or the next cricket match or the next picnic on the beach. A lot of the whites have come out here to get rich quick and enjoy

the life, never mind any other consider-
ations. Nobody, including our military commanders, believes the Japs are capable of
causing any serious trouble for us. The Nips
are generally held in contempt, and that
could prove fatal.'

There was a silence. Susan waited.

'Surely the top brass must be aware of the
situation.'

'The consensus of top-brass opinion seems
to be that the Japs are more concerned with
fighting Russia, that they'd never attempt a
landing in Malaya during the monsoon and
that, even if they did, they'd never get
through the jungle. None of those things is
necessarily true. What *is* true is that when
they took Indo-China in July the Japs gained
an ideal base for launching attacks in all
directions – the Philippines, the Dutch East
Indies, Thailand and Malaya. But all the
warning signals are being ignored: Jap
submarines in Malayan coastal waters,
increased Jap military activity in Indo-China
… nobody seems very worried. Heads are
firmly stuck in the sand. I've heard a rumour
that two Royal Navy battleships are being
sent out here but without an aircraft carrier
to protect them, and one of them, the
Repulse, is an old lady built in 1916. Too little

has been done and it's getting much too late.'

There was another silence before her father spoke again. 'I've offered my services to the civil defence here but I must say it's been something of a let-down. I speak the native languages pretty fluently and I hoped they'd put me to some good use but, so far, all I've done is fill in forms. The sort of thing any fool could do.'

'There's been a lot of that, I'm afraid: valuable men being wasted. And there's another problem: Singapore's a polyglot hotchpotch of races who don't seem to mix with each other or have any special allegiance to the British Crown. I can't see them pulling together under attack.'

'Even so, Lawrence, I still can't believe the Japs capable of taking Singapore.'

'Let's hope you're proved right. But if you want my advice, Tom, you'll send your wife and daughter away. Get them a passage on a ship sailing for Australia – they'd be reasonably safe there.'

'They wouldn't think much of the idea.'

'Better than falling into Jap hands. They have a very uncivilized way of dealing with prisoners. And if they treat Europeans any-thing like the way they treated the Chinese in Nanking, it's going to be very unpleasant indeed. Jap soldiers have been conditioned not to value any life except for that of the Emperor. They're not troubled by a conscience and they'll have no mercy.'

Another silence.

Her father said, 'Well, thanks for the warning, Lawrence... I'll certainly bear it in mind. How about another *stengah?*'

Susan stopped listening and went back to her room. The *amah* had put the mosquito netting in place and sprayed round with the Flit gun. She undressed and lay down on the bed, limbs draped over the bolster to keep cool. Lawrence Trent had seemed rather nice at first but he wasn't. He was one of those people who took a delight in scaremongering, and there were quite a few of them in Singapore. Her father would take no notice, so there was no need for panic. The idea of sailing off to Australia, of all places, was ridiculous. She'd say so at breakfast if it wouldn't give away the fact that she'd eavesdropped.

Better than falling into Jap hands ... they'll have no mercy. No need to think about that because it would never happen.

A mosquito must have somehow escaped the Flit gun. She could hear it whining and dive-bombing the netting again and again, keeping her awake. She rearranged her legs round the bolster to get cooler and tried to ignore the maddening sound.

Four

Roger Clark was very sweet but it had been a mistake to encourage him. He took her to the cinema in the Cathay Building to see a rather boring film and to dinner afterwards at the restaurant above, which he probably couldn't afford. During dinner he talked about Esher and his home in Esher Park Avenue. Apparently there was a pub called the Star on the green and another called the Bear in the High Street. There was also an Odeon cinema and a place called the Moor Place Hotel which was rather good for dinner. And a racecourse.

'Sandown Park,' he said enthusiastically. 'I expect you've heard of it. It's rather well known.'

She stifled a yawn. 'Sorry, no.'

'Of course, you've got a marvellous race-course here. And Esher's nothing like Singapore – not nearly as exciting. But, actually, I find I miss it rather a lot. There's still a lot to be said for dear old England, isn't there?'

She thought of the grey skies and the bone-chilling cold, of foggy London and the grandparents' tall and silent house in Kensington.

'I wouldn't really know. I've never spent much time there. I've always lived in Malaya.'

'Gosh, that must be rather odd. I mean, you're English but you don't know England.'

'It doesn't worry me. I love Malaya.'

'Yes ... it's an amazing place. But I don't think I'd want to stay here for ever. I'll probably be jolly glad to get home in the end.'

'And I expect your parents will be jolly glad when you do.'

She could picture the scene: a motherly mother at the doorway of the house in Esher – mock-Tudor perhaps, like some of the black and white colonial ones in Singapore. She would be wiping away her tears, and there'd be a gruff father standing behind her, hiding his emotion. Both so proud of their returning soldier son.

'They don't fuss, thank goodness,' Roger was saying. 'The trouble is I'm an only child,

113

which makes it a bit tricky. Bit of a burden sometimes – being the one egg in the basket.'

'I am, too,' she pointed out.

'Different for a girl. You don't get sent off to war like us chaps.'

She looked at his nice, eager face. 'How old are you, Roger?'

'I was twenty last month, actually.'

'Well I hope you'll be home in time for your twenty-first.'

'So do I. Looks like we'll be going across on to the mainland at any moment, though, so it doesn't seem too likely. I'm not supposed to mention that, of course.'

Later on, he asked if she would mind awfully going out with him again. It would be absolutely marvellous if she would, he said. She could see that he was badly smitten, which was a nuisance because she didn't want to hurt him.

She dodged the issue. 'But you said you'd probably be leaving the island soon. You'll be away on the peninsula.'

He sighed. 'That's true. I suppose we'll have to wait and see.'

Milly was standing on the steps at the entrance to the Tanglin Club, looking worried.

'Geoff and Vin aren't here yet, Susie. They must have got held up at the hospital.'

They sat down in the hall and watched people coming and going. Milly kept jumping up to go and see if the Australians had arrived and Susan was just beginning to hope they never would, when she reappeared arm in arm with Geoff who had brought along, not the expected Vin but the one a called Ray: Mr Know-All himself.

'I'm really sorry,' Milly whispered as they walked over to the courts. 'Vin had to go on duty. But Geoff says Ray's a good player so you'll probably win.'

They won easily because he turned out to be an *extremely* good player and because Milly was pretty hopeless. He had a serve like a cannonball and a forehand to match but he didn't poach like Clive, or shout 'mine' when it wasn't. Afterwards they cooled off with drinks beside the pool and she felt inclined to be gracious towards him.

'Do you play a lot of tennis in Australia?'

'A fair amount. We've got the climate for it.'

'You're rather good.'

'You're not so bad yourself, Miss Roper.'

It was the first compliment he'd paid – if you could call it one.

'Thank you.'

'And this is a nice club.'

'Yes, it is, isn't it?'

'Very English.'

'It would be. It's run by them.'

'No Asians allowed?'

'Not as members. Only as guests.'

'Don't you find that a mite odd?'

'What's odd about it?'

'Not letting the natives in. It's their country, after all.'

'They have their own clubs, actually. They prefer it that way.'

'Can't say I blame them, with the welcome they'd get here.' He was observing her from behind his dark glasses. 'How's the secretarial course going?'

'All right.'

'You don't sound too thrilled.'

'It's hard to be thrilled by a typewriter and squiggles in a notebook.'

'Do something else, then.'

'You've already suggested that I go and drive ambulances.'

'It was a good idea of mine. You can drive, can't you? That's what you said.'

'I can drive a car.'

'Then you could drive an ambulance. And you've plenty of spare time.'

'But why would I want to?'

'To do something useful for a change.'

'Learning shorthand and typing *is* useful.'

'I bet you're lousy at it. You'll be no help to the war effort.'

Milly said loyally, 'She helps already. She's a Buy a Bomber girl.'

'A what?'

'A Buy a Bomber girl. They sell programmes whenever there are special performances of the latest films at the Cathay cinema. Everyone wears evening dress and all the money from the programmes goes towards buying bombers. It's a big social event. They always report it in the *Tribune*.'

The dark glasses turned on her again. She couldn't see the eyes behind them but she had a fair idea of their expression.

'My word. Fancy that.'

She stood up. 'If you'll all excuse me, I think I'll go for a swim.'

When she came out of the pool the Australians had gone.

'They had to get back to the hospital,' Milly said.

'Good riddance. Just don't ask me to play tennis with any more of them.'

'There is a telephone call, *missee*. A gentle-

117

man wishes to speak to you. He did not say a name.'

'Thank you, Soojal.'

She picked up the receiver in the hall. 'Hallo.'

'Ray Harvey here.'

'Oh. What do you want?'

'Are you busy?'

'It's Sunday. I'm going to church this morning.'

'How about this afternoon?'

'I'll be going swimming at the club.'

'That's a shame.'

'Why?'

'Well, I could probably pinch one of the ambulances for an hour. If you came over to the hospital we could take it out for a run. See how you get on.'

'No, thank you.'

'It's not that difficult.'

'I dare say. I'm just not interested.'

'OK. No worries. If you change your mind, you can find me here at the hospital.'

St Andrew's cathedral was packed for the Sunday morning service and sunlight was streaming down from the high windows like a divine benediction on the congregation. Lady Battersby was sitting directly in front of Susan. Her grey hair, coiled beneath the brim of her straw hat, looked like a large snail's shell; her husband, beside her, had a small head on the end of a long wrinkled neck, just like a tortoise. They sang 'Soldiers of Christ arise' and 'Lead us, heavenly Father, lead us', plodded through Psalm 11 and the endless *Te Deum laudamus*. The sermon was something to do with trusting in God and seemed equally endless. *Be strong ... have faith in the Lord ... put your hand into His and He will guide and protect you.* Susan hardly listened.

Afterwards, Ghani drove them to the Harrisons in Ridley Park for curry tiffin. Several young English army officers had been invited, fresh off the boat; and there was also Denys.

'You turn up everywhere,' she told him. 'Are you on the scrounge, as usual?'

'A fellow has to eat and the food here's always excellent. Also the drink. You're looking absolutely stunning, by the way.'

'I'm not in the mood for sweet talk, Denys.'

'What's the trouble? Has somebody ruffled your feathers?'

'I've been told that I ought to be doing something useful for the war effort.'

'Such as?'

119

'Driving ambulances.'

Denys grinned. 'I must say I can't imagine you behind the wheel.'

'Actually, I can drive, you know. I got our *syce* to teach me.'

'But you're not really the sort, are you?'

'What exactly do you mean by that? What sort?'

'Well, the ambulance ladies I've seen are usually a pretty fearsome lot. Biceps like prizefighters. Who on earth suggested it to you, anyway?'

'An Australian doctor.'

He waved his spoon over his plate of curry. 'You don't want to take any notice of Aussies; living upside down gives them funny ideas.'

She said, 'You don't think I'd be capable of it, do you?'

'Capable of what?'

'You don't believe I could drive an ambulance. I can see it by your face, Denys. And you think it's all very amusing.'

'Now, I didn't say that, sweetie. I just said I couldn't *imagine* you doing it. Leave that sort of thing to the battleaxe *mems*. Plenty of those around. You make a gorgeous Buy a Bomber girl – much more up your street. I'd stick to that, if I were you. I'll always buy a programme from you, I promise.'

'Is that all you think I'm capable of, then? Selling programmes?'

'Hang on ... no need to get so steamed up.'

'I'm not joking, Denys.'

'No, I can see that. There's an enormous bee buzzing around in your bonnet – put there by that big bad Aussie.'

'Have you still got the MG?'

'It awaits without.'

'Good. You can drop me at the Alexandra Hospital.'

The British military hospital had been built in the thirties – a large, three-storeyed white building with red-tiled roofs and verandahs and surrounded by lush tropical gardens. Denys drove the MG up to the main entrance.

'Want me to wait?'

'No thanks.'

He said, 'Look, there's no earthly need to do this, Susan. You don't have to prove anything to me.'

'I'm not proving it to you, Denys.'

'Or to anyone else, for that matter.'

She said, 'Actually, I'm proving it to myself. Thanks for the lift.'

She got out of the car and went inside the

building. The high ceilings and whirring fans made it nice and cool but the sourpuss at the reception desk was anything but welcoming.

'Captain Harvey? He's not on duty today.'

'Where could I find him?'

'I'm sorry but I have no idea.'

'I was supposed to meet him here at the hospital.'

'Well, he left no message to that effect.'

'Do you have his phone number?'

'I'm afraid not.'

She walked down a corridor and stopped a starchy nurse who was as unhelpful as the receptionist, and another who was in too much of a rush to speak at all. She went on, passing wards where white mosquito nets hung at the heads of long rows of beds, like ready shrouds. The beds were full of men with things wrong with them. She saw bandages and plaster casts, tubes and drips, pulleys and weights. There was a nauseating hospital smell. She went back to the entrance to see if Denys had waited, after all, but he hadn't and she was just wondering what to do next when she caught sight of the Australian walking up through the gardens. She waited until he reached her.

'I thought I'd give it a try, after all.'

He looked her up and down. 'You're not exactly dressed for it.'

He was wearing khaki shorts and an open-necked khaki shirt, sleeves rolled up, while she was still in her church frock, high heels, white cotton gloves, a smart little veiled straw hat perched on her forehead, handbag over her arm.

'Does it matter? Where do we go?'

The ambulance, parked round the back of the hospital, was much larger than she had expected: more like a small lorry and with big red crosses painted on the roof and on each side.

'An Austin K2Y,' Ray Harvey said. 'Better known as a Katie. Steel-framed, with wood floor, canvas roof and sides and doors. Three tons, but you ought to be able to manage her. I used to drive one like it as a student. It's not hard.'

He opened the double doors at the back which were painted with two more red crosses. 'Folding steps for getting in and out.' He unfolded them. 'Come and take a peek inside.'

'Is that necessary?'

'Too right, it is.'

She clambered up after him and listened to the lecture.

'Two bunks on each side, as you see, with rails for stretchers. Room for four lying or ten sitting patients. The top bunks crank up and down. That door at the far end connects with the driver's cab. The window in it's so you'll be able to see what's going on back here. Electric lights, air vents up front and a vented window on both sides that slides shut, if necessary.' He tapped a locker on the wall. 'Drinking-water tank housed in this one – here's the tap below.' He opened the second locker. 'Dressings, bandages, all the basic medical kit in this one.' He reached inside. 'Morphine. A quarter grain ready to inject in an emergency.'

'Morphine?'

'A very strong painkiller.'

It looked rather like a small tin tube of toothpaste with a needle stuck on the end. He held it up before her eyes. 'Easy to work, see. You take the cover off, get hold of this wire hoop at the end of the needle and push down to break the seal. Then you chuck the loop away and stick the needle in – the best place is the back of the upper arm, other-wise a thigh or buttock will do. It goes in all the way. Then you squeeze the tube from the bottom till it's empty. By the way, don't forget to pin the empty tube to the patient's clothing after, to show it's been given. Or you can write an M on their forehead.'

She shuddered. Injections, needles, pain...

'I thought I was supposed to be doing the driving.'

'You are.'

'Then I wouldn't have anything to do with all this, would I?'

'Would it bother you?'

'Yes, it would. I'm not very good with blood and gore. Or with needles. That sort of thing makes me feel quite sick.'

'Well, you needn't worry too much, Miss Roper. There'd always be a nurse or medical orderly with you.'

He said it in a dry sort of way, looking down at her, and he was standing very close because there wasn't much room. To be fair, she could see what Milly had meant about his eyes. She turned away. 'Shall we get on with the driving, then? Isn't that what we're here for?'

'That's right. You get in on the passenger side. I'll drive the first part.'

There was no proper door to the cab, just a piece of canvas that had been rolled back and tied with leather straps, and it was tricky getting on board. She put one foot into the iron stirrup but her skirt hampered her and so did her high heels, and there was nothing inside the cab to grip hold of.

He leaned across from the driver's seat. 'Take my hand.'

He hauled her in like a sack of rice and she landed on her knees on the wooden floor, hat askew.

'Where do I sit?'

He pointed to a sort of cushioned box against the wall. 'On there.'

She sat down, straightening her hat, smoothing her skirt.

'I'm used to a left-hand drive, like our Buick.'

'It shouldn't make too much difference.'

He started the engine and there was a peculiar whining sound from under the bonnet as they moved off, nothing whatever like the soft well-bred purr of the Buick. From the corner of her eye, she watched the Australian driving. He had those brawny, bronzed arms that all Aussies seemed to have and he would have been a lot stronger, physically, than she was, but, even so, it looked fairly simple.

'We'll find somewhere quiet, Miss Roper,' he said. 'Then you can take over.'

Somewhere quiet was a rough and winding track through an old pepper plantation.

126

The monsoon rains the day before had turned the earth to mud and the ambulance churned its way along between the pepper trees, rocking and lurching over the uneven ground. She clung to a leather strap, to her hat and to her handbag. They came to a halt and he switched off the engine.

'Your turn now.'

'Why couldn't we have stayed on a decent road?'

'You're a learner, Miss Roper. Remember?'

'You can call me Susan. Miss Roper's making me nervous.'

They changed places, which meant her clambering down backwards, groping blindly with one foot for the stirrup. She missed it and fell into the mud.

'It's easier getting in on the driver's side,' he said. 'You'll have the wheel to grab hold of.'

He stood by, no help at all, while she clambered in awkwardly and settled herself in the driver's seat.

'I can't reach the pedals.'

He fiddled with a catch and manhandled the seat forward. 'Strewth, don't you ever wear sensible shoes, Susan?'

'Not if I can help it.'

She waited while he went round to the

other side and swung himself in, easy as pie.

'Ready?' he said.

'What about the gears? How do they work?'

He leaned over and pushed the stick around. 'First is forward – but you almost never use it. Second is back towards you, third across and forward, top straight back down. OK?'

'Where's reverse?'

'Forget about that for the moment. Clutch, brake, throttle, just like on a car. You'll need to double-declutch when you change gear, by the way.'

'Double what?'

'Put your foot down on the clutch, the gear into neutral, take your foot off the clutch and get the revs up with the throttle. Then right foot off, clutch down again, move the stick into gear, foot off the clutch and step on the throttle.'

'I can't possibly remember all that.'

'You'll soon get the hang of it. Start her up and I'll put her in second for you. No need for any revs, just bring your foot slowly off the clutch and away she'll go.'

The ambulance stayed still.

'You forgot the handbrake,' he said, releasing it for her.

128

They jolted slowly down the track and she moved the stick in the general direction of third gear. There was a hideous shrieking noise.

'Foot down hard on the clutch.'

'It *is*.'

He put his hand over hers and pushed the stick forward. 'Get the revs up. Left foot down again.' He pushed the stick across and further forward. 'That's in third now. More revs *quick*.'

Fourth was no easier. She drove on, crashing her way through gears, stalling the engine and having to restart and go through the whole exhausting process again. The steering, when she managed to get going at all, was hard to control and she had to keep correcting to avoid trees. Her left leg was trembling with the constant effort of stamping on the clutch, both arms ached and her left palm had been rubbed raw by the gearstick. Also, her church frock was soaked in sweat and her white gloves were black. At a sharp bend in the track, she braked, swerved and stalled. Almost burst into tears.

'Start her up again.'

'I can't.'

'Yes, you can.' He took off her veiled hat and tossed it on the floor. 'And you'll see a lot better without that.'

She drove on sulkily, ignoring the shrieks of protest from the gearbox, until they reached a clearing at the end of the track.

'Turn round here,' he said. 'You'll need to reverse.'

'How am I supposed to see behind me?'

'Use the side mirrors. To get into reverse, lift the gearstick, push over and pull back towards you to the right.'

She pulled and pushed in vain, the sweat running down her face.

'You might at least help.'

He reached across again and guided the stick, his hand over hers.

'OK, you're in reverse now.'

The clearing wasn't very big and turning round meant going backwards and then forward, then backwards and forward again and then backwards and forward some more, the engine howling, the gears shrieking, the wheels spewing out great arcs of muddy water. She could hardly see a thing in the mirrors.

'Well, at least you missed the trees,' he said when they were finally facing the opposite way.

He took over when they reached the road, which meant changing places and him hauling her on board again. She rescued her hat and her handbag, checked her reflection in her compact mirror, wiped away the splatters of mud and got out her lipstick.

He was lighting one of his squashed cigarettes with a match. He blew the flame out and chucked the match over the side. 'By the way, Susan, the patients won't give a damn how you look. It's how you drive that counts.'

She snapped the compact shut. 'So, how was I?'

'No flaming good. You'd never pass the test.'

'Test? What test? You didn't tell me anything about that.'

'Well, you didn't think you'd be let loose on the road without one, did you? It takes weeks to train an ambulance driver.'

'*Weeks?*'

'Only we don't have that much time, so you'll have to learn a lot quicker.'

'I don't *have* to do anything, thank you very much.'

'That's right, you don't. You can go back to selling your society programmes, if you like.'

'Yes, I certainly can.'

He drove her to Cavenagh Road and her anger simmered and bubbled like a volcano all the way. When he stopped outside the house, it erupted.

'You're a rotten stinking Aussie bastard, Ray Harvey. You never meant to give me a chance. You just wanted to make a fool of me.'

He shook his head. 'You've got me wrong there, Susan. I thought you'd be a whole lot tougher. And I didn't reckon on you giving up so easily.'

'Who said anything about giving up?'

'You did.'

'I did *not*.'

'It sounded just like it.'

'Well, I'm not.'

She jumped down from the ambulance, straight into a muddy puddle. He leaned out.

'Here, you forgot your handbag.'

He lobbed it over but she fumbled the catch and the bag fell into the puddle. She stood, fuming, as she watched the ambulance speeding away.

Five

'Good morning, *missee*.'

'Good morning, Soojal. Good morning, Daddy.'

She took her place at the breakfast table; Rex was in his place, under it and waiting for titbits. Her father looked over the top of the *Straits Times*.

'Sleep well, poppet?'

'Not very. The storm woke me up.'

'Yes, it was a bad one.'

As a rule she slept through thunderstorms, but the one last night had been unusually ferocious. Torrential rain, wind tearing at the chicks, blinding flashes of lightning, ear-splitting claps of thunder. This morning, though, everything was as calm and peaceful as a lotus pool: the sun filtering through the mist, trees and bushes and plants perfectly still, the only sounds sweet birdsong, cicadas and the clinking spades of the *kebuns* working over by the tennis court.

Soojal brought her coffee and a plate of fruit – slices of pineapple, mangosteens, rambutans, little bananas. She picked out a mangosteen, her favourite, and started to peel away the hard purple skin.

'What are Arjun and Kumar doing?'

'Digging a shelter.'

She stopped peeling. 'A shelter? What on earth for?'

Her father turned a page. 'Just a precaution, poppet. In case the Japs should take it into their heads to drop bombs on us.'

Her stomach fluttered – a chilly, silly little flutter of fear. 'How could they? They're thousands of miles away from Singapore.'

'They might come nearer.'

'But we could easily stop them if they tried, couldn't we?'

'I'm sure we could, but I think it's sensible to be prepared.'

He smiled at her, making light of it, but she could tell that he was serious. He had believed Lawrence Trent. He must have done.

'It'll ruin the look of the tennis court. Can't it go somewhere else, out of sight?'

'It's in a very good place up against the bank. And you can still have your tennis parties, if that's what's worrying you.' The newspaper was lowered and folded firmly. 'I've been thinking, poppet, that it might be sensible, too, if you and Mummy were to go somewhere safer – just for the time being.'

'Where do you mean?'

'Away from Singapore. And Malaya.'

'But *why?* We're perfectly safe here.'

'We don't know that for certain. I wouldn't want to take the risk – not for you and Mummy.'

'Where on earth would we go?' She knew very well.

'Well, I'd thought of you both going to England, but the voyage would be too long and too dangerous. Australia would be a better choice.'

They'd have to drag her, kicking and screaming, up the gangplank. Better not to say that, though. Better to think of a good reason for staying.

'I could be quite useful here, actually. At the Alexandra Hospital.'

'You mean like your friend Milly? I've no objection to your lending a hand there for the moment, if that's what you want. In fact, I'm all for it.'

'Not exactly like Milly. I've thought of volunteering as an ambulance driver. Remember I told you about that army chap who gave me some driving lessons?'

'Very irresponsible of him – whoever he was.'

135

'These other people give you proper lessons, apparently, and a test. Make sure you're up to it. After all, you do your civil defence thing, Daddy. It's only fair to let me do my bit too, don't you think?'

She smiled at him sweetly – the same smile she had used ever since she had been a little girl, the one that usually got her what she wanted. It worked, but not completely.

'Well, you can give it a try, if you like. For the time being. But I warn you, poppet, I'm serious about sending you and Mummy away. If things get any worse, you'll go. Grandmother too.'

'She'd never leave Penang.'

'She might not have any choice.'

He gave Rex the last of his toast, patted her shoulder as he left the table. 'Just remember what I've said.'

When she had finished breakfast she walked down the verandah steps and across the lawn towards the tennis court. Sweep appeared from nowhere particular to say hallo and wound himself round her ankles. She picked him up and cradled him in her arms; he purred loudly. A dozen or so cats had come and gone over the years – Persians, Siamese, Burmese, moggies of all colours and kinds – but Sweep, the stray, beat them all. Not for looks – he was still a skinny little thing – but for character. She had come across him, a miserable scrap of matted black fur crouched in a doorway, and when she had picked him up he had started purring at once in her arms. She had taken him home, fed him, bathed him, got rid of the fleas and the worms, combed the matted fur, given him a whole new life.

The *kebuns* looked up from their digging to smile their betel-nut-stained smiles. When she had been very small the sight had scared her because it looked like a mouthful of blood.

'*Tuan* want earth house, *missee*. We dig big hole.' Arjun pointed to sheets of corrugated iron lying beside the mound of soil. 'We make very strong.'

Behind the smiles they were puzzled, but they would do exactly as the *tuan* had ordered; it wasn't for them to question a white man's whim. She set Sweep down and stared into the hole while the cat peered curiously over the edge. Water was already seeping in at the bottom. Singapore, after all, was built on a swamp.

Arjun spat out a gobbet of red. 'We work very quick, *missee*. *Tuan* say very important.'

She left them digging and Sweep watching them.

The sun had broken through, the mist had vanished and the day was already hot. A lovely day with no clouds in the sky. No sign of another storm or more rain. Too nice to spend indoors pounding away at a typewriter and making squiggles. A swim at the club would be a much better idea and a lazy day lying by the pool, doing absolutely nothing. The Campbells were giving a party in the evening which might be quite fun. No need to think about the horrible shelter; no need to think about the horrible Japs; certainly no need to think about horrible Australia. The only thing she needed to think about was what to wear.

The examiner said sharply, 'Slow down. You took that corner much too fast. You'll have sick patients in the back, remember. If you drive like that, you'll throw them about. You should treat them like eggs.'

Silly old duffer – he was even more of a fusspot than Ghani. Next time he ticked her off like that she'd stop dead, get out and stalk off.

After all, she was getting the hang of things much better. She could change gear quite smoothly now and she could reverse perfectly well. She'd proved it, backing round a corner and all the way up a side street.

'Let's see you stop and start on this hill – without running back an inch.'

It was a steep hill, the handbrake was a pig and there were three tons of ambulance to hold steady. Not easy. She made a mess of it: ran backwards at least two feet.

The examiner clicked his tongue. 'That won't do at all. You'll have to do a lot better than that before I can pass you.'

She drove on, turning left and turning right, as he issued orders. Finally they were back where they'd started.

He looked at her with his cold fish eyes. 'You're not up to the required standard, I'm afraid. And frankly, I doubt you ever will be.'

She said indignantly, 'What's wrong with my driving?'

He opened the door between them and pointed to the drinking glass he had placed earlier on one of the bunks, filled to the brim with water. It was lying on its side, empty. 'That's what's wrong with it, Miss Roper.'

Clive Godwin was at the Campbells' party with a new girlfriend – a shy mouse who looked at him adoringly. Just the sort he needed. Denys was there too, which had been no surprise. She told him about failing the ambulance-driving test.

'I shouldn't worry about it, sweetie. It wasn't your sort of thing, anyway.'

'Oh, I'm not giving up, Denys. Not now.'

He invited her sailing – someone had lent him a boat.

'The same person who lent you the MG?'

'No, this is a different chap. One of those intrepid Volunteers. They've sent him off to play soldiers upcountry.'

He collected her in the MG and they drove out to the sailing club at Changi where the boat was moored – a rather smart little dinghy called *Kittiwake*.

She watched him fiddling about with the sail. 'I hope you know what you're doing, Denys.'

'I was born and brought up by the sea, I'll have you know. My misspent youth was spent going up and down the Solent.'

'In England?'

'Of course. The best country in the world, in my opinion.'

'What made you come to Malaya, then?'

'Adventure. Loot. The call of the mysterious East.'

'But you'll go back to England – in the end.'

'Lord, yes. Eventually.'

'Marry some nice girl and settle down?'

'That's the general idea.' He pulled on a rope and the sail rose, billowing and flapping in the breeze. 'You, I hope.'

'Me? I wouldn't do at all, Denys. I don't like England. I'm staying put in Malaya.'

'You'll change your mind, mark my words. Hop in quick. We're all set to go.'

They sailed along the east coast, weaving in and out of little islets that were no more than mangrove swamps. Denys, she soon saw, had spoken the truth about knowing how to sail. All she had to do was sit back, watch the scenery and duck her head whenever the boom went over.

'That beach looks lovely, Denys. Can we go and swim there?'

'Anything you say, O Princess. But you'll have to take your clothes off.'

'I've got my bathing costume on underneath.'

'Drat.'

He ran *Kittiwake* gently on to the shore. The beach had pure-white sand edged with palms and the whispering casuarina trees, and it was completely deserted. They walked along its length and she kept stopping to pick up pretty shells. At the far end she shaded her eyes with her hand to look out across the shimmering sea.

'My father's convinced the Japs are going to drop bombs on us.'

'Not much likelihood of that.'

'I didn't think so either. But some newspaper correspondent came to dinner the other night and I overheard him talking to my father afterwards.'

'Eavesdroppers never hear anything good.'

'That's true. And this wasn't good at all. He thinks we're in deadly danger. He said the Japs will certainly attack us and that we aren't properly defended or prepared.'

'Newspaper chaps make it all up.'

'But my father believed him. He's having an air raid shelter built in the garden and he's thinking of packing my mother and me off to Australia. Isn't it ridiculous?'

They turned to walk back.

Denys said, 'Maybe it's not such a bad idea, though, sweetie. Just to be on the safe side.'

She stopped, staring at him. 'You don't really imagine I'd leave, do you, Denys? Like a meek little lamb?'

'Well, no ... not actually.'

They walked on; she picked up another shell – a pretty pink and white one. 'The newspaper man also said that the Japs will know everything about us from the ones that have been living in Singapore. They've been spying on us, apparently.'

'No need to worry about that any more. A lot of the Nips scarpered back in July – haven't you noticed how few there are around these days?'

She frowned. 'The Jap who runs the camera shop near us has closed down but I hadn't thought much about it.'

'He'll have popped off back to Japan. And we'll soon be rounding up the rest and booting them off the island.' He grinned at her. 'Forget about the Japs. How about that swim to cool off? Race you in.'

She ran after him and they splashed into the water and swam around and then came out and lay on the sand. He leaned over and kissed her.

'Your moustache always tickles, Denys.'

'Well, you know what Kipling said.'

'No, I don't. What did he say?'

'A kiss without a waxed moustache is like eating an egg without salt.'

'What a peculiar idea! Anyway, yours isn't that sort of moustache and I don't take salt

143

with eggs.'

'They taste much better.'

'Hmmm.'

After a while, she said, 'We ought to go, Denys.'

'Why? It's very nice here. Like being ship-wrecked on a desert island.'

'We've got a perfectly good seaworthy ship waiting for us over there. And it's getting late. Come on.'

He called after her, 'You forgot your shells.'

'Leave them. They belong here.'

She helped him push the dinghy out into the water and turned to look back over her shoulder as they sailed away. At the beautiful stretch of white sand with no guns or trenches or ugly barbed wire to spoil it.

The fish-eyed examiner had been replaced by a much nicer man and there was no nonsense about putting glasses of water in the back. Susan gave him her best smile, hitched up her skirt a notch and did her very best driving. She took the ambulance sedately through bends, up and down steep hills and backed it round corners, and only crashed the gears once.

'Well done, Miss Roper. You did very well.'

'You mean I've passed?'

'Indeed you have.' He patted her bare knee. 'Keep on like you did today, my dear, and you'll be fine.'

The sourpuss at the hospital reception desk said, 'I'm afraid I've no idea where Captain Harvey is at the moment. He's on duty and he'll be very busy, in any case.'

'I'd like to leave a message for him.' She scrawled on a scrap of paper, handed it over. 'Would you see that he gets this?'

He phoned that evening. 'I got your note, Susan. Congratulations. How about a drink to celebrate?'

'All right.' It would be a pleasure to see him grovel.

She'd half-expected him to collect her in an ambulance – wouldn't have put it past him – but it was an ordinary old car. Nothing special at all. Instead of taking her to one of the usual watering holes he drove out of town to a stony hillside overlooking the sea. The bar was only a tin shack but it had a spectacular view of the lights of Singapore and a three-piece Hawaiian band was strumming away softly. A nice little warm breeze fanned her hair as she listened to the South Seas music and watched the lights twinkling below. Ten thousand miles away in freezing cold, winter London there wouldn't be any lights at all.

She sipped her drink through a straw. 'I bet you were surprised that I passed.'

'No. I knew you would – if you wanted to. Now, let's see if you can stick it out.'

He wasn't exactly grovelling. Quite the contrary. She'd imagined him apologetic, at the very least. Impressed by what she'd done.

She poked around in her glass with the straw, hooked out a chunk of pineapple and chewed on it. 'You don't think much of me, do you, Ray?'

'I reckon you're pretty spoiled.'

'You've got a nerve. You don't know me at all.'

'You don't know me either, Susan. So let's call it quits.'

She fished out another piece of pineapple. 'Does this dump serve any food? I'm absolutely starving.'

'No. We go somewhere else for that.'

It was another out-of-town shack, but Indian this time. There were bare wooden tables, rusty ceiling fans clattering overhead, and instead of plates, wet banana leaves. The food was very hot and very spicy.

'Makes a change from Raffles,' he said,

'It's certainly different.' Her mouth felt as

though it was on fire.

'Food too hot for you?'

'Not at all.' She took a gulp of lemonade. 'Tell me, what do you eat in Australia? Kangaroos?'

He smiled. 'Kangaroos are tough. We eat beef. Lots of steaks.'

'I've heard you even have steak for breakfast.'

'Too right. With a fried egg on top.'

'How revolting.'

'We don't think so. We eat lots of seafood, too.'

'What sort?'

'Barramundi, snapper, salmon, prawns, oysters, lobsters – sharks, sometimes.'

'*Sharks?*'

'They taste pretty good and we've got plenty of them in the sea.'

'We have them here, too.'

'They're tiddlers compared with ours. Ours are a lot bigger and meaner. They ride right in on the surf and grab hold of you in a few feet of water, if you're not careful. When I was a student on the wards there were always patients with terrible shark bites – they were the lucky ones.'

'Lucky?'

'The others were dead.'

She said, 'You come from Sydney, don't you?'

'Born and brought up there. Biggest and best natural harbour in the world, wonderful sailing, wonderful beaches, wonderful surfing–'

'Wonderful everything?'

'That's about it. I reckon I feel about Sydney the same way you feel about Singapore.'

'Have you ever been to England?'

He shook his head. 'I'll have to go one day to take my Fellowship exams in London. We can't do those in Australia.'

'Don't all you Aussies have a huge chip on your shoulder about the English? That's what I've always heard. We're bloody Poms.'

'Too right you are.'

'I suppose you think we're frightfully stuck-up.'

'In Australia Jack's as good as his master.'

'Well, you're all descended from convicts, so he would be.'

She'd hoped to annoy him, to get under his thick skin, but not a bit of it. He only smiled.

'Sorry to disappoint you, but my grandfather came from a respectable and law-abiding family in Devon. His father kept a chemist's shop.'

'How fascinating.'

'He emigrated to Australia when he was eighteen.'

'What on earth for?'

'Adventure. He didn't like the idea of staying put in Devon for ever.'

'I can't blame him for that. I don't like England that much either. It's got a horrible climate. What's the weather like in Australia?'

'Depends where you are. It's a big country so it's got different climates. The further north you go, the hotter it is.'

'Well, you're upside down, aren't you? So everything would be the wrong way round.'

'True enough. We have summer in winter, and winter in summer.'

'It sounds awful.'

'It isn't.'

She gulped some more lemonade to put out the fire in her throat. 'My father thinks my mother and I ought to go there – to be safe from the Japs. Rather a joke, really.'

'Nothing to joke about. It'd be a whole lot safer than staying in Singapore.'

'You're the one who said I ought to be doing something useful here.'

'But you don't want to stick around too long if the Japs ever land on Malaya.'

'They wouldn't get very far, even if they did.'

He set down his beer glass, wiped his mouth with the back of his hand. 'That's what everyone here believes, but I wouldn't count on it, Susan. Not if you're smart.'

'You think I should run away, then? Personally, I don't think that's a very decent thing to do.'

'It may not be decent, but it'd be bloody sensible. Look at it like this. If Malaya turns into a battleground, you white women are going to be in the way and in big danger. You'd be doing the men a favour by getting out.'

He drove her back in the ordinary old car and without stopping in a secluded spot which most men did, if they could. She half-hoped that he'd try to kiss her when they reached the house so that she could have the pleasure of giving him the brush-off, but when he leaned across, it was only to push open the passenger door

She put on her gracious, being-very-nice-to-colonials voice. 'Would you like to come in and have a drink?'

'If I thought you really meant that, I might.'

'I do mean it.'

'No, you don't, Susan,' he said in his maddening way. 'Goodnight and good luck with the ambulance.'

Soojal met her in the hall. 'Good evening, *missee*. The *tuan* is on the verandah. I bring lime juice there for you?'

'Yes, please.'

Her father was sitting in one of the rattan armchairs, drinking his whisky *stengah* and smoking a cigar. He smiled at her but she could tell that he was in a bad mood.

'Nice evening, poppet?'

'Nothing special.'

'Who were you out with?'

'That Australian doctor from the Alexandra that I told you about.'

'Oh yes, the one who said we ought to be worrying more about the Japs.'

'He's still saying that. It's awfully boring.'

'It may be boring but he's absolutely right.'

She flopped on to the divan and Soojal brought the ice-cold lime juice. Her father drained his glass and held it out to the houseboy for a refill.

'I telephoned your grandmother earlier. She's refusing to leave Penang. Being very stubborn about it.'

So that was the cause of the bad mood. Susan could imagine the conversation –

hear her grandmother's voice. *Leave Penang! Certainly not, Thomas. Your father and I spent nearly fifty years together here. The Japs don't frighten me one bit.*

'I told you she would be.'

'It's absurd. The servants would look after the house. They've all been with her for years and they're completely trustworthy.' He flicked the ash off the end of his cigar 'And she'd be much safer down here with us in Singapore.'

Soojal brought another *stengah*. She waited for a few moments for it to take effect before she said casually, 'By the way, I passed the test.'

'What test?'

'Driving an ambulance. I told you about it, Daddy. They've been teaching me.'

'Oh yes, I'd forgotten about that – what with everything else going on. I'm still not too keen on the idea but at least you'll be doing more good than me filling in my wretched forms. For the time being, anyway.'

'The time being?'

'I'm afraid you won't be able to stay here much longer, poppet. It's getting too risky.'

'I'm not going to Australia, if that's what you mean.'

'You may not have any choice. And it's not such a bad place, from what I hear. Why don't you ask that Australian doctor of yours over to dinner one evening? He can tell us all about it.'

'He's not mine.'

'I'd like to meet him, though. He sounds interesting.'

'He isn't.'

'Ask him, just the same. I'd like to meet him.'

The uniform was better than she'd expected: khaki cotton slacks, a khaki shirt and a cloth peaked cap which she bashed around a bit and arranged at a fetching angle. By the time one of the *amahs* had taken in the slacks at the waist and darted the shirt, it looked quite reasonable and a bright-red lipstick worked wonders.

Her first job was to collect six army patients who were being sent down by train from the mainland. A Chinese medical orderly went with her to the Keppel Road railway station and everything was plain sailing. She stayed at the wheel, eyes front, window blind pulled down behind her, while the soldiers were carried out on stretchers and loaded into the back of the ambulance. She didn't have to see them and, for good measure, she dabbed some *Je Reviens* on her wrists so that she couldn't smell them either. Once the patients were on board, she drove them to the hospital. One of them groaned a lot – she could hear him above the engine noise – but the rest were quiet.

On the next trip she picked up a group of ten soldiers from their barracks in Dempsey Road. They had minor ailments and were far more trouble than the ones on stretchers, wolf-whistling as she drove up and shouting cheekily to her through the cabin door on the journey.

But, as she told Milly when they met over a cup of tea in the canteen, there was nothing to it, really, and there was still plenty of time to play tennis or go for a swim. Still the time and the energy to go to parties or out to dine and dance. Best of all, it was a wonderful excuse to skip lessons at Pitman's. She scarcely bothered to turn up for them any more.

She met Ray when she was waiting by her ambulance outside the hospital and he happened to come along.

'How's it going, Susan?'

'Fine. By the way, my father wants you to come to dinner one evening.'

'That's nice of him.'

'He wants to talk to you about Australia. I can't think why. How about tomorrow?'

'I'm on duty.'

'The day after? Eight o'clock.'

'OK. I'll be there.'

He walked on without a word said about the uniform or how she looked in it. Not that she cared.

'Susan tells me you come from Sydney, Captain Harvey?'

'That's right, sir.'

'A fine city, from all accounts. I hear the harbour is magnificent and that bridge of yours must be an amazing sight.'

'We think so, but then we're prejudiced.'

'I'd like to go to see it for myself one of these days.'

'It's worth the trip.'

Her father liked Ray, she could tell that. So did her mother, who was hard to please. He'd done all the right things, said all the right things, used all the right knives and forks. Her father went on asking questions about Australia and after dinner, when they sat out on the verandah, he said to Ray, 'I'm thinking of sending Susan and her mother to your country, if the Japs take it into their heads to try attacking us.'

'It makes sense to me, sir.'

'Of course they won't want to leave, but it might come to that. What do you think of the situation here in Malaya?'

'I think it's very bad.'

'So do I. Most people wouldn't agree with us – only a few have grasped the real truth. Everyone else has their head stuck firmly in the sand. They can't see how dangerous the Japs are. *Refuse* to see it.'

Her mother said, 'Oh, do stop going on about the wretched Japanese, Thomas. I'm sure Captain Harvey would far sooner talk about something else. Tell me, Captain, what is the weather like in Australia?'

She listened to him answering her mother, explaining to her about their upside-down temperatures and opposite seasons. And she watched him while she listened. Dishy, Milly had called him, but she couldn't see it herself – except for the eyes. A sort of green-grey and with smoky depths so that you couldn't exactly tell what he was thinking. Well, she knew what he thought of her because he'd told her. Pretty spoiled.

At the end of the evening she went to the

front door to see him out.

'You weren't much help,' she told him. 'My father's more determined to send us off to your ghastly country than ever.'

'Would you sooner he didn't care about what happened to you?'

'He's in a flap because some newspaper correspondent keeps telling him scary stories. That's all.'

They were standing out on the step beneath the portico and it was raining.

'I bet they're true.'

'I'm sick of hearing about the Japs,' she said. 'It's spoiling everything.'

'You'll be hearing a lot more, I reckon.'

Ghani was bringing the ordinary old car round, driving it under the portico out of the wet, stopping by the steps, getting out, standing at ramrod attention as he held the driver's door open.

She said, 'Your carriage awaits, sire.'

'Yeah, I'd noticed.' He looked down at her. 'Well, thanks for the evening.'

'It was my father who invited you.'

He said drily, 'I know. But you were there.'

He gave her one of those Aussie swatting-away-flies salutes as he drove off. The rain was coming down in torrents.

When she went back into the hall, Soojal

was still hovering. He would have heard the conversation at dinner and afterwards on the verandah and probably what had been said just now. Nothing was secret from him.

'You wish for anything, *missee?*'

She sighed. 'What I wish for is that everything could stay just as it's always been, Soojal.'

He nodded gravely. 'I understand, *missee*. I also wish the same.'

She rubbed the Buddha's fat tummy as she passed him on the way to bed. He smiled but it seemed to be a sad smile.

November turned into December. Roger Clark had been sent somewhere on the mainland and kept writing her letters that she didn't answer. It was kinder not to.

The usual scare-rumours were circulating. A Jap submarine had been spotted surfacing in the Johore Straits. Jap warships had been sighted off the southern tip of Indo-China. Jap planes had been seen in the skies over the peninsula. Nobody took them any more seriously than before, least of all the men that Susan transported to and fro in her ambulance.

'Don't you worry, love. We'll see them Nips off all right,' one of them told her breezily.

'Nothin' to it.'

Two big Royal Navy ships arrived from England. The new and reputedly unsinkable battleship, the *Prince of Wales*, and the battle cruiser, the *Repulse* – Lawrence Trent's 'old lady'. They steamed majestically into Keppel Harbour, their great grey bulk magnificent against the blue sky and the misty green islands. They were greeted by crowds of sightseers, loud cheers and a lot of patriotic flag-waving.

On the first Sunday of the month Susan went with a group of friends to the Sea View Hotel for the customary pre-lunch drinks – a dozen or so of them squashed into two cars, careering along the coast road to Tanjong Katong.

The hotel was even more crowded than usual but they commandeered a table and chairs and the Chinese boys brought drinks – cold Tiger beers, gin slings, iced lime juice. The laughing and the talk drowned out the orchestra's selection from *The Desert Song* and rounds of drinks were called for as though it was some big party – a grand celebration. She caught sight of fat, sweaty Paul and rabbit-toothed Marjorie, Clive's dreary friends from the time she'd been there before – still in Singapore and probably still feeling guilty about it.

Once again, the orchestra played a loud chord and there was a dramatic roll of drums. The singing began. Not so much singing as yelling.

There'll always be an England
And England shall be free...

Later, they went to swim at Tanglin where there was a lot of horseplay in the pool and shrieks of laughter. They spent the afternoon lounging idly in the shade of the trees and, afterwards, there was an impromptu party at someone's house with smoochy dancing to gramophone records. When Susan finally got home it was dark, a full moon shining down brightly on the city.

'*Missee* look very happy.'

'It's been rather a jolly day, Soojal.'

'That is good, *missee*. I bring lime juice?'

'No thanks. I'm off to bed.'

She rubbed the Buddha's fat tummy, skipped up the stairs and danced along the corridor

At first she thought it was another violent thunderstorm that had awoken her during the night. But the noise wasn't a storm. It was the staccato firing of guns, the distant

160

drone of aeroplanes, the muffled boom-boom of explosions. She ran out on to the upstairs verandah to see searchlight beams sweeping to and fro across the sky. The planes came closer, their engines louder. A high-pitched, whistling sound was followed by a deafening explosion that made the verandah shake beneath her bare feet.

Over in the servants' quarters, an *amah* started screaming hysterically. Much later, the air raid siren began its warning wail.

Six

At breakfast the *kebuns* were beavering away at the shelter by the tennis court, but otherwise everything seemed quite normal, as though the bombing raid had been nothing more than a bad dream. Amith brought orange juice, fruit and coffee, Rex was stationed under the table, Sweep stalking some quarry on the lawn. The sun was shining, the songbirds twittering, cicadas chorusing, her father calmly reading the *Straits Times.*

When Amith had gone her father said, 'It's

important to carry on as usual, poppet. To set an example to the servants. Show them there's nothing to worry about.'

'What if there's another raid tonight?'

'The Japs will find it much more difficult if they try it again. We made it easy for them last night. Lights blazing, no air raid warning until much too late, not one of our fighters in the air. And it wasn't only Singapore that they attacked, I'm afraid. They bombed Hong Kong and the American fleet in Hawaii, at the same time.'

She stared at him. 'How do you know?'

'They said so on the wireless this morning. There was a special news bulletin. No details yet but it means that the Americans will have to come into the war.'

'Then they'll help us.'

'I doubt if they'll be able to help Malaya. They'll have too much else on their plate. We'll have to fight our own war. You and Mummy will leave as soon as I can arrange it. There's to be no argument now from either of you – or from your grandmother either. She must get out of Penang and come down here to Singapore, whether she likes it or not.'

She fed the doves after breakfast, sitting on the verandah steps while they fluttered round her and perched on her shoulders, cooing in her ears. When she phoned Milly later, Milly didn't sound a bit alarmed.

'Daddy says the Japs tried to land in the north but we soon got rid of them. They'll never manage it.'

'They managed to bomb Singapore.'

'He says we'll be ready for them next time.'

'I hope he's right.'

'I'm on duty at the hospital later. How about you?'

'Not till tomorrow. And the good news is that Pitman's has closed down until after Christmas because of the bombing. No more typing, no more shorthand. I'm rather grateful to the Japs.'

Susan went with her mother to buy blackout material. It was a shock to see the bomb damage in Raffles Place – shops wrecked, glass and rubble in the streets, and Robinson's had been hit. The front of the store had been badly damaged, windows blown in. Tamil labourers were clearing away the rubble, and crowds of people had come to gawp – European, Eurasian, Chinese, Indian, Malay – gathered to stare at what the Japs had done.

Inside the store, there were long queues

and a shortage of assistants. Lady Battersby was complaining to a harassed floor manager.

'How much longer do you intend to keep me waiting?'

'I'm very sorry, madam. So many of our staff are busy clearing up, and everything has to be moved down from the restaurant.'

'Whatever for?'

'The top floor was bombed in the raid, madam. We're planning to reopen the restaurant temporarily in the basement, as soon as possible. Rest assured that refreshments will still be available to our customers.'

'I'm not concerned about your refreshments – only what I came for: a large quantity of your best blackout material to be delivered immediately to my address.'

The woman queueing in front of them said, 'I don't know what all the fuss is about. My husband says the Japs won't dare do it again.'

They went onto the Cold Storage where the glass shelves were intact and as well stocked as ever, but Maynards the chemist had boarded up its shattered windows against looters.

In the car, going home, her mother said, 'Daddy is insisting on us leaving Singapore.'

'Yes. I know.'

'I'm more than happy to go home to England but he wants us to go to Australia. He thinks it's safer there.'

'I'd far sooner stay in Singapore.'

'He won't let you, Susan. Not if the Japs go on bombing us. He wants Grandmother Penang to come with us too, but she's being very difficult about leaving her home. And I must say I don't much like the idea of coping with her on a long sea voyage. We've never exactly seen eye to eye.'

Denys telephoned in the early evening. 'Just wanted to make sure you were all right, sweetie.'

She was touched. 'Of course I'm all right. What have you been up to?'

'I've been busy rounding up Jap civilians and bunging them in a camp.'

'Do you think the bombers will pay us another visit tonight?'

'If so, we'll be ready for them.'

'We weren't very ready last night.'

'Well, apparently the ARP headquarters weren't manned so nobody could get a message to them to sound the siren, and the chap with the street-lighting master key was at an all-night cinema.'

'How pathetic.'

'Yes, isn't it? If they do come back, go and sit in that shelter of yours.'

'It's full of water at the moment; the mosquitoes love it.'

The blackout curtaining made the house unbearably hot and escaping to the verandah after dinner was a relief. In the moonlight, the lallang grass was a silver carpet, the palms giant black fans. She curled up on the divan and kicked off her shoes. The house-boys brought out coffee and her father's *stengah*.

He lit his cigar. 'If there's another raid tonight, we'll go to the shelter.'

Her mother said, 'Don't be ridiculous, Tom. I'm not sitting with my feet in muddy water, being bitten to death by mosquitoes.'

'The *kebuns* drained it today. It's all right now.'

'The water will come back again. It always does in Singapore. We live in a swamp.'

There was more argument about the shelter and, finally, her mother went off to bed. Her father went on smoking in silence for a moment, drinking his *stengah*.

The blackout curtain twitched and a shaft of yellow light showed at the edge of the doorway. 'There is a visitor, *Tuan*. Mr Trent. You wish him to be admitted?'

'Yes, certainly, Soojal. Show him out here.'

After a moment the blackout moved again like a stage curtain, and the newspaper correspondent emerged.

Her father stood up. 'Come and join us, Lawrence. You remember my daughter, don't you?'

'Of course. Good evening, Susan.' He bowed in her direction.

'You'll have a *stengah*, Lawrence?'

'Thank you. I could do with one. It's been a long day, one way and another. I'm sorry to disturb you, but I thought you might like to hear the latest news.'

'Bad, I take it?'

'It rather depends on your interpretation.'

'Wait till the boy has brought your drink – he'd better not hear it.'

Soojal came and went on silent feet. The ice tinkled in the *stengah* glass.

'Mind if I smoke my pipe?'

'Go ahead, Lawrence. You don't mind, do you, poppet?'

'Not at all.'

The acrid smell of pipe smoke joined the cigar's rich aroma.

'I don't want to alarm your daughter, Tom.'

'I should much prefer her to be aware of the facts. Carry on.'

'Very well. The press was issued with three communiqués today. The first said that the Japanese army landed at Singora and Patani in south Siam during last night and met with no resistance.'

'That doesn't surprise me. The Thais were never going to put up much of a fight.'

'It didn't surprise me either. But, unfortunately, the Japs have also landed men on the Malayan peninsula.'

'My God! Where?'

'At Badang and Sabak beaches, near the Siam border. Eight miles north-west of Kota Bahru.'

'I know the region. Sandy, no swamps – they chose a good place.'

'So it seems. According to the official report, they came ashore from troop ships in armour-plated barges. There was confused fighting and some of the Japs retreated. A spot of bother, as one British officer described it. Mopping-up operations are, apparently, in hand.'

'Mopping-up operations?'

'A nice soothing phrase used by our military to imply that a situation is well under control.'

'Is it?'

'I don't think so for a moment. Apparently

a considerable number of Japs managed to force their way inland. Our chaps are trying to cover up the bad news. Talking about regrouping and massing a counter-offensive. And there's worse. The Japanese air force have also been bombing and strafing our aerodromes in the north of the peninsula, including the one at Kota Bahru. They've destroyed more than half our planes in the process. And they bombed Penang, by the way.'

'Penang? My mother lives there. Do you have any details?'

'Not yet, I'm afraid. As I said, they're trying to keep a lid on everything. I take it you've seen the message from the commanders-in-chief posted up all over town?'

'Yes, I read it.'

'*We are ready; we have plenty of warning and our preparations have been made and tested,*' Lawrence Trent quoted drily. '*Japan will find that she has made a grievous mistake.* I think that was the general gist of it.'

'Most people seem to believe it.'

'And they'll go on believing it and trusting the commanders. I wish I could but I'm just a sceptical old hack, especially after what's just happened at Pearl Harbor and to Hong Kong.'

'The Governor sounded very confident.'

'He's a decent and honourable man but he's got both feet in the past. He was a schoolmaster once, you know, and he still plays by school rules, especially the cricket ones. Not the sort of tough leader you need in a war of this kind against people like the Japs. Anyway, I'm off upcountry first thing tomorrow, so I shall be seeing for myself what's going on. When I get back to Singapore, I'll let you know what I've found out.'

Her father said, 'Even if the Japs have got on to the peninsula, Lawrence, it's still inconceivable that they could make very much headway. There are surely more than enough of our troops up there to drive them out and I know the Malayan jungle – most of it's virtually impassable.'

'Not to the Japs. They'll know how to make full use of it. To infiltrate. Their objective will be first capture the north of the peninsula, and then progress steadily south to the Johore Straits and Singapore.'

'You're forgetting that we now have the *Prince of Wales* and the *Repulse* anchored in the Straits.'

'What *you're* forgetting, Tom, is that those ships have no proper air cover. The aircraft carrier that was supposed to accompany them from England is still back there under-going repairs. The Japs must know that perfectly well. Meanwhile, there will certainly be more bombing raids on Singapore.'

'We can take it.'

'Like the Londoners in the Blitz? But this isn't London. And this isn't England and the English standing united. This is a Far Eastern country with a big Asian population who think quite differently from us. They don't much care whether there'll always be an England. Of course, with the Americans in the war we'll win in the end. The Japs gave the sleeping tiger's tail a great big tug at Pearl Harbor and they'll regret it. But it's all going to take time and there's not enough of that left to save Malaya.' Lawrence Trent looked at her. 'I'm sorry to talk like this, Susan. I don't mean to frighten you.'

'I'm not frightened,' she said. 'I don't believe the Japs could ever take Singapore.'

'I believe they will. Which is why you and your mother should leave as soon as possible. Your grandmother, too.'

Her father said, 'I've been telling them that. My mother refuses to leave Penang, my wife wants to wait for a passage to England. And my daughter is too busy driving ambulances.'

'I'm afraid she'll be busier than ever.'

'How long do you think we've got left, Lawrence?'

'Two or three months – if we're very lucky.'

The air raid siren went again that night and they sat in the shelter being attacked, not by Japs, but by mosquitoes, before it turned out to be a false alarm and the all-clear was sounded. Rather than go back to bed, Susan sat for a while on the verandah steps in the heat of the night, watching the fireflies and listening to the croaking of bullfrogs. Sweep came out of the darkness to sit quietly beside her.

'I bring you something, *missee.*'

She turned her head. 'No, thank you, Soojal.'

'News not good, *missee.*'

'No, not very.'

'Japanese very bad people, *missee.* Better you not stay here.'

He'd been listening, of course. The servants always knew everything.

'I don't want to leave, Soojal.'

'I know, *missee.* But better you go.'

The *Prince of Wales* and the *Repulse* were both sunk by Japanese bombers two days later as

172

they patrolled the Malayan coast. A long convoy of ambulances drove to the docks to collect injured survivors being brought down to Singapore by ship. The orderly with Susan was a talkative little Welshman called Delfryn and, on the way, he gave her his unasked-for opinion of the disaster, his sing-song voice lifted above the noise of the engine and the whine of the gears.

'There'll be no hope for us now, miss. The Nip navy can do what they like, see. We've no decent ships left to stop them.'

It was pouring with rain and water was trickling through the ambulance air vents and running down her back.

'That's nonsense. We've still got other ships and we've got planes too.'

'Might as well be rowing boats. And all we've got for planes is a lot of old crates. The Japs have got those Zeros, haven't they? Much better than any of ours, so I hear. We don't stand a chance against them. Look how they sunk those two big ships – no trouble at all. Went down in a few minutes. And all those men drowned.'

'A lot of them were rescued.'

'Terrible burns, though – that's what I was told. And all kinds of nasty injuries.'

The destroyer *Electra* was already moored

at the docks, the gangplanks down to bring the wounded ashore. Susan stayed in the front cabin, keeping her eyes averted, the blind over the communicating door lowered. She could hear the bumps and bangs and the cursing that always went on when the stretchers were loaded. And she could hear the moans and cries of the injured men and smell the horrible stink of oil and another much more sickening smell which she realized, revolted, must be of burned human flesh. She poured several drops of *Je Reviens* on to her handkerchief and held it to her nose, breathing in deeply. After what seemed a very long time the orderly opened the door behind her and poked his head through.

'All aboard, miss. We can go now. Better get a move on but for God's sake don't bump this lot about.'

Treat them like eggs, that nasty driving examiner had said. She did her best but nervousness made her do some jerky gear changes and every time this happened, there were pitiful cries and moans from beyond the door. At the hospital she waited, shaking, while the stretchers were being manoeuvred out of the back. The Welshman stuck his head round the door.

'Can you come and keep an eye on this

one for a moment, miss, he's in a real state.'

'Can't someone else do it?'

'They're all busy. Come on, miss, he needs someone to hold his hand, that's all.'

She got up slowly and went through the doorway into the back of the ambulance. The orderly had gone, so had the three other stretcher cases. The fourth man was on a lower bunk. His face was swathed in bandages and he was scrabbling at them and sobbing hysterically. His arms were bandaged too and what little skin remained visible was black. The smell of burned flesh made her retch.

She managed to speak. 'It's all right. You're at the hospital. They'll take care of you. It's all right.'

His hands stopped their frantic scrabbling and he turned his head towards her. She saw that his hair, visible above the bandages, was thick and fair and curly. Nice hair. Somehow that made it all the more terrible.

'Who's there? I can't see you. Who's that?'

He sounded very young – perhaps her own age. Not much more.

'I'm the ambulance driver.'

He clawed again at his face. 'My eyes ... my eyes... Have I gone blind? I can't see anything.'

175

'It's just the bandages,' she said and heard her voice shake. 'That's why you can't see.'

To her horror, one of his hands shot out and fastened tightly round her wrist.

'I'm blind, aren't I? Tell me the truth, for God's sake ... *tell me.*'

She should have told him lies – any lies to comfort him. Held his hand, like the orderly had asked. That was what she was supposed to do. Instead, she panicked and tried to pull her arm free. He clung to her even tighter – tight as a vice – and in the struggle she'd dragged him off the stretcher before he finally lost his grip. He started to shriek and flail around.

'I'm blind, I'm blind ... oh God, oh God, oh God.'

The orderly returned, bringing Ray Harvey with him. The Australian took one look at her, backed up against the door, the man flailing and shrieking on the floor at her feet.

'Get the hell out of here, Susan.'

She went and sat in the cab and leaned her forehead on the wheel.

After a while the orderly climbed in beside her, patted her arm.

'You'll get used to it, miss,' he said. 'Don't fret.'

They went backwards and forwards to the docks many more times that day. At the end of it she went home, stripped off the uniform that stank of oil and burned flesh and sweat and lay down on her bed, exhausted. Her wrist was still red and sore where the burned sailor had clung to it.

Seven

Grandmother Penang came down to Singapore by train, accompanied by her equally aged *amah*, Zhu, and much against her will. After the heavy air raids by the Japanese air force, all white European women and children had been evacuated from Penang Island on military orders. She arrived at the railway station wearing her white solar topee, her black widow's weeds and a furious expression. The train had been crowded with hundreds of other evacuees. Englishwomen in crumpled cotton frocks, flushed scarlet with heat, clutched tearful children and howling babies and struggled with suitcases and bags and boxes.

Susan, who had been sent with Ghani to

meet her grandmother, received a sharp peck on the cheek and an equally sharp reproof.

'Far too much lipstick for a young girl ... and its not as though you need it. And I don't approve of painting fingernails and certainly not toenails. Only trollops paint their feet. Zhu, don't bump Hector about like that. You know how he hates it.'

Hector, Grandmother's parrot, acquired from the jungle many years ago by Grandfather, was making indignant squawks from under the cloth covering his cage. The Chinese *amah,* tiny and bent, could barely lift it off the ground. Ghani was dispatched to deal with the luggage – a massive cabin trunk hooped with steel bands and plastered with faded steamship labels bearing witness to many voyages across the oceans, and several suitcases and heavy crates containing Grandmother's collection of Georgian silver.

'They wanted us to leave with next to nothing – barely the clothes we stood up in. Ridiculous! The whole affair is a shameful disgrace. We've abandoned the natives without a word. Run away like cowards to save our own skins. I never imagined the day would come when I'd see the British in Malaya do that. Thank God your grandfather isn't alive.'

The luggage couldn't possibly fit into the Buick and had to follow behind in three rickshaws. On the journey to Cavenagh Road, her grandmother expressed her views on the shortcomings of the Royal Navy, the army, the Royal Air Force and the Government.

'Useless, the lot of them. First they let the Japs sink those two battleships, then they let them land on the beaches, and then they start retreating. *Retreating!* What's the good of that? The Japs came and bombed us and flew their aeroplanes up and down the streets, just as they pleased. Corpses lying everywhere, fires blazing, gangs looting and no police stopping them. No control, no organization, no leadership. Scandalous! Where's your mother, by the way? Lying down with one of her headaches, I expect.'

Her mother was doing exactly that and would probably stay in her room for hours, or even days, to avoid Grandmother who had never had any patience with her migraines, or with her dislike of Malaya. Soojal was on the steps, bowing and smiling, as they arrived, and Grandmother issued peremptory instructions about her luggage and about Hector. She swept up the staircase, Zhu tottering in her wake, the household amahs scurrying behind.

Her mother stayed firmly in her room, but when her father came back from his office tea was served under the jacaranda tree. The conversation was constantly interrupted by Hector, whose cage had been put nearby. Sometimes the parrot squawked in English, other times in Malay or Chinese, or Tamil.

'He picks it up from the servants,' Grandmother said, like a fond mother with a precocious child. 'He's remarkably clever. He was also a vicious old bird with a razor-sharp beak capable of cracking knuckles as well as nuts, as Susan had discovered on visits to the bungalow in Penang.

Her father put down his teacup. 'I'm afraid he'll have to stay behind, Mother'

'Stay behind? What *are* you talking about, Thomas?'

'When you leave Singapore. There's no alternative now – you must realize that. I'm arranging for the next available passages out for you, Helen and Susan. To Australia, preferably.'

'*Australia?* I'm not going *anywhere*, least of all Australia. I have just arrived in Singapore where I intend to remain until the British regain their senses and the Japanese army is routed. I shall then return to my home in Penang, where I should still be if it weren't for this disgraceful and humiliating situation.'

'Penang is expected to be taken by the Japs within the next few days – that's why the evacuation arrangements were made.'

'I refuse to believe it. Surely our army can deal with those little men.'

'The British army is in retreat, Mother. It seems incredible, I know, but apparently it's true. The Japs have already taken Jitra and are advancing south.'

Hector shouted something unintelligible in Tamil and marched to and fro excitedly on his perch. For once, Grandmother ignored him.

'That may be, but sooner or later they're bound to overreach themselves. I can see no cause for panic – certainly no necessity to go rushing off to Australia. Singapore Island is perfectly safe.'

'No, it's not, Mother. We've already had one bad bombing raid and the Japs are bound to carry out more.'

'You have a shelter here, don't you? That place over there by the tennis court. We can go and sit in it until they go away.'

'They won't "go away", as you put it.

They're here to try and take the Malayan peninsula and then to capture Singapore. That's their general plan, I believe.'

'Capture Singapore! What an absurd idea! Impossible!'

'It once seemed so, I agree, but not any more. Not the way things are going. So, I want the three of you to leave as soon as possible. It's what Father would have wished me to arrange for you. His first consideration would have been your safety.'

Hector, peeved at being ignored, poked his head through the cage bars and tried some Malay.

Grandmother still took no notice; she drew herself up in her chair.

'I was forced to run away from Penang, Thomas; I don't intend to run any further. We have a duty to set an example to the Asians. They would spot any sign of weakness on our part, which would be disastrous. British prestige is at stake. Send Helen and Susan by all means, if you wish, but I shall stay here. I have lived in Malaya for more than fifty years and no Jap is going to make me leave.'

There was loud squawking from the corner. Hector spoke in clear English this time and in a good imitation of Grandfather's voice.

'God save the King! God save the King! God save the King!'

Grandmother smiled grimly.

'Exactly.'

Apart from some hit-and-run visits by Japanese fighters, there were no more bombing raids over the next days. Preparations for Christmas went on; so did the parties and the dinners and the dancing, though there were fewer young men present and, for once, no sign of Denys. Eventually Susan spotted him at the railway station when she was making yet another ambulance trip to collect yet more wounded. When the orderly had gone off to wait on the platform for the train to arrive, she had powdered her nose, repaired her lipstick, dabbed some *Je Reviens* on her forehead and wrists and gone to sit on a bench in the shade. It was then that she caught sight of Denys talking to an army officer He saw her, too, and after a while he came over.

'What are you doing here, Susie?'

She indicated the ambulance parked nearby. 'Collecting patients.'

'Still driving them? Good Lord, I never thought you'd stay the course.'

'Well, I have – so far.' She fanned herself with her cap. 'What have you been up to, Denys? Still rounding up Jap civilians?'

'No, they were all in the bag long ago. We've packed most of them safely off to Ceylon. It's the other kind of Jap that we have to worry about now.'

He looked rather tired and very un-Denys-like. Not at all his cheery self. He sat down beside her and groped in his breast pocket.

'Cigarette?'

'Yes, please.' After it was lit, she said, 'What's the latest news?'

He shrugged. 'Who knows? By the time any news reaches Singapore it's two days out of date. Penang's been taken, but I expect you already knew that.'

'Oh, yes. My grandmother was evacuated from there and she took it as a personal insult. What's going to happen next, do you think?'

'The last thing I heard was that we've retreated as far as Grik. Next stop Kuala Kangsar, after that Ipoh, I'd say. It's anybody's guess. And it's not just the army retreating, it's the civilian chaps, too – rubber planters, tin miners, administrators – all those sort of bods turning up in Singapore. They've had to set fire to rubber stocks, flood mines, smash up machinery – everything they've left behind, rather than let the Nips get their hands on it. Hell of a mess.'

'You never believed they'd attack us, did you?'

'I never thought they'd have the nerve. The thing is once they got a foothold in northern Malaya, we've been on the slippery slope. They're outsmarting us at every bloody turn. Made fools of us, so far. We simply have to stop the rot somehow.' He shook his head. 'I didn't think you'd still be in Singapore, Susie. I thought you'd be on one of the ships taking women and children out. Wasn't your papa going to pack you off?'

'He's been trying to but my mother's been ill. We thought it was one of her migraines at first, but it's some sort of fever. The doctor says she's not fit to travel.'

'The sooner she is, the better, I'd say. You should leave, Susie. While the going's good.'

'There's nothing good about it. I feel like my grandmother feels – it would be running away, letting the Asians down. I don't want to do that. And I'm not afraid of the Japs.'

'You should be. They're frightening people.'

She heard the sound of the train approaching – the puffing of steam, the clank of metal wheels. 'I'd better get ready.' She put her cap back on, ground out her cigarette in the dirt. They both stood up. 'Good luck, Denys.'

He bent to kiss her cheek. 'Good luck, Susie. I'll give you a ring ... see how things are going.' He grinned at her, more like the old Denys. 'By the way, you look terrific in that get-up.'

She climbed into the ambulance and waited for the wounded to be brought out – four more gruesome stretcher cases. They only sent the bad ones down. Men with chest wounds, head wounds, stomach wounds, mangled and missing limbs, transported in sweating heat. The smell of putrefaction was permeating the air vents behind her seat. She shut them and got out the bottle of *Je Reviens* again, sprinkled some on her handkerchief and waved it to and fro under her nose.

On Christmas Day her mother was still confined to bed, but Susan went to St Andrew's cathedral with her father and with Grandmother, who had exchanged her white topee for a veiled black straw. They sang carols about snow and ice, holly and ivy, and frosty wind making moan while the sun beat down from a cloudless sky. After the service, people stopped outside to talk. Nobody mentioned the fact that Hong Kong had just fallen to the Japanese.

At the Christmas lunch at the Tanglin Club extra tables had been laid for evacuees who had arrived from the peninsula. Everybody was smiling and laughing, eating and drinking as though nothing whatever was wrong.

Susan came across Milly at the swimming pool, but without Geoff.

'I've hardly seen anything of him lately. He's too busy at the hospital. Still, Daddy says things are bound to get better soon. The Japs won't have it their own way for much longer.'

'They've just had it their way in Hong Kong – or haven't you heard?'

'Yes, but Daddy says Singapore is quite different. Hong Kong hardly had any troops, whereas we've got lots.'

Susan could picture Colonel Benson saying nice, reassuring things to his daughter but she wondered what he really thought. And how bad it really was on the mainland. Denys hadn't been very optimistic but nobody seemed to know for sure. There was no official information given out and lots of different rumours were flying around: the fighting was going well and hundreds of Japs had been killed; or, the British army was retreating steadily southwards with heavy losses and the Japs were now bombing Kuala Lumpur; or, there was no need for alarm because help was on its way from England ... more ships, more planes, more men.

'Lucky your brothers are in England, Milly.'

'*They* don't think so. They'd far sooner be here. Anyway, I don't think Mummy and I will be for much longer. Daddy says the army's arranging for wives and children to leave. That's the latest news. Actually, I'll be rather glad if we do go. I thought it was all rather exciting at first, but it isn't any more. It's frightening. Don't you think so?'

She had told Denys that she wasn't afraid of the Japs – but it wasn't strictly true. The ones she'd encountered in Singapore had always seemed rather sinister, hiding their feelings behind a mask of politeness. The man in the local camera shop, for instance, had always bowed and scraped but he had never smiled. She had sensed his scorn: even his hatred.

'Yes, it is a bit. When would you be going?'

'Quite soon, I think. Mummy told me to pack a suitcase and have it ready. I can't take much, though; we have to leave almost everything behind. The worst is that we'll have to leave Bonnie.'

Bonnie, Milly's pet spaniel, was as overweight as her mistress.

'The servants will look after her.'

'*If* they stay. Our *kebun's* already disappeared; we think he's probably gone off to hide in the jungle. They're all scared stiff.' Milly rubbed some sun oil on to her legs. 'You'll have to leave, too, I expect, Susie.'

'Not if I can help it.'

'But your father won't let you stay if the Japs get anywhere near Singapore, will he? I suppose he'll stay behind, though, like Daddy has to, being in the army.'

On the opposite side of the pool there was a woman with her son. Very English – fair-haired, fair-skinned, dressed in sensible English swimming costumes. She'd never seen them at the club before. They were probably one of the evacuee families from the peninsula that had been allowed in. Susan watched as the boy lowered himself into the water and struck out boldly across the pool. He reached the side and held on to the edge. He was quite near where they were sitting and she saw his face clearly: greenish eyes, a snub nose, freckles.

Milly said, 'Have you been out with Ray again?'

'No, thank you. Once was quite enough.'

'I'll probably never see Geoff again after we leave.'

'You might if you go to Australia.'

'Only he won't be there, will he? Not if the war goes on. He'll be here. And anyway, we're supposed to be going to England and that couldn't be further away from Australia. What if the Japs get as far as Singapore, Susie? What do you think will happen to everybody that gets left behind?'

'They'll go on fighting and stop the Japs landing.'

'Do you really think they could?'

'Peter! *Peter!*'

The woman was beckoning anxiously to the boy.

'Coming, Mummy.'

She watched the boy doing a very splashy sort of crawl back to the other side.

'Susie? Do you really think they'd be able to stop them?'

She said firmly, 'Yes. Of course they will, Milly.'

Towards the end of December Japanese aircraft returned at night to drop more bombs on the city. As well as bombs, they dropped leaflets which said *Burn all the White Devils in the sacred White Flame of Victory.*

On New Year's Eve Susan went to a party. Some of the leaflets had been pinned up on the walls as a joke and everyone laughed. They all linked arms at midnight and sang 'Should auld acquaintance be forgot' extremely loudly. Everybody kissed everybody else and several of them, herself included, ended the party by jumping into the swimming pool, fully clothed.

During early January the Japanese bombers came back again and again – in broad daylight now as well as at night. They flew over the city in big and perfect formations, sometimes of almost a hundred planes. Most of the bombs fell on the docks and the airfields and on the poorer districts so that the native workers fled, leaving ships unloaded, shelters undug, bodies unburied. Black smoke billowed from burning oil-storage tanks and the city began to stink of the rotting corpses trapped under rubble.

Lawrence Trent came back with news of the fighting on the mainland. The Japanese were, he said, moving steadily south. They had brought ashore armoured carriers and tanks and rumbled down main roads, all guns blazing, with only useless British rifles being fired in return. The Japanese infantry followed in their wake while Japanese planes covered them from the air, some battalions on bicycles. Exhausted British troops were being ambushed, massacred, outflanked. They were being beaten back by sheer weight of numbers as more and more Japanese troops poured on to the peninsula and advanced in hordes over swamps and ricefields, along roads, through rubber plantations, on rafts down rivers, infiltrating the jungle armed with tommy guns and hand grenades, concealing themselves among the trees to attack behind the British lines.

They had no standard uniform, and to add to the confusion they sometimes dressed themselves as Malays. Ipoh had been captured, then Kampar. There had been ferocious fighting with terrible losses at the Slim River where the Japanese had seized the road bridge intact. Kuantan had fallen and the last British troops had withdrawn from Kuala Lumpur, which had been occupied by the Japs without even a fight. The official communiqués spoke of British troops falling back on previously prepared positions, as though the retreat had been of their choice rather than forced upon them.

They listened to all this sitting out on the west verandah at Cavenagh Road, as the sun sank behind the jungle and the bullfrogs began their nightly chorus.

Susan's father said, 'On *bicycles?* Are you serious, Lawrence?'

'Perfectly. I told you the Japs were resourceful.'

'It still seems ludicrous. *Bicycles,* for heaven's sake!'

'They're an excellent means of transport and they can go more or less anywhere. And the Japs travel light. Have you ever seen a British Tommy setting off for war? He's weighed down like a pack-horse with a ton of equipment.'

'But if we can regroup our forces in the south, there must still be a chance of stopping them.'

'There might be – if we can hold the Johore line.'

'And if we can't?'

'Then the game's up and I don't believe anything will save Singapore. The Lion City is going to be brought to its knees.'

Her grandmother said icily, 'That's

defeatist talk, Mr Trent, and I won't allow it. I have rather more faith in the British soldier than you. I consider him second to none.'

'There's nothing wrong with the British soldier, Mrs Roper. He's been fighting with tremendous courage. So have the Indians, the Gurkhas, the Australians and the Malays. But, unfortunately, the Japs seem to have gained the upper hand in almost every respect – numbers, tactics, equipment, manoeuvrability, cunning, military intelligence ... pretty much everything. They've simply outsmarted us. Added to that, Singapore's totally unprepared. No tanks, hardly any aircraft, no navy to speak of, not enough weapons, the big guns pointing the wrong way, no defences on the north shore. People living in cloud cuckoo land. The military and civilian authorities at loggerheads. When the army wanted to site a defence post on a golf course recently, the secretary said nothing could be done until the committee had met. I think that about sums it up.'

In the silence that followed Hector squawked triumphantly from his cage.

'Rule Britannia! Rule Britannia! Rule Britannia!'

Lawrence Trent said, 'Not for much longer, I'm afraid.'

Milly came to the house to say goodbye. She brought Bonnie with her and her eyes were full of tears.

'We're leaving tomorrow. Daddy says we've been ordered to. The army want the women and children out of the way.'

'Where are they sending you?'

'I don't know. They won't tell you where the ship's going. I don't even know its name.' She tugged at the spaniel's lead. 'Would you do me an awfully big favour, Susie? Daddy says he won't have time to look after Bonnie and I don't trust the servants. If you're staying on for a bit, could you look after her for me? Make sure she's all right?'

'I'll do my best.'

'She likes three good meals a day – one in the morning, one at lunchtime and one in the evening – and she simply loves liver. You can mix it with dog biscuits.'

'I'll tell Soojal.'

'She adores chocolate, too. Milk chocolate's her favourite. I give her two squares after lunch and then four more after dinner, as a treat.'

'I'll remember.'

'Thank you, Susie. I'm *awfully* grateful.' Milly wiped her eyes. 'I managed to see

Geoff at the hospital yesterday and said goodbye to him. He'll be staying – just like I thought. All the doctors are. They've got hundreds of patients to look after. He says the wounded keep arriving every day. It was horrible saying goodbye ... wondering if I'd ever see him again.'

'You will, when the war's over.'

'That's what he said, but I'm not so sure about it. I expect you'll have to leave soon, Susie.'

'My mother's still not well enough to travel.'

'You'll go as soon as she is. Then what will happen to poor Bonnie?'

'Don't worry, I'll tell Soojal to look after her with the other animals. I can trust him.'

Milly sighed. 'It's been such fun, hasn't it? We've had a wonderful time in Singapore.'

'Yes, we have.'

'Do you think this is a sort of judgement on us, because we've been having such a lovely time? A judgement for enjoying ourselves too much?'

'No, I don't think so, but we probably deserve it.'

As she waved goodbye to Milly, the spaniel tried to follow her mistress and began to whimper.

Eight

The Welsh orderly, Delfryn, sat beside her in the ambulance, shouting above the engine noise.

'I don't mind telling you, miss, I'd just as soon not be doing this run. Those Nips don't have respect for red crosses. They don't believe in them, see. If any of their planes catch sight of us, they'll shoot. You mark my words.'

She would sooner not be doing the trip either, but it had sounded straightforward enough. Drive across the Causeway into Johore, pick up some wounded from an army casualty station and drive them back to the Alexandra Hospital. Simple as that. Normally, they would have gone in a convoy, but there had been a bad air raid the night before and the other ambulances were still busy moving the dead and injured.

She took the Bukit Timah road across the island, past plantations and patches of jungle and native *kampongs*. The orderly kept leaning sideways out of the ambulance,

197

holding on to his steel helmet and scanning the skies for Japanese aircraft. She had taken hers off because it was so heavy and hot.

'You ought to keep it on, miss,' he'd told her disapprovingly. 'If the Nips catch us on the Causeway we'll be in all sorts of trouble.'

No Jap planes appeared as they crossed over the Johore Straits and they reached the mainland safely. The road leading through the jungle to the casualty station was full of ruts and holes and the cab felt like an oven even with all the vents wide open. Delfryn started to sing loudly – to keep their spirits up, he said. He had a rather good tenor voice and the song was all about Welsh valleys and hills.

'Do all Welshmen sing?' she asked.

'Most of us do. It's in the blood, see. We can't help it. And we get homesick.'

'I don't suppose Wales looks much like this.'

'Nothing like it at all.' He sounded shocked, as though she'd said something blasphemous. 'Wales is beautiful.'

'Don't you think Malaya is?'

He shook his head. 'I think it's a terrible place. Much too hot and very unhealthy. I don't know why anyone would want to live here.'

The dressing station was a large army tent, pitched close to a native village. The medical officer came out as they arrived.

'I've picked out the worst cases,' he said. 'The sooner you can get them to hospital, the better. I'm afraid we can't do much more for them here.' He looked at Susan, frowning. 'It would have been better if they'd sent a man.'

'I'm a perfectly competent driver.'

'I'm sure you are. But it's just too dangerous for a woman. The Jap planes come over all the time.'

'They do in Singapore, too.'

'Not quite like here.'

He went back into the tent and the orderly followed. Susan parked the ambulance in the shade near some native huts, switched off the engine and jumped down. The huts had been built on stilts against floods and stone water jars were stored in the open spaces beneath. Tethered goats grazed, chickens pecked and scratched. In the surrounding jungle, insects chorused, birds sang, monkeys chattered and parrots screeched – all making a big racket. She leaned against the front mudguard, powdering her nose, re-applying lipstick. Some small boys who had been busy playing a game near the huts had stopped to stare at her. They wore brightly-coloured sarongs and shirts and their limbs were smooth and brown, their feet bare.

She put her lipstick and compact away in her pocket and beckoned to them, smiling. *'Mari sini.'*

The tallest and boldest boy edged forward.

She smiled some more. *'Jangan takut.* Don't be afraid.' She groped in her other pocket, found some mints and held them out to him. *'Hadiah gula-gula untok adek.'* It was important that he understood that they were a friendly gift. He advanced, step by step, like a nervous animal. Asians, she knew, were suspicious of Western sweets which might contain forbidden ingredients.

'Jangan takut,' she repeated, still smiling. 'OK.'

He reached out to take them from her hand but at that moment the first stretcher was carried from the tent and he backed away. The children retreated to a safe distance and stood watching as the ambulance was loaded up. Susan climbed in behind the wheel and held her scented handkerchief to her nose. Delfryn would ride in the back with the patients, perched on the attendant's tip-up seat on the other side of the closed door. All she had to do was drive.

The MO came round to her side and stood looking up at her, fists on hips.

'You've got some badly wounded men back there – try not to jolt them about too much, if you can help it.'

'I'll do my best.'

He stared at her doubtfully and she knew that he was taking stock of the powdered nose, the fresh lipstick and the scent of *Je Reviens*.

'Haven't you got a helmet?'

'It's awfully heavy.'

'I'd put it on, if I were you.'

It was an order, not a suggestion. She found the helmet on the floor and arranged it on her head, not bothering to tighten the strap.

He said, 'Stay out of sight as much as you can – stick close to the trees. If you see any Jap planes overhead drive off the road and hide till they've gone.' He slapped the mud-guard with the flat of his hand. 'Off you go, and good luck!'

It was impossible to avoid all the ruts and holes, to stop the ambulance from lurching and rolling. Delfryn opened the door a crack and shouted through it.

'You'll have to slow down, miss. It's too

bumpy for them back here.'

'Sorry.'

She crawled on, gears whining. The jungle pressed close on each side, dense and dark. Lawrence Trent had spoken of the Japs creeping stealthily through the jungle. They were supposed to be miles away to the north, but she kept imagining them in there, among the trees, watching and waiting to pounce.

The plane came from behind, flying very low and very fast. There was a sudden and terrifying stutter of gunfire and the ambulance juddered and rocked violently. She wrenched at the wheel and careered off the road towards the shelter of the trees. The plane had gone past and was turning to come back; she could see it clearly as it banked – the Japanese red circle on its side and on the tips of its wings. It was aiming straight for them again, guns blazing. She sent the ambulance plunging headlong into the jungle. It scraped between the trees, burst through a tangle of vines and came to a dead stop with its nose embedded in a thicket of bamboo.

She found herself sprawled over the steering wheel with her head up against the windscreen. Her helmet had been knocked off and blood was trickling down the side of her face; it seemed to be coming from a cut on her forehead where she could feel a lump the size of a small egg.

The Jap plane must have gone away because she couldn't hear it any more and there was no more gunfire – no sound except the loud jungle chorus. Nothing at all from the back. She rolled up the blind on the window and peered through. Delfryn ought to have been sitting on his seat with his back against the door, but she couldn't see him; in fact, she couldn't see anything much at all because it was too dark in there. And when she tried to open the communicating door it seemed to be stuck.

'Delfryn!'

No answer She climbed out and went round to the back, forcing a way through broken branches and knotted vines, scratching her arms and face, tearing her clothes. The canvas sides of the ambulance had been ripped open and there were rows of holes, neat as stitching, across the back doors.

'Delfryn!'

Still no answer.

She fumbled clumsily with the handle and tugged at the right-hand door. It swung back on its hinges and locked into place. She made herself look inside. The orderly lay slumped against the communicating door at the far end and his chest was covered in blood – very bright red and glistening. The blood had also run down on to the floor, between his legs, and formed a big pool. She had never seen so much blood, never realized there was so much in one body. He was dead, of course. He must be. She wanted to slam the door shut quickly and not look any more, but she knew she had to make sure.

The steps refused to unfold for her so she hauled herself up into the back. Delfryn was dead all right. His eyes were wide open and staring upward at the roof and flies were already buzzing around, feasting on his blood. The sick came up in her throat and she turned and vomited out of the open doorway. As she was wiping her face with her handkerchief and trembling violently, a voice whispered.

'I say, could I possibly have some water?'

She had forgotten about the four stretcher cases – been too shocked to think about them. The whisper had come from the lower bunk, right by where she was standing.

'Just a moment.'

Thank God, Ray had shown her where the

water was stored in a tank in one of the lockers, and how to work the tap below. She found a cup, filled it and crouched down beside the bunk, held the cup to the man's mouth. He drank a few sips, stopped and stared up at her

'Susan … *Susan?*'

'Yes. I'm Susan.'

'It's Roger … you remember. Roger Clark. We went out together in Singapore.'

She recognized him now – beneath the stubble and the ghastly pallor.

'Yes, of course. I didn't realize it was you.'

'Afraid I'm a bit of a mess.'

'Do you want some more water?'

She tipped the cup again. He took more sips but it kept running out of the sides of his mouth and down his chin, so she had to support his head while he drank. Touching someone badly wounded revolted her but she forced herself to do it. He sank back on the pillow; the effort seemed to have exhausted him.

'Where are we?'

'Hiding in the jungle at the moment. A Jap plane was shooting at us. I think he's gone away.'

'But what are *you* doing here?'

'I was driving the ambulance. I didn't

205

know you were inside.'

He gave her a ghost of a smile. 'I didn't know you were driving.'

She said, 'I'd better see how the others are.'

The man in the bunk above Roger was still alive. His eyes were open and his lips moved when she looked at him, but she couldn't make out what he was saying. The two men in the opposite bunks were as dead as Delfryn and she could see that the Jap pilot had got them too. She pulled the blankets up over them, grabbed a spare one and threw it over the orderly's corpse. She must have trodden in the blood because it was spattered all over her shoes and the soles were slippery. She clambered out of the back and wiped them, shuddering, on the grass. After a moment, when she had taken some deep breaths and got a bit of a grip on herself, she went round to the front. Both wing mirrors had been smashed by the branches and the windscreen wiper torn off, but the ambulance's engine seemed un-damaged.

One of the men was calling out. She went back and climbed in again. It was the man in the top bunk. He was crying and moan-ing and pleading.

She bent down to Roger

'What's he saying … do you know? What does he want?'

'Very bad pain … needs morphine.'

Morphine? Ray had talked about that, too, when he'd shown her over the ambulance. She searched frantically in the other locker, pulling out dressings and bandages, scissors, bottles and tubes and, finally, a box of ready-filled morphine syringes – the ones that looked like toothpaste tubes with long needles on the end. What had Ray said? Something about the wire loop on the top … why in heaven's name hadn't she paid more attention?

The man was screaming now – horrible animal-like screams of torment. She grabbed one of the syringes, took the cover off, trying frantically to remember. Push the wire bit down to break the seal … that was it. Then take it off and stick the needle in … all the way. The man was still screaming and writhing about. She caught hold of him.

'Keep still! *Keep still!*'

She couldn't hold him down on her own – he was too strong and thrashing about like a madman, arms going everywhere. She grabbed hold of one arm, stabbed the needle in as far as it would go and squeezed the tube.

After a moment, he stopped screaming and lay still with his eyes closed. Dear God, perhaps she'd killed him? Done it all wrong? Given him too much? Dear God... Then he opened his eyes again, whispered.

'Thank you.'

Ray had said something else, too – about pinning the empty syringe to a patient's clothing – only the man wasn't wearing any shirt or jacket. Instead she used the lipstick in her pocket to write a big M on his forehead and left the syringe stuck into the blanket.

She crouched down beside Roger. 'I think it worked.'

'Yes. He'll be OK for a bit.'

She said, 'I'm going to get you to the hospital. It won't take too long. Will you be all right?'

'Rather... It helps, just having you here.'

Apart from the water and the morphine, she'd been no help at all. Just the opposite. The MO had said the patients were all badly wounded and asked her not to jolt them around. Instead, she'd driven too fast and then gone careering wildly off the road, bumping and bouncing and crashing through trees. Delfryn and the other two must have been killed by the Jap pilot but if

Roger and the man in the top bunk died, it would be all her fault.

'Any more water?'

'No … thanks. I wanted to ask you, Susan … did you get my letters?'

'Yes. I'm very sorry I didn't answer you.'

'It's all right. I didn't really expect it.'

He looked dreadful. Whatever had happened to him, it must be very serious. And he was trying so hard not to make any fuss. She took his hand gently in hers.

'I expect they'll send you home to England, Roger, as soon as you're better.'

'That'd be jolly nice.'

'Back to Esher. What was the name of the road?'

'Esher Park Avenue.' It sounded like a long sigh.

'That's right. Your parents'll be so pleased, won't they? And you'll be able to go for a drink at the Bear.'

'And the Star. They both do awfully good beers.'

'Yes, both of them. One after the other. Several pints.'

He said, 'You've cut your head.'

'I bumped it, that's all. Nothing to worry about.' Her uniform, so clean and crisp when she'd set off, was covered in blood, torn and filthy.

'I have to go back to the cab now, so we can get going. The sooner the better.'

He lifted a thumb, smiled up at her. 'OK.'

The engine refused to start. It coughed and died several times before it faltered into life. She waited for a few moments until it had settled to a steady note and then backed the ambulance carefully away from the bamboo thicket. The smashed side mirrors were useless, so she had to lean out sideways to see behind. She kept hitting a tree or a bush, having to stop, go forward, then reverse around it – again and again until she reached the road. It was already getting dark.

The rain started then: a monsoon deluge bursting from the skies. Without a windscreen wiper, she was forced to stop. She opened up the top half of the windscreen as wide as it would go and drove on slowly, peering out into the rain. The road became a river, hard to follow; several times she had to halt, climb down and splosh ahead to test the ground to know which way it went.

The Causeway lay before her – more than a mile of it over the Straits to Singapore. No cover, no protection and she would have to switch on the headlamp or risk going into the sea. There must have been another bombing raid because huge orange fires were raging on the island. Go-downs at the docks, most likely, with their stores of rubber ablaze.

She said a prayer to God as she drove on to the Causeway, and then another prayer to the green glass Buddha, in case he could do anything too. Both of them must have listened and done something because the Jap planes kept away. On the other side she followed the Bukit Timah road across the island, drove up the hill to the Alexandra Hospital and stopped outside the main entrance.

People came hurrying out, the double doors at the back were flung open, the steps lowered. She stayed in the driver's seat, fingers still gripping the steering wheel. After a while, a nurse stuck her head in.

'You all right?'

She found her voice. 'I gave one of them morphine.'

'Yes, we saw. Well done, you.' The nurse leaned in further. 'Hey, you've been hurt. I'll fetch a doctor.'

The doctor, when he arrived, was Ray. He didn't ask any questions. He reached in, prised her fingers one by one away from the wheel, lifted her in his arms and carried her into the hospital.

She lay on a couch in a cubicle and the same nurse stripped off all her sodden, blood-stained clothes and wrapped her in blankets.

'My word, you're wet through. Have you been swimming in the sea?'

Another Aussie. They were everywhere.

Presently Ray came back. He leaned over and took a look at her forehead. 'Seems like you cracked your head hard on something. It needs cleaning up and a couple of stitches.'

He did the cleaning and the stitching – rather more than a couple, judging by the time it took.

When he'd finished, he said, 'Sorry, I've had to cut some of your hair away but it'll soon grow again. Feeling any better?'

'I'm perfectly all right, thank you.'

'That's good.'

She said, 'The man in the top bunk – I gave him morphine from one of those things in the locker. Is he OK?'

'He's fine. Don't worry.'

'Did I do it right?'

'You certainly did.'

'Roger Clark ... the one in the bunk below?'

'Did you know him?'

'We'd met before, in Singapore. Is he all right?'

'I'm sorry, Susan. He died soon after you got here.'

She put her hand over her eyes.

'I killed him. And the other one will probably die as well, because of me. I drove like a lunatic, trying to get away when the Jap plane attacked us. It was all my fault.'

Someone rattled the cubicle curtain and a voice said, 'Doctor, you're needed urgently, please.'

'In a moment.'

He sat down on the edge of the couch, took her hands in his.

'Listen, Susan. You didn't kill Roger. Get that into your head. He was going to die in any case. He was in a very bad way. You did a hell of a good job getting the ambulance back at all, and thanks entirely to you, one of them has survived. He's going to pull through all right.'

But she thought of nice Roger and his nice parents in the house in Esher Park Avenue, and the Bear and the Star and the awfully good beer that he would never drink again.

She started to cry.

Nine

Singapore was swarming with troops. Shiploads of them arrived at the docks as hordes more retreated across the Causeway. They were camped in parks and gardens and among rubber plantations. Convoys of lorries blocked the roads and servicemen filled the streets, hanging round the bars, crowding the cinemas and the dance halls, monopolizing the taxi girls.

More civilian refugees poured in from the peninsula and some of them arrived on the doorstep at Cavenagh Road. Cousin Violet turned up like a bad penny from Tampin, the Atkins and the Murrays, old friends from Kuala Lumpur, the Randolphs from Kuantan. A spinster aunt had fled in terror from Yong Peng.

The air raids had become much worse: the Jap planes attacked round the clock and bombed and machine-gunned anything and everything they chose – civilian as well as military. Rumour had it that there wasn't a serviceable RAF airfield left on the island

and that the only planes were biplane Tiger Moths. Meanwhile, Raffles still advertised dinner dances in the *Straits Times* and a government poster exhorted people to grow their own vegetables.

The Australian nurse at the Alexandra took the stitches out of Susan's cut a week later. Her name was Stella and it turned out that she knew Ray Harvey rather well.

'His family lived near us in Sydney and I trained at St Vincent's, same as him. All the nurses were dotty about him, including me. He never looked my way, though, more's the pity.' She snipped on. 'Only two more to go. Looks like it's healed up nicely. When your hair's grown back you won't see a thing. You were lucky.'

Luckier than the badly wounded she'd passed lying on stretchers in the hospital corridors. And much luckier than the hundreds of dead lying in the morgue.

The next stitch came out.

Stella said, 'That bloke you brought back in the ambulance is doing fine now. I thought you'd be glad to hear that.'

'He seemed so badly hurt.'

'He was, but he's being taken good care of. He'll be OK. The ambulance was in a real mess, you know. Riddled with bullets.

It's a wonder any of you survived.' Another snip. 'There you are, that's the lot.'

On the way out of the hospital Susan ran into Geoff, who wanted to know if she had heard any news of Milly. She hadn't. Milly would be somewhere on the high seas, sailing away to safety – if her ship hadn't been sunk by the Japs.

She said, 'When you see Ray, would you thank him from me?'

'What for?'

She pointed to the cut. 'He stitched this for me.'

'Looks like he's done a good job. He's pretty handy with a needle.'

He'd been kind too, as well as handy – she had to confess that. Very kind, actually. Sat with her and held her close while she'd sobbed away like a hysterical idiot. She seemed to remember weeping all over his white coat. She also seemed to remember the blankets falling down.

At sundown, the Cavenagh Road refugees assembled on the west verandah where Soojal and Amith served the drinks – iced lime juice for Cousin Violet and the spinster aunt, Singapore Slings and whisky *stengahs* for the others, except for Grandmother who preferred her *gin pahit*. Hector walked up and down his perch and interrupted rudely in several languages. Her father, when he joined them, brought the latest news and none of it was ever good. Japanese soldiers were now said to be within sixty miles of Singapore.

Mrs Atkins shivered. 'We heard what they did to people in Ipoh and KL, especially to the Chinese. They cut off their heads and spiked them on stakes, and they raped the women and bayoneted the children. And if the Malays refused to work for them, they were thrashed and tied to trees so the ants got them and they died of thirst.'

Grandmother said coldly, 'Those sorts of rumours are invariably exaggerated.'

'Oh, I'm afraid these are true, Mrs Roper. A friend of ours saw Japanese propaganda photographs. It was even worse when they took Hong Kong, you know. They drank all the whisky and went on the rampage. Shot fifty British officers and raped and murdered European women and nurses from the hospitals–'

Grandmother interrupted firmly. 'We should much prefer not to hear about it, thank you, Mrs Atkins.'

After dinner there was bridge. Her parents made up a four with the Atkins, the Murrays took on the Randolphs. Grandmother and Cousin Violet played mah-jong while the spinster aunt retired to a corner with her embroidery. Susan went out into the garden. It was a clear, star-lit night which meant the bombers would probably come and they would have to sit in the shelter again. It was a real squash with all of them, including Rex and Bonnie and Hector in his cage. She had tried taking Sweep too but he always refused. Not many people had home shelters and the only public ones were muddy dugouts or open slit trenches, half full of water and mosquitoes.

The Atkins and the Murrays queued for long hours outside the P&O shipping office and eventually left on the ironically named *Empress of Japan,* heading for England. The Randolphs hired a launch from Collyer Quay and were taken aboard a Chinese coastal steamer bound for Colombo, and Cousin Violet and the spinster aunt sailed away on a cargo boat going to South Africa. Susan's mother was finally well enough to travel and her father came home with embarkation papers for a liner sailing to Australia. There was another argument with Grandmother, who eventually gave way when told bluntly that she would be nothing but a hindrance and a liability if she stayed.

A 'useless mouth', her father said, not mincing his words. 'It's your duty to leave, Mother. Surely you realize that.'

Zhu, her old *amok*, was to go too, but Hector would have to stay behind. There was more argument about that.

'I couldn't possibly leave him here, Thomas.'

'You'll have to. The shipping line won't let him on board. No pets are permitted.'

'I fail to see why. They have parrots in Australia, don't they?'

As it happened, the liner in question was bombed and sunk by the Japanese before it even reached Singapore.

Their cases – only one small one each – stood ready in the hall while they waited for the next available ship. Susan had packed her memories: her first evening gown, her photograph album, her favourite doll, the childhood books that Nana had read to her.

Ray Harvey telephoned.

'Geoff gave me your message. Glad you've healed up OK.'

'Yes, it's fine, thanks.'

'Sorry I couldn't see to the stitches myself. There's been a hell of a lot going on here.'

'I can imagine.'

'I hope you'll be getting out of Singapore soon.'

'In a few days. We're waiting for the next ship.'

'That's good news. To Australia?'

'Worse luck.'

'You never know, you might like it better than you think.'

'How long will it take us to get there?'

'Depends where you're going.'

'No idea.'

'Probably Fremantle, in which case it'll be about a week.'

'I expect you'll be staying on at the hospital?'

'Have to.'

A pause. It cost her, but it had to be said to him.

'I'm sorry to have made such a stupid fuss, Ray. I'm afraid I just went to pieces in the end.'

'I don't blame you. It was pretty grim. You did bloody well.'

'I must have been a perfect nuisance.'

'No,' he said. 'You weren't. I promise you that.'

Somebody started speaking to him at the other end. He said, 'Hang on a minute.'

She waited till he came back on the line.

'Sorry, Susan, but I've got to go now.'

'Well, thanks again.'

'Let me know what you think of Australia when you get there.'

'It could be difficult to keep in touch.'

'Try writing me a letter. It might even reach me.' She went out into the garden and sat on the verandah steps and, presently, Sweep came silently out of the darkness and sat beside her.

'I want to talk to you, Daddy.'

'What about, poppet?'

'About me staying in Singapore.'

'Out of the question.'

'I could help.'

'It's a man's job now.'

'I've been doing a man's job.'

'And I should never have let you. Lawrence Trent tells me that the Japs are nearly at Johore Bahru. There'll soon be nothing but the Causeway between them and us. Singapore will be under siege.'

'We can hold out against them for ages. There are thousands of troops on the island.'

'You heard what Mr Trent said about the situation.'

'Why do you always have to believe *him*?'

'Because he knows the truth.'

'England will send reinforcements.'

'There are none to spare. And Churchill's given us up. He's said as much. In any case, it's too late now.'

'Then can't you come with us?'

'I've work to do here, poppet. Not just filling in forms any longer. Those days are gone. We can't let the people of Malaya down, whatever happens. We have to fight on to the end.'

They were given passes for another ship – a liner bringing more Australian troops to Singapore and returning to Fremantle. Ghani drove them to the docks and her father came to see them off. Susan sat in silence with her mother and grandmother in the back of the Buick. Zhu was huddled in the front between her father and Ghani. It was a beautiful day, the sky a cloudless blue.

She had said goodbye to the servants in turn: to the *amahs*, to Cookie and the kitchen boy, to the *kebuns*, to Amith. They had all looked sad and bewildered, the *amahs* frightened too. Soojal had been the last and she had clasped both his hands in hers and seen the tears in his eyes.

'Safe journey, *missee*. I take care of everything here for you.'

Finally, she had said goodbye to Rex and

Bonnie and given them each a piece of chocolate, and goodbye to wicked old Hector who shouted something rude at her. To her great sadness, Sweep was nowhere to be found.

'You'll look after him till I come back, won't you, Soojal?'

'Yes, *missee*. I look after him for you.'

She gave the Buddha's tummy one last rub for luck, and placed a pink hibiscus flower behind his ear.

On the way to the docks she stared out of the car window, twisting and untwisting the string of pearls round her neck. Ruined streets and rubble, deserted marketplaces, shuttered shops and burned-out cars went by. A Chinese family crouched pathetically in the ruins of their home and some Tamils stood watching at the roadside as the Buick swept past. What must they think of the white *tuans* and *mems* now? What price the great British Empire that had claimed to be protecting them? She thought, ashamed, we've betrayed them all.

Closer to the docks, Ghani had to weave in and out of bomb craters. Troops were wandering about and a group of drunken Australian soldiers were smashing shop windows and waving beer bottles. A military truck tore past, scattering the soldiers; some of them jeered and shook their fists.

The Governor had broadcast on the wireless to the people and spoken of the battle to be fought for Singapore and the need to write a glorious chapter in history. None of it seemed very glorious so far.

At the docks their way was barred by dozens of empty cars, abandoned by their fleeing owners. Ghani found a handcart to take the luggage and they walked the rest of the way to the wharf and joined the end of a long queue. There was no shade from the glaring heat of the sun, no shelter of any kind.

Before long the air raid warning sounded and Jap planes screamed overhead. They wheeled to fly low along the wharf, guns firing, and the queue went down before them like standing corn before a reaper's scythe.

When the planes had gone those who had survived rose from the ground. Susan helped Grandmother to her feet while Zhu retrieved the solar topee. Her father was comforting her mother. Children and babies were crying, women screaming. The woman who had been standing immediately behind Susan had been hit in the head and lay dead, half her face shot away. When the dead and the injured had been carried away the queue inched forward once more, stepping over the blood.

After nearly three hours they reached the officials' trestle table where their papers and passports were checked and stamped. At the foot of the gangplank, her father kissed her goodbye and hugged her.

'Off you go, poppet.' He pushed her firmly towards the gangplank. 'Godspeed!'

Halfway up, she turned round to see him walking away, and when she turned again at the top he had already vanished.

There had been no time to clean the ship after the troops had disembarked. Her mother and grandmother's cabin had no porthole and the fan was broken, the heat appalling. Her mother lay down on a bunk and closed her eyes.

'Well, at least we're getting out of this horrible country at last.'

Susan said, 'What about Daddy?'

'It was his choice to stay.'

'We may never see him again. The Japs might kill him. Don't you care?'

Grandmother put a hand on her arm. 'That's enough, Susan. Go and find your berth.'

The purser had allotted her a bunk in a cabin further along the deck but someone else was sitting on it – a fat, ugly woman, mopping her sweaty face.

'I've taken this bunk and I'm not moving. I've got a bad heart. You'll have to find somewhere else.'

She carried her suitcase out on to the deck again and went over to the rail. The men who were being left behind were standing on the quayside, looking up at the ship – some waving, some calling out, some smiling, some grim, some just sad. There was no sign of her father.

Nobody tried to stop her as she started down the gangplank. She pushed past passengers struggling up with their baggage and they grumbled and swore at her. At the bottom, a ship's officer said, 'Hey, where do you think you're going, miss? The ship will be sailing soon.'

She took no notice of him and walked away down the wharf. The abandoned cars were being pushed over the side into the sea – Chryslers, Vauxhalls, Cadillacs, Buicks, Morgans, Jaguars, Fords, Morrises ... splash, splash, splash, splash, splash. Further on some policemen were taking bottles of whisky from a pile of crates and pouring the contents into the harbour. She went on past them, out of the dock gates and back on to the streets of Singapore.

There were no taxis. No rickshaws either. She started to walk, lugging her suitcase, handbag over her arm.

She had reached Alexandra Road when a military vehicle drew up beside her with a screech of brakes. Denys leaned out.

'What in Christ's name are you up to now, Susan?'

'Going home.'

'Are you mad? What the hell for? You were supposed to be leaving before the Japs arrive.'

'I changed my mind and walked off the ship. I'm going to stay in Singapore with my father.'

'Christ Almighty! Does he know?'

'Not yet.'

'Well, you'd better get in.'

She slung the case on the back seat and climbed in beside him.

He said furiously, 'I ought to drive you straight down to the docks again.'

'It wouldn't do any good. The ship's about to sail. And I'm not leaving anyway. You can't make me, Denys.'

'You're crazy, Susan. Absolutely stark,

raving mad. Singapore's going to fall, don't you realize? The Causeway's been blown up, but that won't stop the Nips for long. Do you know what'll probably happen to you when they get here?'

'What'll happen to you, come to that?'

'It doesn't matter what happens to me. But *you* should have gone with the other women and children, while you could. You're a complete idiot. And a damned nuisance as well.'

She sat in chastened silence until they reached Cavenagh Road.

'Thanks, Denys, anyway.'

'Don't thank me for bringing you back here. I just hope your father can persuade you to see some sense. Maybe it's not too late to get out. If it isn't, for God's sake, *go!*'

She hauled her suitcase out of the back and went indoors. Everything was silent. None of the usual household sounds: no click of mah-jong tiles, no clink of sundowner glasses, no twittering of the songbirds in their cages, none of Hector's harsh squawks or Rex's barks. Only silence. But the glass Buddha smiled at her kindly from the table beside the stairs.

'*Missee?*'

Soojat looked as shocked as Denys, but

anguished instead of angry.

'Why are you here, *missee?* What has happened?'

She put down the suitcase and her handbag. 'I decided to stay, that's all. Is the *tuan* home?'

'No. He came back but then he is gone. This is a very bad thing, *missee*. It is dangerous for you here.'

She looked round the hall. 'Where are the other servants?'

'The *tuan* send everyone away to their families. Everyone. Safer for them, he says. Only me and Ghani to stay. We look after the house and the *tuan.*'

'Where is Rex? And Bonnie?'

He spread his hands. 'The *tuan* gives orders to me. Before you leave this morning.'

'Orders? What orders?'

'I cannot say.'

'What orders, Soojal? *Tell me.*'

'The animal doctor comes here. He gives the dogs very strong medicine.'

She stared at the houseboy. 'You mean, he put them down?'

'Yes, *missee*. They die at once. Very quick. Amith helps me to bury them. We must do as the *tuan* says.'

'Show me where they are.'

She followed him out into the garden and he led her to the two small mounds of earth side by side in the pet cemetery beneath the frangipani trees. Poor old Rex, poor fat Bonnie. No more toast under the table at breakfast, no more pieces of milk chocolate.

Soojal said quietly, 'Better for them, *missee*. Japanese soldiers not kind to animals. They suffer. And the *tuan* says to let the birds go. I open the cage doors, so they can fly away. The parrot, also. The doves and the fish I will feed as long as possible. I am very sorry. Very, very sorry.'

She swallowed. 'It's not your fault, Soojal. I understand. You did what the *tuan* told you.'

'Yes, *missee*. The *tuan* knows best.'

'Yes, the *tuan* knows best.' She wiped her eyes. 'And Sweep? Where is Sweep?'

'I cannot find him, *missee*. The *tuan* gives order for him too but I think he hides. Cats are very clever. They know things. Perhaps he will hide from the Japanese when they come.'

'You said you would look after him.'

'I cannot disobey the *tuan*.'

'You could for my sake, Soojal. Please look after him if he comes back. Give him food.'

'Very well – for your sake, *missee*. If he

230

comes back.'

'You promise?'

'I promise.'

'Thank you.' She turned away from the graves. 'Where did my father go?'

'To help with the fighting, *missee*. I do not know where.'

'I'm going out to find him.'

'Ghani is not here. He drives the *tuan*.'

'I'll take my bike.'

She rode up and down the streets and drunken soldiers kept trying to stop her, standing in her path, waving their arms, grabbing at her, shouting after her as she escaped them. The siren went again and another air raid started: the drone of Jap bombers, the whistle of bombs falling and the deafening boom that followed. She jumped off the bike and flung herself into a ditch at the side of Tiong Bahri road just as another one exploded close by and the earth rocked around her.

The bomb had landed on a Chinese settlement in a coconut grove across the road – a cluster of rickety shacks built from timber and matting and sheets of corrugated iron. It had raised a great cloud of dust and flames were already crackling in the wreckage. After a moment a fire engine came tearing round the corner, bell clanging.

She climbed out of the ditch and stood at a distance as the firemen pumped water on to the flames and air raid wardens began searching through the rubble with shovels and picks. They dug up an old woman and an old man, then a young boy, and then a tiny baby – all of them dead – and laid them out in a row. Then they dug further and brought out another Chinese woman, quite young and also dead. She was holding a child in her arms, protecting it with her own body.

'This one's alive,' one of the rescuers said, lifting up the child. 'It's a miracle.'

He caught sight of Susan. 'Here, look after her, will you? There may be more trapped.'

She put the little girl down on the grass and wiped away the dust from her face. She looked like a little doll, with straight black hair and almond eyes beneath a fringe. She was dressed in a cotton frock but barefoot.

Susan said in Cantonese, 'Do you hurt?'

The child nodded, pointing to her arm. It looked awful – swollen and bleeding. Very probably broken.

The child whispered, 'Where is Mummy?'

'We'll find her in a minute.' She lifted the little girl in her arms, shielding her from the sight of the bodies. 'We must wait here for now.'

An ambulance arrived and the men started to load the back with the dead. She stepped forward. The little girl had wound her good arm tightly round her neck. 'This child's injured. She ought to be seen by a doctor.'

The ambulance driver said, 'You can bring her in the cab. That way she won't see any of this lot.'

'But she's nothing to do with me.'

'Where's her mother?'

She nodded towards the bodies. 'Over there.'

'Looks like you're stuck with her, then.'

She climbed up into the passenger seat with the little Chinese girl clinging to her like a limpet. As they drove away, she realized that she had left her bike behind.

The air raid was still going on and there was another terrifying noise now as well as the bombs and the ack-ack guns – a high-pitched screaming sound followed by ear-splitting explosions.

'The bastards are sending shells over,' the driver said. 'They can't be far away.'

The road ahead was choked with refugees: Chinese families burdened like beasts with pots and pans, bedding and sacks of rice, Tamil women following their men, their possessions balanced on their heads. The ambulance driver was cursing and yelling at them as he tried to get through but they took no notice.

At the Alexandra, the injured – soldiers and civilians – were everywhere: in the hallway, on verandahs, along passages, propped like rag dolls against walls, lying groaning on stretchers. The fans had stopped working and the heat was horrible, so were the flies and the stench.

Susan grabbed at a nurse. 'What shall I do with this little girl? She's been hurt.'

'You'll have to wait. Find a place somewhere.'

'She's not mine. I can't stay.'

The nurse shrugged. 'Give her to somebody else, then.'

'Do you know where I could find Captain Harvey?'

'No, I don't. It's chaos, can't you see?'

She carried the child down a passageway where dirty linen lay in piles, covered with flies. A shell screeched over and exploded in the gardens outside; the little girl started to cry, tears rolling down her cheeks.

'It's all right,' Susan told her. 'It's all right.'

She found Ray at last. He was at the end of a corridor packed with wounded. She fought a way through, calling out his name, and when he turned round she thrust the child into his arms.

'She's been hurt ... her arm. I think it's broken. Can you look at it?'

He felt the arm, moved it gently. 'It's not broken. It's bruised, with a few bad scrapes. Needs cleaning up, but she's OK.' He handed the child back to her. 'I thought you'd left, Susan. What the hell happened?'

'I changed my mind. Got off the ship.'

He stared at her. 'Well, you're a bloody fool. And what in God's name are you doing with this Chinese kid?'

'A bomb killed her mother. I brought her to the hospital.'

He said harshly, 'Well, you'd better get yourself out of Singapore flaming fast, Susan, and take the kid with you before the Japs finish her off with a bayonet. And while you're at it, you can take this English boy, too. His mother here has just died. A bomb got her as well.'

She hadn't noticed the boy. He was standing, white-faced and silent, gazing down at a woman lying on a stretcher. Very English in his grey shorts and white Aertex shirt.

'I can't do that, Ray.'

'Why can't you?'

'Because I'm staying here with my father.'

'What the flaming hell for? He wanted you out, didn't he? The Japs'll be here in a couple of days. They hate the Chinese and they like you Poms even less. Think about these two kids. One's a Pom and one's Chinese. They're on their own and the Nips aren't going to be nice to either of them. Give them a break and get them out.'

'They're nothing to do with me.'

'They are now, whether you like it or not. They both need you.'

'I can't leave my father.'

'Yes you bloody can. He won't want to have to worry about you, as well as everything else. That's not going to help him. You've still got a last chance to leave. The Australian nurses here have been ordered to get out. They're going now and you can go with them. Get out of Singapore, Susan, and take the kids with you. And hurry up about it, for Christ Almighty's sake.'

The little Chinese girl whimpered and tightened her stranglehold round her neck; the English boy went on staring blankly down at his dead mother. *The Nips aren't going to be nice to either of them.*

236

'If I must.'

'Too bloody right, you must. I don't know the boy's name – he won't tell us.'

The same boy had been splashing around happily in the Tanglin pool on Christmas day, and his mother had called to him.

'I do,' she said. 'His name's Peter.'

She carried the Chinese girl on her hip and dragged the boy along by his hand. Outside, ambulances were arriving with more dead and more injured, stretchers being rushed to and fro. Another shell screamed over, exploding in the gardens below. A small army truck was parked down the driveway, Australian nurses in their grey uniforms sitting in the back. She hurried over, pulling the boy after her.

'Can you take us with you? Is there room?'

The one called Stella leaned over the tailgate. 'Pass the kids up. *Quick!* We're leaving.'

Hands reached out to snatch the girl, then the boy and, lastly, to haul Susan on board just as the truck roared off.

They made room for them on the bench. She held the girl on her lap and put her arm round the boy as the truck hurtled through the streets. At Clifford Pier, crowds of people were fighting to embark while troops with tommy guns struggled to keep order. Her suitcase and her handbag were still in the hall at Cavenagh Road. She had no luggage, no passport, no money and no papers to show either for herself or the children, but the Australian nurses formed a ring of steel round them and swept them through.

A tug carried them out across the harbour, a gentle breeze rippling the surface of a deep indigo sea, the noise and fury on the shore dying away in the distance. When they had boarded the ship Susan went to the stern, carrying the girl on her hip, holding the boy's hand.

The evening sun had thrown the city into sharp relief – the Cathay Building and the spire of St Andrew's rising above the rest. Fires were still blazing, flames leaping into the sky, and an immense pall of thick, black smoke hung over the island.

At dusk the crew weighed anchor and the ship sailed. Susan stayed at the stern with the children, watching Singapore vanish from sight.

Part Two

CAPTIVITY

Ten

The ship was an old freighter that had probably spent its days plying up and down the South China Seas and the Indian Ocean. It creaked along, laden with more than two hundred evacuees – white European women and children, a few civilian men, a handful of military and the Australian nurses. There was no room below and Susan found a corner for the children on the deck. Stella washed the little girl's arm with clean water and rubbed in some ointment taken from her kitbag.

'Looks OK to me but you never know in this climate. I've got a bar of chocolate, would they like some?'

The girl nibbled at her piece but the boy turned his head away. He hadn't uttered a word since the hospital.

'How did you get landed with them?'

'Their mothers were killed in the air raid. I didn't seem to have much choice.' She didn't mention the scene with Ray.

'Same with us. No choice. We all refused

241

to go at first but Matron said it was an order. We feel really bad – walking out on the patients and the doctors like that. None of them complained but that didn't make it any easier. We'd come overseas to do a job and they stopped us doing it.'

She said, 'I wanted to stay, too.'

'Well, I suppose we should be grateful that we couldn't. Everyone knows what the Japs are like – that's why they packed us off. Those kids of yours wouldn't have stood much of a chance – specially the little Chinese girl. What's her name?'

'She won't say. The boy's name's Peter.'

'Poor kid. Looks like he's in shock. I wonder where his dad is.'

'I don't know. I don't know anything about either of them. Do you have any idea where this ship's supposed to be going?'

'Java – at least that's what somebody said.'

They were given dry biscuits and tinned bully beef to eat; the boy, Peter, still refused to touch anything, or to speak. The nurses lent coats to put over the children and made pillows for them with their kitbags. Susan lay on the deck, watching the stars and listening to the throb of the ship's engine and the steady slap of the waves against the sides.

When dawn came up, they saw that they were trailing after a motley flotilla: big ships, small ships, ships of all shapes and sorts. More biscuits and bully beef were served, with rations of water. In the afternoon, a Jap spotter plane appeared and flew over.

'He'll go and tell all his friends,' Stella said. 'They'll be here soon. By the way, it's Friday the 13th today, in case you hadn't realized.'

They were ordered below deck and lay huddled together in airless heat as the spotter's friends swooped in from the east – forty or more of them forming up to bomb and machine-gun the ships. Susan had one arm round the girl, the other round the boy. Some woman started reciting the Lord's Prayer loudly and when she got to the Amen, she began all over again.

A second wave of planes arrived and bombs fell closer to the ship, making it shudder and roll. One of them exploded against the side and seawater rushed in through a gaping hole. People were screaming and stampeding to get up on to the deck when a second bomb hit and the ship began to list heavily to starboard and to fill with smoke. In the panic and confusion, Susan lost sight of Stella and the other nurses. She picked up the girl, gripped the boy's hand and fought her way up the stairs.

The bridge had been hit and was in flames; people were throwing themselves overboard in panic. The Jap planes came back, very low, and their guns raked the deck from bows to stern, mowing down passengers and blasting lifeboats from their moorings into the sea.

Susan kicked away her shoes and wrenched off the boy's sandals. Holding the girl in her arms and the boy by the hand, she jumped over the side.

When she surfaced she still had the girl but she had lost her grip on Peter and he had disappeared. She trod water, shouting his name, and had almost given up hope of finding him when she saw him swimming towards her, doing the same splashy crawl he had done in the Tanglin pool. A ship's raft floated past and she grabbed its rope, heaved both the children up on to it and hauled herself up after them. There was another person already lying there – a woman.

The ship, enveloped in flames and black smoke, had rolled on to its side and was sinking fast. Within a few minutes it was gone, leaving behind a film of black oil and a scene of carnage: wrecked lifeboats, overloaded rafts, people floundering and choking in the water – some clinging to lifebelts, some swimming for their lives, others slipping away beneath the surface. And all around – drifting along with the current – there were dead bodies, parts of bodies and dead fish. Soon there would probably be sharks.

The raft floated with the current, too. There was nothing to paddle with – not that Susan would have known which direction to take. No land was in sight – only sea and, far away now, the few flotilla ships still left unsunk.

The woman on the raft had been badly hurt and was barely conscious. She managed to speak but so feebly that Susan could only make out the name Duncan, which she kept repeating. Her husband? Her son? There was no way of knowing and nothing she could do for her.

They drifted on, carried by the current, and lost sight of the other survivors. The woman had stopped speaking or moving and Susan realized that she was dead. As darkness fell, she gathered the children into her arms and stayed awake while they slept.

During the night a storm blew up and the waves tossed the raft up and down and round about, making them violently sick; her arms ached from clinging on to the children to stop them sliding overboard. The dead woman had vanished.

At sunrise, she saw land – a small hill rising out of the sea several miles away. The current took them steadily towards it and soon they were near enough to see a beach and palm trees. The raft floated closer and closer but suddenly, and cruelly, the current took hold again and swept them on past the beach.

They drifted on, following the shoreline. There were no more beaches, only a mangrove swamp along the water's edge. But land of any kind was better than letting the current take them far out to sea again. The sea had never frightened her before. It had always been lovely to look at from the rails of a P&O liner, pleasant to swim in, fun to sail on. Now, it was none of those things.

She said to the boy, 'Peter, could you swim with me as far as those mangrove trees? Do you think you could do that?'

He nodded.

She smiled at him. 'That's lucky, because that's what were going to have to do. Can you swim breast stroke? It won't be so tiring as crawl. Can you do that?'

He nodded again.

'Right. We're going to get off the raft now. Stay very close. You can hang on to me if you get tired.'

She swam on her back, pulling the girl, the boy swimming beside her The water was calm after the storm but it was a long way to the trees and Peter soon grew tired and slipped behind. She trod water with him for a while but she could see that he was almost exhausted.

'Hold on to the belt of my frock, Peter. Hold it very tight and I'll pull you along too.'

She dragged the two children through the water, using all her remaining strength. Just as she thought she could go no further and that all three of them would drown, a friendly little current took pity and carried them gently towards the trees and the swamp.

They clung to a half-submerged branch. The mangrove roots – twisted and sinister – grew deep down into dark and stagnant water, too deep for Susan to stand. Fish kept plopping up to the surface and skittering along spookily on their tails, while crabs scuttled about between the tree roots. Something slithered heavily into the swamp nearby. A crocodile?

She said calmly to the girl in Cantonese and to the boy in English, 'We must climb up into the tree. We can rest there. You go first, Peter.'

He scrambled upwards and she followed with the girl. There was no place to sit comfortably and so they had to wedge themselves between branches, but it was better than being in the swamp, and the mangrove leaves gave them some shade. They had all been badly sunburned on the raft – especially Peter – and their skin was raw and peeling.

The girl whispered, 'I'm thirsty.'

Susan was thirsty as well, and Peter must have been too, though he hadn't complained, or uttered a word.

'This water is too salty to drink. We'll stay here until it isn't so hot, then we can try to swim on a bit and see if we can find some fresh water.' She smiled brightly at the little girl as she spoke, to show her that there was nothing to worry about. 'You haven't told me your name yet. Let me guess. Is it Lee?'

A shy shake of the head.

'Is it Yim?'

Another shake and a giggle.

'Is it Chua?

From his perch on a higher branch, the

boy spoke suddenly: his first words to her.
'It's Hua.'

'How do you know, Peter?'

'She told me when we were on the boat. It means a flower.'

'So it does. Do you speak Cantonese, then?'

'My *amah* taught me some. I can speak a bit of Malay, too.'

'That's useful. Do you know what your name means in English, Peter?'

'It means a rock.'

'Quite right. Everyone can depend on you.'

At the moment, though, they were depending on her. If they didn't find fresh water, they would die of thirst. And if they couldn't find a way out of the mangrove swamp, they'd die anyway.

'How old are you, Peter?'

'Seven. I'll be eight in May.'

'And how old are you, Hua?'

'I think she's four,' Peter said. 'But I'm not sure. She doesn't speak very clearly.'

The sun was still high in the sky and it would be an hour or two before it was cool enough to move on. To pass the time for the children, she began reciting some of the nursery rhymes that Nana had taught her and Hua listened entranced, even though she couldn't understand a word. Susan recited 'Sing a song of sixpence', 'Dame Trot and her cat', 'Jack Sprat', 'A wise old owl'. Sometimes she pretended to forget the words.

'The man in the wilderness asked of me,
How many strawberries grew in the sea.
I answered him, as I thought good – Oh dear, I can't remember the rest.'

Peter was always able to finish it for her. *'As many as red herrings grew in the wood.'*

'Well done, Peter! You know them all.'

'Mummy used to read them to me at bedtime. When I was little.'

She progressed to A.A. Milne and he knew those words, too. 'King John', 'Bears', 'The Dormouse and the Doctor' ... 'Which is your favourite, Peter, do you think?'

'I'm not sure. "King John" perhaps. I feel a bit sorry for him because people wouldn't speak to him for days.'

'So do I. He wasn't such a bad man, was he?'

'Not really. He only wanted a red ball for Christmas.'

'And he got it in the end when one bounced in through the window. I don't think it was from Father Christmas, though, do you?'

'No, I think somebody else kicked it in by mistake.'

They went on solemnly reciting and discussing English nursery poems, while clinging to a tree in a mangrove swamp on an unknown island somewhere in the China Seas.

Peter said later, 'I'm awfully thirsty.' It was a quiet statement, not a whine.

'Me too. We'll wait a little bit longer, then we'll go and find some drinking water.'

The tide was going out, leaving a band of stinking mud around the edge of the swamp. When they climbed down from the tree, they sank up to their knees in its horrid sliminess. Clouds of sandflies attacked them and the mud teemed with crabs, running about and snapping their claws. The sharp mangrove roots cut their bare feet when they tried to walk so there was nothing for it but to take to the dark and sinister water and swim again.

The water ended, not in a nice sandy beach, but in dense jungle. There was a small patch of boggy green grass above the waterline and Susan made a bed of palm leaves there for the children. The thirst was very bad now and it was getting dark.

'In the morning we'll find fresh water,' she

promised them. 'As soon as it gets light.'

Peter said suddenly, 'What's that thing on you?'

'What thing? Where?'

'On your leg. There.'

She looked down and saw the leech fastened to her calf – black, glistening, disgusting. Sucking her blood. It was all she could do not to scream.

'It must have been in the water.' She pulled it quickly off her leg and threw it into the swamp. 'Can you see any more on me anywhere, Peter?'

'No. That's all.'

'Let's look and see if you and Hua have got any on you.'

Thank God, they hadn't.

She settled the children down. As darkness fell they went to sleep and she sat beside them, keeping watch for a crocodile, a snake, a tiger. Whatever danger there might be. The noise of the insects was so loud that it filled her head in a pulsating roar, and every so often an unearthly cry or a shriek came from the depths of the jungle. With the heat and the thirst and the exhaustion, her mind kept wandering crazily. She was back in Singapore, sitting on the west verandah in the evening. Her father was sitting in his chair, *stengah* in hand, and Soojal was smiling as he came towards her with the silver tray. She could see him very clearly and reached out to take the iced lime juice – the glass frosted, a pretty slice of lime decorating its rim but when she raised it to her lips there was nothing there.

During the night, something woke her. She heard the rustle of leaves, the sound of a large animal close by, so close that she could feel the warmth of its breath. She lay motionless and petrified, sensing that the animal, which could easily have been a tiger, was watching her. After a while, whatever it was went away.

By morning a cold and clammy mist had settled over the swamp, blotting out the rising sun. They were a sorry sight – shivering, faces swollen and eyes half-closed from mosquito bites, more bites all over their arms and legs, the cuts on their feet festering, the leech bite on her calf angry and itching.

She made them dip their feet and legs and arms in the salt water – it was worth the risk of more leeches if it helped heal the bites and cuts.

'We must leave now,' she told them. 'We'll

go into the jungle and find a stream with fresh water.'

She wielded a dead branch with both hands to beat a way through the under-growth. Giant leaves slapped her painfully in the face, sharp stems tore at the flesh of her arms and creepers wrapped themselves round her legs. The jungle floor felt merci-fully soft beneath her feet – a spongy carpet of rotting leaves and vegetation. And there was beauty, too: golden sunlight filtering through the emerald-green canopy a hundred feet above, brilliant butterflies dancing on the air and brightly coloured birds flying through the trees. It was better not to think about other creatures that might be crawling about – giant red ants, poisonous snakes, deadly spiders, scorpions.

She found some fruit for them to eat – durians, rambutans, large fleshy berries – which slaked their thirst a little, and she let the children rest while they ate. Peter looked feverish.

'We must go on now,' she told them after a bit. 'We're bound to come to a stream soon.'

The heat was dreadful now. The bites itched and the cuts hurt and there were new insect stings to add to the misery. Pinpricks of red over their ankles and legs – probably from ants. Around noon she let them rest again for a while, sitting guard while they lay asleep on a mat of bamboo leaves like the lost Babes in the Wood.

Tormented by the discomfort and the thirst, she imagined herself beside the Tanglin pool. Imagined diving into the cool, clear, blue water, swimming its length. Then another length and another. And another.

The boy, Peter, stirred restlessly. He looked worse than ever, poor little chap. Give them a break and get them out, Ray had told her. Well, what chance had the children now? Ship sunk, lost in mangrove swamps and jungle on some unknown, uninhabited island. Thanks to him, they were in this terrifying mess and facing a horrible and slow death. She buried her face in her hands.

And then she heard a dog bark. Not a wild jungle animal but a domestic dog, just like Rex.

She roused the children and they struggled on in the direction of the sound. The undergrowth thinned out and they stumbled out of the jungle into a clearing.

The *kampong* was only a few hundred yards away – a group of atta huts built on bamboo poles beside a river. Chickens and goats, fish laid out to dry in the sun, fishing boats drawn up on the bank. The barking dog was by the river and some native boys were throwing a stick for it. When the boys threw the stick into the water the dog would paddle off, fetch it back in its mouth, drop it and then bark for them to do the same thing again.

Susan held the children by the hand, one on each side of her, and they walked towards a hut where a woman was sitting on the steps stirring something in a bowl. When she saw them she put down the bowl, ran to another hut and disappeared inside. Presently an old man appeared. The headman, Susan decided, judging by the *kris* tucked into his sarong and the *tanjak* folded round his head, as well as by his very dignified bearing. She let go of the children, stepped forward and bowed to him politely, addressing him in Malay.

'*Tuan, boleh tolong kami? Anak-anak lapar, hendak chari maken minum dan tempat tidor.*'

She had asked his help for the children – food and water for them and a place to sleep. He was unlikely to refuse – the unwritten law of the East obliged him to help a stranger in need – but one could never be absolutely certain, especially in such a remote place. He looked at them for a moment and then nodded.

'*Yah, saya boleh tolong.*'

She bowed again and thanked him. '*Terima kaseh, tuan.*'

The woman fetched a jar of water and coconut-shell cups which she filled and refilled several times until they had drunk enough. A little crowd had gathered round to stare – other women and children, the boys who had been playing with the dog. Dark-skinned, soft-eyed, curious. They kept pointing and whispering behind their hands.

The headman spoke sharply and they retreated. The woman beckoned to Susan and she took the children by the hand again and followed her up the steps into the hut. Inside, the floor was strewn with rushes. Women brought water for washing and green ointment to rub into all the cuts and bites and sores. The first woman, whose name was Salmah, returned with rice and fish in rough wooden bowls. Hua fell asleep over her bowl and Peter ate nothing. Susan tried to coax him but he turned his face away. When she felt his forehead it was burning hot.

Salmah put her hand on it too. '*Budak ini sakit.*'

'*Ya, budak ini ada demam.*' There was no doubt about the fever.

The woman went away again and came back with a coconut shell full of liquid which she held to Peter's mouth, urging him to drink. '*Minim La! Obat ini yang bagus.*'

He took a sip at a time, screwing up his face at the taste, but she made him go on and when he had finished it all she lowered him gently to the floor.

When Peter had gone to sleep, Salmah padded softly away down the steps and Susan lay down on the rushes between the two children. Very good medicine, the native woman had said. It was probably made from something disgusting like ground cockroaches, but that didn't matter so long as it made Peter better And whatever the green ointment had been, it was certainly helping the soreness and itching already. But Peter's breathing sounded frighteningly fast and harsh. She had no idea what was wrong with the boy, other than some kind of fever. It was very easy to be struck down suddenly by sickness in Malaya. A spider could have bitten him during the night, or a scorpion, or a snake? Or was it malaria? Or perhaps dengue fever? Without a proper doctor he might easily die.

The dog was barking again and she could hear the boys shouting and laughing by the river. It was a comforting sound – the sound of human beings close at hand. She rested her cheek on her palm and slept.

Peter was no better the next day, but at least he was no worse. Salmah came again with the evil-tasting medicine and other women carried in more food and took away their clothes to wash them, leaving sarongs and *bajus* instead for them to wear. Hua went outside to play with the village children while Susan stayed with Peter, sponging his burning face with water. There was little else she could do except be there whenever he woke up so that he could see her and she could smile and say encouraging things to him and urge him along. You had to fight a fever or it would win. She had seen that happen with one of the *amahs* at home who had lost interest in the struggle to live and so had died. When Peter opened his eyes, she talked to him – recited more of the nursery rhymes and poems and asked him about his lessons at school. What was his favourite subject? Who was the nicest teacher? Who was the horridest? And so on. It was a very one-sided conversation but it seemed to do some good because by evening he looked better and his breathing was easier. By the next morning she could tell that the fever had passed, and when Salmah brought more of the medicine he refused to drink it.

'You must, Peter,' she insisted. 'It's wonderful medicine. It's making you better.'

'It's disgusting,' he said in very clear and determined English. 'I'm not going to.'

Between the two of them they persuaded him to take a little more and then, while he slept again, Susan went outside the hut. Hua was playing happily in the shade with the village girls, the women were busy at the cooking pots, preparing food, and the boys and the dog were down by the river where the men were gutting a catch of fish. She wandered over in their direction. The native clothes felt cool and comfortable – much more so than constricting Western garments – and walking barefoot felt nice, too, now that the cuts on her feet were beginning to heal.

The dog came running up to her, stick in mouth, and dropped it at her feet. When she threw it in the river it went dashing off and plunged into the water, paddling furiously, nose above the surface. The boys laughed, the men smiled. Peace-loving, gentle people.

There was nothing to fear from them. She walked along the bank and one of the men called after her to beware of the crocodiles. The river was wide, the water muddy brown and slow-moving – she had seen many like it on the Malay peninsula.

They were on Bangka Island, Salmah had told her, which she knew was off the east coast of Sumatra about three hundred miles from Singapore. She wondered what had happened to Stella and the other nurses: whether they'd drowned or survived and, if they had survived, where they were now. Perhaps on another part of Bangka, or on a different island? There were many small islands off Sumatra and if they had been in a lifeboat or even on a raft, they would have had a good chance of reaching one.

Within a few days Peter had recovered completely, and spent his time playing with the boys and the dog. Sometimes the men took him fishing in their boats. His fair skin tanned to a deep brown but his English hair bleached to white-blond. He could never be taken for a native villager, any more than she could, or Hua either, but they could all adapt to life in the *kampong*. She thought, if we could stay here in the *kampong* we'd be safe. Then we could go back to Singapore as

261

soon as the Japs were defeated. The children would be no trouble to the villagers and I could work with the women – learn how to cook like them, make myself useful. It wouldn't be for long.

She went to see the headman who was sitting talking with the other men under some trees away from the women and children. She asked if she could speak with him and when he nodded, she sat down at a respectful distance. The men watched her intently with their dark eyes, waiting for her to speak. She had the uneasy feeling that she had been the subject of their discussion. In Malay, she asked the headman's permission to beg a favour

'*Tuan, boleh saya minta tolong?*'

He gestured for her to continue. '*Boleh.*'

She was very humble, very aware how important it was for a woman to show proper deference.

'I wish to ask if you would permit us to stay in the village with you – myself, the English boy and the Chinese girl. If we have to leave we will probably die because we do not know our way or how to survive in the jungle. May we stay with you until the Japanese have been driven out of Singapore and we can safely return there?'

He was silent for a moment, very grave.

'I cannot allow you this.'

'Please, *tuan*. For the children's sake.'

He said, 'The Japanese are already on Bangka Island. Soon they will come here and when they see that we have given a white *mem* and boy and a Chinese girl shelter, they will punish us severely. We have learned that this is so. All white people must surrender to them. They have made a prison camp on the island and we will take you and the children safely there so that you will not die in the jungle.'

'But we might die in the prison camp, *tuan*. It is said that the Japanese hate the English and the Chinese.'

'If an English *mem* and boy and a Chinese girl stay here, *we* may die, and all our women and children. We must take you to Japanese officers at the prison camp. It has been decided.'

She saw from the men's faces that the decision would not be changed, no matter how much she pleaded.

She said, 'Do you have news of Singapore, *tuan*?'

'Only bad news. The Japanese are in Singapore now. Many English *tuans* are dead and many are in prisons.' He nodded to her. 'Tomorrow morning you must go by boat with the boy and the girl, soon after sunrise.'

They were given a supper of curried chicken and rice and on the next day everyone in the *kampong* gathered at the river to say goodbye. Peter and Hua were dressed again in their own clothes and Susan had given back the sarong and *baju* and put on her blue cotton frock. The night before Salmah had sewn her pearl necklace, her gold watch and her gold charm bracelet into the hem of the frock.

'To hide from the Japanese,' she said. 'They will take everything.'

She had given them parcels of food wrapped up in banana leaves, and coolie hats of plaited palm leaves that the women had made specially for them. Susan made a polite little speech of thanks in Malay, and as the boat drew away from the bank the villagers smiled and waved and they smiled and waved back. The two natives paddling the boat beamed at them too. Anyone would have thought they were on a pleasure outing instead of going to surrender to the Japanese and be put in a prison camp.

She had tried to prepare Peter and Hua without alarming them. She had told the children that they would get the villagers into trouble if they stayed and so they must go, instead, to a camp where other Europeans were living until the war with Japan was over. Hua had said nothing but Peter had been very upset to leave the *kampong* and his new friends.

'Why do we have to go? It's nice here. Why can't we stay?'

'I told you, Peter,' she had said. 'The villagers may be punished if the Japanese soldiers find they have been helping us. You wouldn't want that to happen to them, would you?'

'No. But we could go and hide in the jungle if the soldiers came.'

'It's too risky, and, besides, the head of the *kampong* says we must leave. His word is law. It has been very kind of him to let us stay so long.'

'What will the camp be like?'

She had said truthfully, 'I don't know. But whatever it's like we must make the best of it.'

He was sitting in the prow of the boat all on his own and she could tell by the sag of his shoulders that he was still upset. Poor Peter, it must have seemed as though everything good was being taken away from him.

The river wound its sluggish way through the jungle and the sun grew hotter and hotter. The hats helped to keep them cool and, where possible, the natives steered the boat in the shade of overhanging trees. They passed crocodiles lying like logs on the muddy banks – huge jaws, scaly backs, long tails, clawed feet. One of them slid into the water and she could see its hooded eyes just above the surface, watching them.

Around noon they ate the rice and dried fish that Salmah had given them. She had told Susan that the journey would take all day and that they would reach the place by sundown.

'*Apa tempat itu?*' she had asked Salmah. What place?

'*Tempat itu orang Jipun suda bikin camp.*' The place where the Japanese have made a camp.

They came to it after a long bend in the river – trees felled on the bank to make a clearing, a wooden jetty, a crude hut. A Japanese soldier walked out on to the jetty as the boat approached. He was carrying a rifle with a bayonet fixed on the end which he brandished at them, yelling in Japanese.

Susan refused to be hurried. She said goodbye to the natives and told them to go at once, then she took each child by the hand and stepped on to the jetty. The soldier stuck the sharp point of his bayonet in the belt buckle on her frock and went on jabbering.

She said coldly in English, 'I can't understand a single word you are saying. Where is your officer?'

More jabbering and then an officer, of sorts, appeared – an ugly little yellow man in a crumpled, dirty uniform, unshaven and wearing thick glasses. The sort of Jap that people had mocked in Singapore.

She said, 'I am Miss Susan Roper. This is Peter and this is Hua. Our ship was sunk by Japanese bombs. The natives rescued us from the sea in their fishing boat and brought us straight here to you.' At all costs, nothing must be said about the *kampong*.

He answered her in bad English. 'You very lucky. Many die.'

'Yes, we were lucky. Would you mind telling this man to remove his bayonet. It's quite unnecessary. We have come to surrender.'

The officer barked an order and the bayonet was lowered.

'You British?'

'Yes, I am British. From Singapore.'

'The boy?'

'He's British too.'

'Not girl. She Chinese.'

'Yes, she is Chinese. Her mother was killed by your Japanese bombs in Singapore. I am looking after her.'

'You run away in ship?'

'We left Singapore by ship, yes.'

'Not Singapore now. Name is *Syonan*. Light of the South in Japanese.'

'Oh, really?'

'The British defeated. They surrender to Imperial Japanese Army. All British are prisoners. You, too, are prisoners. You go to prison camp.'

'Where is the camp?'

'You walk there with this soldier. No escape or he kill you. You understand?'

'I understand.'

'English women learn to be very humble now. Very obedient. Your Empire is finished.'

The Japanese soldier walked close behind them, bayonet fixed and jabbing at them if they slowed. *Lakas, lakas*, he kept saying. *Lakas, lakas.*

Susan turned on him. 'We're going as fast as we can, you stupid man.'

She held the children firmly by the hand, one on each side. There was no road, only a track with a rough surface that cut into their bare feet and opened up old wounds. After a while, she picked up Hua and carried her. They walked for a mile or more through the jungle and, as the day was beginning to turn into night, they reached the prison camp.

Eleven

Susan had expected some sort of grim grey building, like Changi on Singapore Island; instead, the prison was an old native *kampong* surrounded by a barbed-wire fence. The attap huts had presumably been abandoned, or else the former inhabitants had been forcibly removed to make way for the prisoners.

She and the children entered through a gateway guarded by two Jap soldiers, also wielding bayonets on the ends of rifles. There was a jabbering exchange between their escort and the two guards and, with more jabber and some more quite unnecessary bayonet prods and kicks from booted feet, they were taken to a hut set apart from the rest. Inside there was a bamboo table, a chair, a kerosene lamp already lit against the growing darkness, and, seated behind the table, another Jap officer – presumably the camp commandant. More incomprehensible jabber. Susan stood waiting, Hua balanced on her hip, her free hand gripping one of Peter's.

This officer was not quite so ugly as the previous one and his uniform was clean and pressed, his face shaved; she wondered how he managed it in the middle of the jungle.

He stared at them for a moment.

'Take off hats.'

As she hesitated, one of the guards stepped forward and knocked their coolie hats off their heads.

The officer said, 'British peoples must show us respect now. We are your victorious conquerors. Hat must be off head and then you bow.'

She bowed.

'Not enough.'

She bowed lower.

'Children must bow too.'

She told Peter in English, Hua in Cantonese. They both bowed, though she had been afraid that Peter might argue about it.

He said, surprised, 'You speak Cantonese, then?'

'A little.'

'Malay also?'

'A little.'

The interrogation started, the questions barked in staccato Japanese-English.

'Your name?'

'Miss Susan Roper.'

'Names of children?'

'This girl is called Hua, the boy Peter. I don't know their surnames.'

'Why do you not know?'

'Their mothers were killed by Japanese bombs in Singapore. I haven't asked them their other names yet. We've been too busy surviving.'

It went on. Nationality, address in Singapore, or *Syonan* as he insisted on calling it. Name of her father, his occupation, name of the ship that had sunk, how they had managed to reach Bangka. The answers were all written down. Her arms were aching with Hua's weight so she put her down and held her hand tightly instead.

When the questions were finished, the officer said, 'You do not look like English woman.'

What did he expect – a flowery frock, a veiled hat, white gloves, white shoes? After the shipwreck and the raft and the swimming, the sunburn, the bites and the cuts and the sores, not to mention the time spent in the other *kampong*, yes, she must look very un-English.

'Well, I am.'

'Those are not English hats. Those are native hats. You hide on island with natives. They help you.'

'No. They brought us straight here. The hats are from Singapore. They sell them in the markets there. We often wear them against the sun.'

He stared at her some more.

'You lucky to live.'

'Yes, I know. We're very lucky.'

'Many English die.'

'So I hear.'

'The White Devils are being driven from the East.'

She said nothing, looking at the hut wall over his left shoulder. There was a gecko clinging to it, motionless. It seemed to be listening to the interview with great interest.

'You stay here in camp now. Japanese soldiers treat women and children well. We are not savages. We give you food and water. Then you sleep.'

'Thank you.'

He leaned back in his chair, running his fingers along the edge of the bamboo table. 'I learn English in England. I stay two months in London to learn.' He was obviously very proud of the fact.

'How interesting.'

'London very foggy. Very cold.'

'Yes, it can be.'

'Perhaps I return one day, but in summer.'

'Perhaps you will.'

'I have not yet seen *Syonan*. I hear it is very nice place.'

'Yes, it is.'

'The English build good buildings. Make parks and gardens. In Japan we have very beautiful gardens, also. More beautiful than in England.'

'Really?'

She kept her eyes fixed on the gecko on the wall, who was still listening. She might have to bow to this man but she didn't have to be chummy to him. After a moment's silence, he snapped something to the guards and with more bayonet brandishing and kicking they were hustled out of the hut, retrieving the coolie hats from the floor as they went. They were given some water and a bowl with a little rice in the bottom; the rice was grey and dirty but it was food and she made the children eat it, Peter pulling disgusted faces.

By the time they were taken to one of the huts, it was completely dark. The guard carried a torch and flashed it around as they went inside. White women and children were lying in rows on the bare earth floor and they raised their heads, blinking like animals disturbed and frightened by sudden light. Before Susan could find a spare space for them to lie down the guard and the torch had gone, leaving them in the dark.

There were over two hundred prisoners in the camp – English women and children who had been shipwrecked in the Bangka Strait fleeing from Singapore, and Dutch women and children from Sumatra, including some nuns. At first there had also been men but they had been taken away; nobody knew where or what had happened to them. There was no sign of Stella or any of the other Australian nurses, and no news of them. Several of the women and children had been wounded in the attack on the ships but there were no doctors, no medicines or antiseptics. Water came from a well, carried in buckets, the lavatory was an open ditch, there was no soap and only one towel. When there was a monsoon downpour they stood out in it, faces uplifted, to let it wash them and their clothes.

The daily routine never varied. *Tenko,* the camp roll call, was at 7 a.m. when the prisoners lined up to be counted and to bow low to the Japanese commandant, Captain Atsuji. Women who had refused to bow at the beginning had been beaten by the guards. Now, everyone bowed.

At midday they queued for the first meal – a few spoonfuls of burned grey rice slopped from a bucket and a cup of tasteless liquid from another bucket that was supposed to be tea. At 4 p.m. they were given more rice with tiny pieces of vegetable or specks of something that might have been meat, or little lumps of pork fat floating in water that was called soup. Some of the Dutch had spoons and forks but the English prisoners had to eat with their fingers. There was nothing to do all day but walk up and down until the evening *tenko* at 5 p.m. Bedtime was at 7 p.m. followed by a seemingly endless night spent lying on the earth floor – the time when mosquitoes and bugs launched their main attack.

The wounded died, one after the other, and were buried in rough graves dug outside the camp: eight women and four children. The Dutch nuns led the prayers, wooden crosses were made and marked with the name and the date, jungle flowers were picked and made into wreaths for each one.

New prisoners kept arriving at the camp so that soon there was scarcely room in the huts to lie down. Sleep, in any case, was very difficult. Apart from the attacking insects, the Jap guards had a sadistic habit of shining their torches into the huts, deliberately waking everyone up and making the babies and young children cry. Sometimes they hit the prisoners on the legs with their bayonets or kicked them with their hard-toed boots, for good measure.

The woman standing next to Susan and the children in the food queue said, 'You're Susan Roper, aren't you? I didn't recognize you at first. I was at one of your mother's luncheons last November.'

She hadn't recognized Mrs Cotton either – last seen all dressed up to the nines and now ragged and barefoot, face burned lobster red by the sun.

'Your mother's not here, is she? What's happened to her? Is she all right?'

'She's on a ship going to Australia.'

'Why aren't you with her?'

'I changed my mind.'

'Oh dear! You should have gone with her. You really should. Australia would have been safe. Mind you I wouldn't have left Singapore at all if my husband hadn't insisted on it. He stayed though. Heaven knows what's happened to him now.'

'Have you heard any news?'

'Only what the Japs tell you and, of course, you can't believe everything they say. They say we surrendered and they've taken over and I dare say that's true. Jim, my husband, always said it was bound to happen in the end. He thought the British in charge were useless and that nobody took the Japs seriously enough. I can remember saying something about it to Lady Battersby at that last lunch of your mother's. Of course she thought I was talking rubbish. She's here too, by the way. She was on the ship with me – her husband stayed behind in Singapore, too. We ended up in the same lifeboat.'

It was hard to imagine Lady B. taking to a lifeboat.

'I haven't seen her.'

'You wouldn't have done. She's been locked up on her own in the punishment hut because she refused to bow to the commandant. We haven't seen her for at least a week. She may be dead, for all we know. The Japs don't seem to care if we live or die. And I don't know how we're going to stay alive on the rations they give us. Who are these children with you, by the way?'

Susan explained.

Mrs Cotton lowered her voice. 'It's the children I'm most sorry for. Poor little things. They haven't got much of a chance in conditions like these.'

She was right about that. The heat, the mosquitoes, the bad food, the filth and the flies. Fevers and all kinds of diseases would spread fast and furiously. One of the babies was the next to die, and the mother's anguished howls could be heard all over the camp. Susan watched Hua and Peter anxiously for signs of illness. They spent the days playing with the other English children, much as they had done with the native ones in the *kampong*.

Hua was learning some English words and Susan kept teaching her more. In Cantonese she asked, 'What is your other name, Hua?'

The almond eyes screwed up. 'I don't remember.'

'Do you have brothers or sisters?'

The child shook her head.

'What does your father do?'

She lifted her small shoulders, giggled.

The Chinese settlement had been a poverty-stricken place so the father would have had a low-paid job – working in hotel kitchens, perhaps, or as some kind of humble servant, perhaps even as a rickshaw-wallah. There were more Chinese than Malays in Malaya and some of the Chinese immigrants had grown very rich, but Hua's family would have been poor.

'Do you have uncles or aunts, Hua?'

This time she nodded. She had an aunt whose name was Su.

'Did she live with you, in the same place?'

Another shake of the head. Aunt Su had lived somewhere else, which was lucky for her or she would probably have been killed too.

She asked the same sort of questions of Peter, but warily because she knew that he found it a painful subject.

'You've never told me your surname, Peter. What is it?'

He dug in the dirt with one foot, not looking at her.

'Travers.'

'Do you have a middle name?'

'Yes, but I *hate* it.'

'It can't be that bad.'

'Yes, it can.'

'What is it? I won't tell anybody else.'

'It's Cecil. I was named after my grand-father.'

'Your father's father?'

He nodded.

'Where does your grandfather live?'

'In England.'

'Well, I think you've got a very nice name. Peter Cecil Travers. That sounds awfully smart. When you're rich and famous you might be *Sir* Peter. What are you going to be when you're grown up?'

He dug away with his toe. 'I don't know yet.'

'Well, you've got plenty of time to decide. Perhaps you'll be the same as your father. What does he do?'

'He's an engineer.'

'What sort of engineer?'

'He builds bridges and things like that.'

'Is his name Peter, too?'

'No.'

She persisted gently. 'What is it?'

'John.'

'Where did you live before you came down to Singapore?'

He dug deeper. 'Lots of places.'

'What was the last place?'

'Kuala Kubu.'

'I used to live in Kuala Lumpur. That's not far away. Did your father stay behind when you and your mother left to go down to Singapore?'

He nodded

'So, that was the last time you saw him?'

He nodded again, biting his lip.

She was as bad as Captain Atsuji with his barrage of questions, but at least she now knew Peter's full name, and she knew that his father was a civil engineer called John who had stayed on in Kuala Kubu and that he had a grandfather in England called Cecil. It would all help to return Peter to his family one day.

Peter dug on with his toe. 'How long are we going to be in this place?'

'I don't know,' she told him. 'Quite a long time, I expect. The Japs will keep us prisoner until the British and Americans win the war and I'm afraid that won't happen for a while. We must just make the best of things. I promise you one thing, Peter.'

He lifted his head and looked at her. 'What's that?'

'When the war's over and we're set free, I'll find your father for you.'

'He might not be alive. He might have been killed like Mummy.'

'He's an engineer, not a soldier, so he'll probably be quite all right. We'll find him. And we'll find your grandfather in England, too. That's a promise.'

He nodded and went off to join the other children, who were making long ropes out of plaited palm leaves. The girls used theirs for skipping, the boys theirs for jumping. Peter, she noticed, was rather a good athlete. Perhaps he took after his father – the father called John who, like her own father, might be alive or might be dead.

After supper – rice again, this time with a piece of half-raw potato and some scraps of rubber that were, apparently, dried octopus – one of the guards came up to Susan. He spoke in bad Malay. Captain Atsuji wanted to see her. A sharp prod with the bayonet. At once.

She went into the hut, took off her hat and bowed.

'You like cigarette?'

A tin full of Players was being offered across the table – obviously filched from the British.

'No, thank you.' She would have loved one, but not from a Jap.

He lit one for himself, blowing the smoke tantalizingly in her direction.

'English cigarette. Very good.'

She waited, fists clenched. What was his game? What was he up to? The kerosene lamp on the table was making little hissing sounds and moths were beating their wings helplessly against the glass. His slit-eyed face looked frightening in the lamplight – like a carnival mask.

'Your name Susan. Susan Roper.'

'I've already told you that.'

'Yes, we have list of prisoners now. All names.'

'Bully for you.'

She saw that he was puzzled by the English slang.

'You talk to me. Good talk.'

'I *am* talking to you.'

'Is bad talk. Not good. You speak to me like friend.'

Like a friend? Oh God...

'I'm not your friend. I'd sooner be dead.'

He scowled. 'I order you as prisoner. You talk and teach me good English. How to use correct words.'

She nearly laughed aloud with relief. The horrible little man only wanted to improve his terrible English. She shrugged.

'If you like.'

'We start now. I say good morning. How are you?'

'Sick as a dog.'

He frowned. 'This is correct?'

'The English use the expression all the time. It means not very well.'

'So... Sick as a dog. Now you ask me how I am.'

'How are you?'

'I am very well, thank you.'

'An Englishman would say I'm in the pink.'

He repeated it carefully.

'We talk about weather now. English weather. Today it is very cold.'

'Yes, it's bloody freezing.'

Again he repeated it. 'Bloody freezing. I ask more questions.'

'Carry on.'

'What is the time, please?'

'I haven't the foggiest.'

'Fog? I do not talk of weather now.'

'It's nothing to do with the weather. It just means I've no idea.'

'I not have foggiest.'

'*The* foggiest.'

'I not have the foggiest.'

'I have not the foggiest.'

'I have not the foggiest. This is correct?'

'Yes. You've got it right.'

'I ask another question. Where is the train stop, please?'

'Not stop. Kennel. You must ask for the kennel. Where is the train kennel, please? That's what you say.'

The ridiculous English lesson dragged on. If he ever got to London again she would love to see people's faces when he tried to ask his way or to strike up a polite conversation. He was looking very pleased with himself.

'Now you ask me things and I answer.'

'All right. Can we have more food? We aren't given enough to survive and what we are given has gone bad. And we need medicines, especially for the children. Some of them are very ill.'

His face darkened. 'This not good talk.'

'You said Japanese people weren't savages but you are letting us die. Only savages would do that.'

He jumped to his feet and hit her across the face so hard that she staggered sideways. Then he hit her again, harder still, and she fell to the ground.

'You very bad woman. Not respect Japanese officer. You go now.'

The guard kicked her with his boot as she struggled to her feet. 'Bow to officer. Show respect.'

In the hut, Mrs Cotton said, 'Are you all right, Susan?'

She touched the side of her face gingerly. Her lip was bleeding and already swollen and a tooth felt loose. 'I'm OK.'

'What on earth did he want?'

'English lessons. He wants to improve his English conversation. It was rather a hoot.'

It hadn't been a hoot, though. To be a captive, to be completely in someone else's power and to fear what they might do if they so chose was the most terrifying thing on earth. She was still trembling, her heart still pounding away as she lay on the floor in the dark. The mosquitoes had started their nightly raid. Some animal – probably a monkey – called out suddenly from the jungle. It sounded like mocking laughter.

Lady Battersby was released a few days later. She tottered out into the compound, blinking in the glare of the sun. Incredibly, her navy leghorn straw hat was still on her head, her gloves on her hands, her stockings on her legs, her white court shoes on her feet, her white leather handbag over her arm, and the snailshell hair in position. Only the pearl choker was missing, confiscated by the Japanese. She waved away all offers of support in the same old peremptory manner, but she looked frail and much older. At *tenko* the next morning all eyes were on her, all breaths held as she stood in the front row. If she refused there would be more long hours standing in the sun for them all. After a long and tense moment, she bowed.

Another prisoner arrived alone – a tall girl in ragged clothes, with wild hair and skin burned deep brown. Susan watched her stride in through the gateway, ignoring the guards and their bayonets. It wasn't until she heard her Australian voice that she realized it was Stella.

Like all new arrivals, she was instantly mobbed by the others and bombarded with questions. Where had she come from? What had happened to her? What news did she have of the war? Stella told her story. When the ship had been sunk she had got onto a raft with other nurses, and they had drifted for several days. Three of the nurses had died before the raft was washed up on a deserted beach, and the rest of them were in very bad shape. After a day or two they had decided to try to find a way through the jungle to reach help. They had set off but she had somehow got separated from the others. She had come across a river and followed it until some Jap soldiers had seen her and brought her to the camp. She had no idea what had happened to the other nurses.

'I didn't realize it was you at first,' Susan told her later.

'Same here. You look like you've been through the wars a bit.'

'How did you manage to hang on to your shoes?'

'I never took them off. And thank God I didn't. I've needed them, I can tell you. What about those two little kids you were looking after?'

'They're here. We were lucky. We all survived.'

'Tell me about it.'

She told her. Stella whistled.

'Crikey, you *were* lucky. I was too. This place might not be five star, but at least we're alive.'

'What about the other nurses that were with you?'

'They're dead.'

Susan stared at her. 'All of them? Are you sure?'

'Certain. Swear you won't ever breathe a word and I'll tell you about it.'

They walked away to a corner of the compound and Stella talked in a low voice. When the raft had been washed up on the beach, they had found other survivors there – British sailors from another ship, one of them seriously wounded. They had done what they could for the wounded man but he had died during the night. The next day a group of Japanese soldiers had arrived. The British sailors had been marched off round a corner out of sight and the nurses had heard shots before the Japs had returned wiping blood from their bayonets.

Stella said, 'We knew what they'd done, of course, the murdering bastards. Next thing, their officer told us nurses to get in a row and made us walk away from them into the sea. Then they machine-gunned us in the back. They missed me but I pretended I'd been hit. I fell face down in the water and floated there, as though I was dead. When they'd gone away, I came out and hid in the jungle. You should havee seen the sea – it was all red with blood. I was the only one to survive.'

'Oh God, how horrible.'

'Yeah, pretty gruesome, isn't it? I didn't

tell the others that part of the story because if the Nips find out that I was a witness they'll kill me. So, swear you won't tell a soul.'

'I swear.'

'You see, I've made up my mind that, whatever happens, I'm going to stay alive so that when we've finally won this bloody war I can see to it that those pigs get punished for what they did. They're going to pay for it one day.'

Soon after Stella's arrival, they were moved across the Bangka Strait to another camp in Palembang in Sumatra. The long journey began in the dark at three in the morning when the women and children walked in a weary line to the quayside, carrying their few possessions and a handful of cooked rice wrapped in a banana leaf to last them for the day. They walked slowly, some of them limping from sores and unhealed wounds, others weak from sickness. After several hours waiting on the quayside they were ferried out in small boats to a dirty old tramp steamer with open decks. There was no protection from either the blazing sun or the drenching rain which came and went alternately on the twenty-mile crossing over the strait into the mouth of the Musi River. There were sixty more miles in steaming heat until they finally reached Palembang in the late afternoon. After waiting for several more hours on the quayside they were transported to the new camp, standing up in open trucks and booed by the natives gathered on the roadside.

It was larger than the previous camp – a rectangular space, surrounded by a wire fence, about a hundred yards long and fifty yards wide and with one well. The prisoners were kept in vermin-infested bamboo huts with rusty corrugated-iron roofs, and they slept on bare concrete floors – thirty or more to each small, airless hut. Rain dripped in through leaky roofs, lizards crawled about the walls, snakes slithered in between cracks and curled up in corners, enormous spiders and rats ran over them at night and lice and leeches and mosquitoes had a human feast.

The daily rations were delivered by truck and thrown out on to the ground for them to retrieve like starving dogs – rotten cabbages, decaying beans, mouldy carrots, sacks of dirty rice full of weevils, fat maggots and bits of broken glass and stones. Sometimes they were tossed a hunk of decomposing wild pig that had to be hacked into fair shares for each hut with a penknife and ended up as a tiny sliver for each person.

Cooking was done in empty kerosene cans and tins over wood fires fuelled by chopped-up doors, all water carried in one bucket from the well. There were no baths or showers and the lavatory was an open concrete drain, used also by the guards – stinking and fly-ridden.

More prisoners arrived in lorries. English civilians, Dutch nuns in their flowing white habits and Dutch families weighed down with suitcases and boxes crammed with their possessions. The men were immediately marched away, the women and children left behind to swell the camp numbers. There were now nearly four hundred crowded into the twelve huts. Natives from the surrounding *kampongs* came to the wire to stare and point at them, the children giggling behind their hands.

The camp commandant, Captain Hatsuho, was a short man with stiff black hair and a voice like a dog's bark. He spoke no English and his screaming harangues at *tenko*, standing on an old packing box, were translated unintelligibly by one of the guards. Punishments were meted out at random – blows to the head, slaps to the face, withdrawal of rations, solitary confinement. If the bowing was thought not low enough at *tenko* all prisoners, children included, were made to stand for hours in the burning sun. The guards were sadistic, stupid, lazy. Their captives gave them names to suit them: Bandy Legs, Squint Eyes, Pig Face, Buck Teeth.

Among the English arrivals there had been a woman doctor and several nurses, and two of the huts were given over to make a camp hospital. There were no beds, no sheets, no equipment, no quinine or other medicines, but plenty of patients to fill it to overflowing. They made *bali bali* for them to lie on – low pallets of rubber-tree branches bound together. Malaria, fevers and dysentery spread throughout the camp and the row of graves outside it lengthened steadily.

Stella had gone to work in the hospital and her hatred of the Japs increased with every death.

'One of the kids went today,' she said. 'That sweet little girl Ruth. We tried everything but we couldn't save her – there was nothing to save her with. I'd like to kill every Jap on this earth.'

The violent Sumatra storms had damaged most of the roofs. In the hut where Susan slept with thirty other prisoners, there was a big hole above her. At night, lying on the hard, cold concrete floor, Hua on one side, Peter on the other, she could look up and see the stars shining above. She thought, the Japs can take away our freedom, our dignity, our comfort and almost everything else that matters, but they can't take away the stars.

Twelve

1942 dragged by. The monotonous days became weeks and the weeks became months. Since the Japs did nothing to improve conditions in the camp, the prisoners did what they could for themselves. Two representatives were elected to deal with Captain Hatsuho – a nun, Sister Beatrix, for the Dutch and Miss Tarrant, a missionary schoolteacher, for the British. Lady Battersby had been much put out not to have been chosen, but Miss Tarrant spoke some Japanese and was a much more tactful negotiator. Lessons were started for the children in a corner of the compound and Miss Tarrant managed to persuade Captain Hatsuho to provide paper and pencils. Committees were formed, rations shared out meticulously. Cooking, cleaning and water-carrying rotas were drawn up in each hut, turns taken with the only axe to chop firewood, cooking pans improvised from empty cans with sticks for handles, utensils from tin and wood, washing lines from bamboo. Life in the camp brought out the best and the worst in people: some were always more willing to help than others, some always had excuses. Some were strong and some were weak.

Volunteers gave language lessons, bridge lessons, dancing lessons, singing lessons. Miss Mumford, a music teacher, formed a camp choir and put on concerts. Lady Battersby bullied people into giving talks on every imaginable subject: Cultivating Orchids, Collecting Teapots, Walking the Pennine Way, Breeding Siamese Cats, Life on a Rubber Plantation. Empty rice sacks were stuffed with grass to make mattresses and pillows, dolls and toys fashioned out of odds and ends for the children, and games made by hand – snakes and ladders, ludo, playing cards.

Bartering was done with the native pedlars who came to the camp wire. Susan took one of the gold charms off her bracelet – an elephant – and exchanged it for four bananas which she gave to Peter and Hua. They were tiny and thick-skinned, the fruit inside no bigger than a finger, but they were food. Hua didn't seem to mind the eternal rice but Peter hated it and he had grown thinner and thinner, his bones sticking out like a starving animal's. That's what we're all doing, Susan thought. Starving to death slowly – if we don't die quickly.

Dysentery and malaria were rife in the camp. Nothing healed properly. Bites and blisters turned to running sores and ulcers, cuts and scrapes festered, rashes itched and spread, and the flies and the red ants and mosquitoes and insects of all kinds tormented them with their biting and buzzing. The rats ate their clothes as well as what little food they managed to save, and made nests for their young in the huts. They all stank to high heaven because there wasn't enough water for washing either clothes or bodies, and no soap to wash with. Susan's hair was like dirty straw, her skin the colour of old mahogany. Everyone had lice and fleas. They were all in the same boat, which was a small comfort, like the stars.

Mrs Cotton lived in Susan's hut and helped her with the children.

'My son Harry's not all that much older

than Peter, but he's safe in school in England, thank God. I cried for days when he went but now I'm glad. The school's been evacuated to Wales and when we got Harry's last letter he said he was having a super time. Heaven knows if we'll ever get any letters in this place. I don't suppose people outside even know if we're alive or dead.'

'The Japs made a list of our names and addresses, so there's always the hope they might pass it on to the Red Cross.'

'I doubt it. They don't care about the Red Cross, do they? Look at what happened to those parcels the other day.'

A lorryload of boxes had arrived outside the camp gates, close by their hut – boxes with American Red Cross in big letters on the side. They had watched excitedly through cracks in the hut walls as they were being unloaded. The guards had wrenched open boxes and pulled out jars of tablets, bottles of medicines, cartons of dressings, cotton wool and bandages. Then they had opened more boxes and fallen on the tinned meat and cheese and milk and butter, the Camels and Chesterfield cigarettes which they stood around chain-smoking.

None of it had found its way into the camp. Not one jar or bottle or carton or tin.

The hospital went without the medical supplies and the prisoners went without the food. Supper that evening had been the same old weevilly grey rice with a few bitter *kang kong* leaves, each tiny spoonful eaten very slowly to make it last as long as possible. There was always desperate, terrible craving for something sweet.

The hunger never left them, especially at night when an empty stomach gnawed away like the rats that lived in the huts, and they rolled around in misery. In the dark they talked about their favourite foods, and what they would eat as soon as they were free. Susan lay awake torturing herself by conjuring up lovely dishes that Cookie had served at Cavenagh Road – noodles and shrimps, kung po chicken, shredded pork, crispy won ton. She thought, her mouth watering, of the Sunday curry tiffins at the Tanglin Club, of the dinner parties, of dining at Raffles, of beach picnics with the hampers of food and wine, breakfast on the east verandah with Soojal bringing fragrant coffee and fresh orange juice and a plate of her favourite mangoes and papayas. She even thought of the Indian meal served on banana leaves at the hut Ray had taken her to – which reminded her again, most bitterly, that it was all his fault that she was where she was.

Sometimes, to stop herself thinking about being hungry, she thought about clothes instead and what she would choose to put on, if only she could. At home in Cavenagh Road she had had at least fifteen pairs of shoes and dozens of evening gowns, cocktail outfits, day dresses, sundresses, skirts and blouses, tailored costumes and frivolous hats. Now she had one ragged frock, no shoes and a palm-leaf coolie hat. Some of the Dutch women still had powder and lipstick but there was nobody to wear it for: certainly not the Japs. Nobody had seen themselves in a proper mirror for many months, or cared any longer how they looked. Nothing could be done about their scabby, sunbaked, scarecrow appearance, so it had ceased to matter.

Occasionally, when the hunger pangs gnawed unbearably at night, she put on one of her favourite dresses, her highest heels, her best jewellery, her brightest lipstick and went out dining and dancing. She ate the most scrumptious dinner at Raffles, or at the Coq d'Or or the Coconut Grove – five courses at least – and danced the night away to gorgeous music with a smoothie like

Denys, or with Bill, or Hugh, or Teddy or Jack. The good-looking sub lieutenant invited her to another dance at the naval base and she wore her pale-pink tulle gown and her silver sandals, stuffed herself to the gills at the supper buffet, drank glass after glass of champagne and danced till dawn.

Once she went out with Ray, but that was a big mistake. She had taken quite a lot of trouble: washed and curled her hair, put on her newest frock, her peep-toe platforms and dabbed herself with *Je Reviens* – all prepared to be nice to him. It had been a waste of time. He took her back to the shack on the hill, the one with the Hawaiian music and the lovely view but no food. She'd eaten all the fruit in the cocktail and they had argued about everything. The only comment he had made about her appearance had been to say that her shoes were ridiculous.

'What do you mean, ridiculous?'

'You'll go and break your ankle if you don't watch out.'

'Do you expect me to wear dreary sensible things?'

'I don't expect you to do anything sensible.'

He'd driven her home in the ordinary old car and stopped outside the house. Then he'd reached across to push the passenger door open, just as he'd done before.

'Gentlemen usually get out to open the door.'

'I'm an Australian, not a gentleman.'

'That's fairly obvious. You're also supposed to kiss me goodnight.'

'Is that an order?'

'It's the custom. Not that you'd be any good.'

She'd got out, slammed the door and stalked off.

She bartered another of her gold charms – a handsome lion with a flowing mane – for a length of brightly coloured cotton from a native at the wire. One of the Dutch women, called Ine, owned a sewing machine and she made a new frock for Hua and a shirt for Peter in return for a third charm – a little gold sampan. There was just enough material over to make a suntop for herself, and Ine gave her an old curtain to wear knotted round her waist as a sarong. The blue frock was hidden away in her rice-sack mattress, with her watch, her pearls and the remains of the charm bracelet concealed in its hem.

Mrs Brook, one of the older women in her

hut, had managed, like Lady Battersby, to cling on to her handbag when her ship had sunk and had saved a little zip-fastened travelling sewing kit, complete with needles, miniature cotton reels, and a pair of scissors. Susan borrowed the scissors to cut Hua and Peter's hair. Her own she left to grow long, tying it back with threads pulled from a rice sack.

She taught the smallest children in the camp school all the English nursery rhymes and poems that Nana had taught her. They sat cross-legged in a circle round her and recited them in a loud chorus.

Sing a song of sixpence,
A pocket full of rye,
Four-and-twenty blackbirds
Baked in a pie.

When the pie was opened
The birds began to sing;
Was not that a dainty dish
To set before the king?

The king counting out his money, the queen eating her bread and honey were acted by the children, and so, with relish, was the maid hanging out the clothes and having her nose pecked off.

She remembered songs to teach them, too: 'Old Macdonald', 'Row, Row, Row Your Boat', 'Widdecombe Fair', 'One Man Went To Mow', 'The Grand Old Duke Of York'.

Hua could speak very good English now – so good that she seldom spoke her own language any more. Susan kept talking to her in Cantonese so that she wouldn't forget it by the time they were liberated, but there seemed no chance of them being freed for a very long time. There were always rumours; the camp lived and died by them. The Americans had landed in Sumatra and were sending the Japs packing. Singapore would soon be retaken. Everyone would be home by Christmas. Hitler had been assassinated and Germany had signed an armistice with England. Nobody knew what to believe but the rumours kept up their spirits and their hopes.

Then Hua, who had seemed immune from the disease, fell ill with malaria. Susan sat beside her in the hospital as she lay semi-conscious on the *bali bali*, trying to cool her face with a rag and a tin of tepid water. The raging fever was followed by the child shivering and shaking with cold beneath the rice sack.

Stella came over. 'One of the Dutch women bought some quinine from a Chinese bloke at the wire. She said it cost a fortune, but then they've got the money. Might be worth a try.'

The Chinaman appeared the next day – a tiny man with a big hat that hid his face. Unlike the other pedlars, he carried no trays or baskets.

Susan spoke to him in Cantonese. 'You have quinine?'

'Perhaps.'

'A little girl is very ill with malaria. She needs quinine. Without it she will die.'

'Very expensive.'

'I have no money.'

He shrugged and turned away.

'I have something else.'

He waited.

She put her closed fist through the wire, opened her fingers slowly to reveal the string of pearls: the ones she had been given for her eighteenth birthday and had worn at her first dance.

'Will these pay for it?'

He put out a hand – his palm small and creased as a monkey's paw. She withdrew hers quickly.

'Give me the quinine first.'

A smoke-coloured bottle appeared like a magician's trick from the depths of the loose garments that he wore. She took it from him. The label said in handwritten English *Quinine* and when she shook it, whatever was inside rattled. It might be the real thing, or it might not. There was no way of knowing.

'Quinine?'

He nodded.

'You swear?'

He nodded again.

She put the necklace slowly into his hand. It vanished immediately.

The Chinaman lifted his head and she saw his face for the first time. It was as creased as his palm, his eyes gleaming slits.

'Quinine very good. The girl will live.'

They were sent to do coolie labour outside the camp, hacking away at the jungle growth with *changkols* – iron hoes so heavy they could hardly lift them and which gave them horrible blisters on their hands. Later on, they used the *changkols* to make vegetable patches in the camp and planted seeds saved from the rotting vegetables dumped off the lorry – seeds from long beans, carrots, cabbages, all watered carefully with the precious water ration. One of the older, kinder guards brought in tapioca and sweet-potato cuttings which they stuck in the earth. The seeds sprouted like Jack's bean-stalk and the sweet potatoes and tapioca took root and flourished. To brighten and civilize their lives they planted flowers.

Every Sunday church services were organized by Miss Tarrant and the Dutch nuns. The women knelt in the dust to pray and stood to sing hymns without music. Except for the sick, every prisoner attended.

A truck arrived at the gates early one morning to deposit more prisoners – dumped out like the rotten vegetables. More Dutchwomen and children and, among them, an English girl called Rita. They had come from a camp at Palembang.

Room was made for Rita in Susan's hut – precious inches given up for extra space. They gathered round her in the hut to hear her story. She had been a typist in an import–export company in Singapore and the Japs had already crossed the Causeway on to the island when she had escaped on a launch with a group of civilian engineers. The launch had left after dark, just as the Japanese aircraft had arrived to drop their bombs. The whole waterfront from Keppel

Harbour to the post office had been a mass of flames, from end to end. They had crept down the coast, following a Royal Navy launch which had guided them through the minefields. By dawn, just when they had begun to think they were safe, the engine had suddenly broken down. None of the engineers could restart it and they had drifted helplessly until they finally ran aground somewhere on the coast of Sumatra and were captured by the Japs. They had been taken to a makeshift camp where there were other Dutch prisoners – men and women kept in separate quarters. After several days, one more prisoner arrived.

'He was a newspaper correspondent in Singapore,' Rita said. 'He'd got out even later than us, on the very day that Singapore surrendered.'

Susan said, 'He wasn't called Lawrence Trent, by any chance?'

Rita shook her head. 'I never knew his surname but his Christian name was Roy. He was an Australian and he said he'd been at the Alexandra Military Hospital when the Japs got there, the day before the surrender. He told us that the Japs had shelled the hospital and then they went in and massacred the patients and the doctors and nurses – shot them and bayoneted them in the operating theatre and in the wards all over the hospital. After that, they ordered more people outside in the gardens and killed them, too. Hundreds of them.'

There was silence in the hut.

Rita went on. 'He managed to escape by hiding in a ditch until it was dark, then he went down to the docks and hired a sampan out to a small ship that was just leaving. It was going through the Malacca Strait when it was attacked and sunk by Japanese bombers. He said he was picked up eventually by a Japanese ship.'

Susan said, 'Did he say who'd died at the Alexandra? Did he give any names?'

'No. He just said it was a whole lot of people. Doctors and nurses and patients. Two hundred, at least. Maybe more. It was a bloodbath, he said. An indescribable bloodbath.'

Mrs Cotton said, 'What else did he tell you?'

'Well, he'd heard that the Japs had murdered thousands of Chinese in Singapore – raped the Chinese women and girls and cut the men's heads off with swords and stuck them up on poles.'

'What about the Europeans?'

'All white European civilians were ordered to go to the *Padang* in front of the Cricket Club and then they were marched off to Changi Prison. Men and women, he said. The troops had already been taken prisoner when they surrendered, of course.' Rita looked round at the stunned faces. 'That's all I can tell you. The Japs moved us women away to another camp soon after. They kept sending us from one place to another and we've spent months travelling round till we ended up here.'

The others went on asking questions. The tiniest new titbit was seized upon, chewed over and digested. Susan didn't listen any longer. Instead, she went outside the hut and walked alone along the compound wire. Stella was on duty at the hospital hut but she'd hear the news soon enough. Good or bad, true or false, it always travelled like wildfire throughout the camp. She passed the old Jap guard who had given them the sweet-potato and tapioca roots and he gave her a toothy grin, but she turned her head away from the hateful sight of him.

Stella said, 'They'll pay for it one day. They'll be punished. When this war's over.'

She'd spoken quietly but Susan knew the

depth of her feeling. They were walking round the compound – fruitlessly round and round. Caged animals in a terrible zoo, ill-treated by brutal keepers, thrown putrid scraps for food, stared at and mocked by onlookers outside the wire fence.

'There's a chance it may not be true, Stella. The newspaper correspondent could have got it all wrong.'

'He was there at the hospital, wasn't he? That's what he told Rita. Strewth, he was an eyewitness. Of course it's true. I've seen the Nips in action too, remember? There's nothing they like better than killing us – the more the merrier so far as they're concerned. And they don't care *how* we die. They can shoot us, bayonet us, cut our heads off, blow us up, starve us, torture us, let us die from disease and neglect – it's all the same to them, just so long as we die. All those people at the Alexandra – doctors and nurses and patients, for God's sake – they must have loved killing *them*. It was easy. They were unarmed, defenceless – the patients lying in their beds, the doctors and nurses trying to save them. The Nips must have had wonderful fun. A real party.'

Ray would be dead. So would Geoff. So would Vincent. So would Denys, almost certainly. Her father would have been marched off to prison with thousands of other civilians. Harmless, hardworking, loyal Chinese, like Cookie, would have been horribly butchered.

Susan covered her face with her hands. 'It's unbearable, Stella. Unbearable.'

Stella put an arm round her shoulders. 'You've got to bear it, old chum. You don't have a choice. None of us do. We've got to keep going, somehow. We've got to learn how to stay alive.'

At Christmas, they gathered to sing carols: 'Once In Royal David's City', 'While Shepherds Watched', 'O Come, All Ye Faithful.'

Miss Tarrant had put on a nativity play with the camp children. Peter, after some persuasion, played the part of Joseph; one of the little Dutch girls was Mary and the baby Jesus was of stuffed sacking. Hua was an angel with palm-leaf wings. Susan had managed presents for them: for Peter a sword made from two pieces of firewood bound together and smoothed with rough-backed leaves, for Hua a doll out of scraps of material begged from around the camp and sewn with Mrs Brook's needle and thread.

There was nothing to celebrate on New Year's Eve – unless it was the passing of 1942. In Susan's hut, they played silly quiz games and charades until midnight, when they linked arms to sing 'Auld Lang Syne'. In the depressed silence that followed, they heard more singing coming from the next-door hut.

> *God save our gracious King,*
> *Long live our noble King,*
> *God save the King!*

The words carried all over the camp, and other prisoners joined in. Nobody cared that singing the national anthem was strictly forbidden by the Japs.

> *Send him victorious,*
> *Happy and glorious,*
> *Long to reign over us;*
> *God save the King!*

As a punishment, they were all made to stand in the sun for four hours after *tenko* next morning. But it was worth it.

Thirteen

The row of graves grew longer and longer as the women and the children went on dying. They died of diseases, fevers, infections, malnutrition, beriberi, heatstroke, heart failure, tropical ulcers ... an endless variety of causes, including losing the will to live. There was no way of isolating infectious cases and no drugs to treat them with. The hospital patients lay on *bali bali* or on the bare floor, with only rice sacks to cover them. And it rained almost every day: hissing torrents that dripped through the holes in the roofs, turned the compound to mud, the latrine drain into an overflowing sewer. The clean rainwater would have been a godsend, but there was nothing to save it in except for a few rusty oil cans.

Stella said grimly, 'All we need now is an outbreak of cholera to finish us off.'

A Welsh woman called Mrs Williams died in Susan's hut during one night. She had seemed perfectly all right the evening before but by the morning she was dead, flies settling on her face and crawling into her open mouth, her corpse already beginning to smell. The guards refused to help or provide a coffin and so they carried her out on a makeshift bamboo stretcher under a rice sack. They walked in a slow procession through the gates to the end of the row of graves, where, sweating in the heat, they dug one more with the *changkols*. By the time they buried her, armies of ants were already swarming over her body. On the way, somebody had stolen her shoes.

Her Christian name, apparently, was Gwyneth. She had been a very quiet, retiring person and they had known very little about her except that her husband was something in the Malay civil service and had been left behind in Singapore.

Miss Tarrant took the service and Lady Battersby, hat and gloves donned as for St Andrew's cathedral, took it upon herself to read from her ivory-bound prayer book in a very loud and clear voice.

'I heard a voice from heaven, saying unto me, Write, From henceforth blessed are the dead which die in the Lord: even so saith the Spirit; for they rest from their labours.'

They marked the grave with a wooden cross and wrote on it in indelible pencil.

Gwyneth Williams, died 12th November 1943.
Nobody knew which year she had been
born. After that they picked wild flowers
and placed them on top of the mound
before they returned to the camp. The next
night they moved up an inch or two in the
hut to make use of the vacant space.

The sweet potatoes and the tapioca and
the vegetables so painstakingly planted and
watered and fed with rotted compost could
not stretch far enough to make much
difference. Other vegetables were sometimes
found among the usual ones thrown off the
back of the lorry – bolting spinach, shrivelled
carrots, hard little soya beans, green peas like
buckshot, squashy cucumbers, yellow leeks.
Like the sweet potatoes and the tapioca,
spinach roots grew well when pushed
straight into the earth. Whenever there was a
ration of palm oil they fried the rice and
vegetables together. The red oil looked
exactly like tinned tomato soup and had an
unpleasant taste but it improved their diet,
and it came in useful for making lamps out
of tins and wire and rags. They lived from
day to day; surviving today was what
mattered, not what might happen next week.
Nothing mattered but staying alive.

A chicken belonging to the guards came

into the compound. It had found its way through a hole in the wire behind the hut, and pecked around in the dirt. They watched it for a while, debating whether stealing and eating it would be worth the punishment. It was Lady Battersby who fetched the camp axe and chopped its head off with one blow. Within minutes, the bird had been plucked and drawn and was simmering away in the cooking pot. The baby monkey that climbed over the wire might have suffered a similar fate if it hadn't looked too human. Lizards were difficult to catch and with so little meat on their bones hardly worth the energy spent. Rats with more flesh ignored the clumsy home-made traps and nobody had the nerve to try to catch a snake.

The native pedlars offered ducks' eggs among their wares and another of the gold charms off Susan's bracelet bought two of them for Hua and Peter, as well as two bananas, a papaya, a coconut and some gula. The papaya turned out to be rotten inside but the eggs and bananas were good, so was the coconut and its milk, and the gula tasted almost like sugar. She kept the papaya seeds and planted them carefully. Within a few weeks a small tree had sprung up.

Every Tuesday evening one of Lady Battersby's talks took place. The prisoners gathered to listen while Mrs Henderson told them about life on a rubber plantation, Miss Mathews, a teacher, talked about Jane Austen. Mrs Vandenberg, a Dutchwoman, knew all about tulips and one of the nuns spoke knowledgeably on Rembrandt. The subject never mattered. What mattered was that it was about the world outside the camp. The world they had been cut off from for almost two years. It helped to keep the hope alive that they would go back one day.

It started with a headache – the worst headache Susan could ever remember. Like knives stabbing away inside her skull. After a while her legs started aching too, and then her stomach. She collapsed on the floor of the hut where Mrs Cotton found her and fetched the doctor from the camp hospital. Dr Lewis took one look at her and another look at the bright-red rash that had appeared on her chest and was spreading over her whole body.

'We'll get you over to the hospital at once.'

'I'd sooner stay here. I'll be all right in a while.'

'I'm afraid you won't, dear.'

She couldn't walk and so they carried her on a bamboo stretcher. One moment she was shivering with cold, the next burning with heat, head splitting, limbs and joints aching agonizingly. She went in and out of consciousness – aware of the nurses tending her and of the doctor's face appearing above her from time to time. She thought, quite calmly, I'm going to die. I'll be put beside Mrs Williams at the end of the row. Lady B. will put on her hat and gloves and read a suitable prayer. I must ask Stella to look after the children. And Mrs Cotton. They'll take care of them. I know they will. She closed her eyes and slept again.

Stella said, 'Feeling better?' She was standing beside her.

'I think so.' Miraculously, the headache had gone, and the pain in her limbs, too.

'You were really crook. We thought you were going to give up on us. Looks like you've decided not to, after all.'

'What have I had?'

'Dengue fever from some bloodthirsty little mosquito. Nasty thing to get.'

'I felt dreadful.'

'Yes, you weren't doing too well. Sometimes it can get right out of hand. But you're OK now. Dr Lewis says you're to stay here for a day or two more until your temperature's normal, then we'll kick you out to make room for the next patient.'

'How long have I been here?'

'Ten days.'

'*Ten days*... What about Peter and Hua?'

'No worries there. The whole hut's been looking after them and they've been spoiled rotten. They wanted to see you, but we wouldn't let them come in here. Too many things they might catch.'

When she left the hospital the children raced up to her. Hua jumped up and down, hanging on to her hand and laughing; Peter said in his quiet way, 'We knew you'd come back.'

More rumours and none of them good ones. The Japs had landed at Darwin in northern Australia; the *Queen Mary* and the *Queen Elizabeth* had been sunk by submarines in Sydney harbour; the Americans had lost hundreds of ships and thousands of men in the Pacific. They were all too easy to believe because the Japs seemed so cocky. They screamed orders, they slapped faces, prodded with their bayonets, kicked with their boots. Hours were spent standing out in the sun, rations withheld, coolie labour with the *changkols* redoubled, pointless and disgusting tasks given like moving a stinking mountain of camp rubbish from one place to another.

Occasionally high-ranking Japanese officials would come in big cars to inspect the camp. They would strut around in preposterous uniforms of red and gold, big swords swinging, and the prisoners would bow low as they passed by, hiding the contempt in their eyes.

The smaller children were outgrowing the nursery rhymes and simple songs. Susan taught them 'It's A Long Way To Tipperary', 'Pack Up Your Troubles', and because the Japs would punish them for singing 'God Save The King' she taught them 'There'll Always Be An England' and 'Land Of Hope And Glory' instead. The children sang them all at the tops of their voices. Stella taught them 'Waltzing Matilda' and they yelled that one out, too.

Susan listened, bemused.

'A swagman sounds like a thief, but what on earth's a billabong, Stella?'

'It's a waterhole. And a swagman's not a thief: he's a sort of tramp who lives on the open road. They carried their bedroll and belongings in a canvas bag slung over their shoulder.'

'And what on earth's a billy?'

'A can to boil water in.'

'What about a tucker bag?'

'That's easy. Tucker's food, so a tucker bag's for carrying your grub in.'

'And jumbuck?'

'It's a sheep.'

'You do have some strange words.'

'A lot of them are from the Aborigines. We've got some lovely Abo place names: Woollamaloo, Wagga Wagga, Katoomba ... names like that.'

She watched the children playing hopscotch, squares marked out in the dirt with a stick. Hua was hopping up and down the squares very fast.

'I remember you telling me once that you'd lived near Ray Harvey in Sydney, Stella.'

'That's right. The Harveys had a house in Mosman. I knew Ray when he was just a kid – older than me, of course, so I was a bit in awe. His sister, Verity, was closer my age. I remember he made a go-kart out of a box on pram wheels and he and some of the other local boys used to go tearing up and down the streets. Of course they never had any time for us girls. Then Mr Harvey died and they moved over the Bridge to the east shore. I didn't run into Ray again till I started training at St Vincent's. He was a wonderful bloke. Well, you met him, so you know what he was like.'

'I didn't know him well.'

'He was the tops. The patients all loved him, specially the kids. So did us nurses.'

'Actually, he took me out once.'

Stella stared. 'You never told me that.'

'There wasn't anything to tell.'

'My word, there would have been if I'd gone out with him.'

Mrs Cotton died early in 1944. She had survived several attacks of malaria but beriberi got her in the end. She died talking about her son, Harry, at school in England.

'He'll be ten next month. Getting quite grown-up. Do you know, I haven't seen him for nearly three years, Susan.' Tears slid down her cheeks; she wiped them away with her hand. 'I miss him so much.'

'Don't worry, you'll see him again soon.'

'Yes, just as soon as this wretched war's over.'

Hua couldn't remember when her birthday was, so they always celebrated it on the same day as Peter's, in May. Susan made a pretty necklace for her out of dried seeds and she gave Peter, who was ten, a cricket bat made from a packing case. She had hacked the wood into shape with the axe, smoothed it with the rough-backed leaves, polished it with palm oil and bound the narrower handle-end with a piece of old string found when they'd moved the rubbish dump.

He handled it reverently. 'Gosh ... Daddy always said he'd give me one when I was ten.'

'Did he play cricket?'

'Yes, he was jolly good. He taught me how to bat and bowl.'

'You'll be able to play it properly when you go back to school, after the war.'

He said, 'I was meant to be going to Daddy's old school in England. They play lots of cricket there – in the summer. In the winter, they play rugger. My grandfather went there too, years ago.'

'The one you were called Cecil after? Your father's father?'

He nodded.

'Where does he live in England?'

'In Hampshire. It's a big house. He and my grandmother have lived there for ages. I've been to stay there.'

'Do you like it?'

'Oh, yes. It's near the sea and you can go sailing. They've got a dinghy.'

'And you like them – your grandparents?'

'Yes, they're jolly nice.'

That's good, she thought. If John Travers turned out to be dead, then Cecil Travers and his wife would be there for their grandson in their house in Hampshire.

One of the Dutch boys had an old tennis ball and before long the boys were playing cricket matches.

Not quite the same as on the smooth green *Padang* at the Singapore Cricket Club, or on English school playing fields or village greens, but cricket none the less.

The coolie labour parties went out early every day to clear away jungle. Armed with the heavy *changkols*, the women hacked and scraped away futilely at dense undergrowth. The elderly Mrs Fooks collapsed and died later in the camp hospital, others fainted from exhaustion or the heat, another was bitten by an angry snake. A poor Dutch-woman who tried to keep a papaya fruit that she had found in the grass was beaten savagely about the head by a guard.

When she returned to the camp after one of these long, weary days, Susan found

Stella waiting anxiously for her by the gates.

'It's Peter,' she said. 'Trouble.'

Her heart started to race. 'What's happened?'

'He was playing cricket and batting the ball hard, like they all do, and it went and hit one of the guards. They've made him stand out in the sun all day as a punishment. The poor kid's been there for hours.'

Peter was all alone in the middle of the open space where they lined up for *tenko*, standing with his shoulders hunched, arms hanging at his sides, staring down at the ground.

Stella held her back. 'Best not to go near him, Susie. Some of us tried to take him some water earlier but the guards say that if we do he'll have to stay there all the longer. It's Hatsuho's orders.'

She shook off Stella's hand. 'I'm going to speak to that bastard.'

'It won't do any good. Miss Tarrant and Sister Beatrix have already been to see him.'

'Now it's my turn.'

The commandant was seated behind his desk, his interpreter at his side. Susan took off her hat and bowed.

'Captain Hatsuho, I have come to ask if you will permit the boy Peter Travers to go free, now that he has been punished.'

She listened to the rant that followed, the Jap talk that sounded like stuttering gibberish.

The interpreter said, 'Captain Hatsuho say punishment not finished yet. Boy very bad. He must stay many more hours to learn respect for Japanese soldiers.'

She said, 'It was an accident. He didn't mean to hit the guard. He was only playing a game of cricket.'

'Captain Hatsuho say not accident. Boy not sorry.'

'I'm sure he is sorry. Very sorry. Peter is only a child. He's ten years old, that's all.' She looked at the commandant. 'Do you have a son, Captain Hatsuho?'

A faint flicker passed over his face. He does, she thought.

'Doesn't your son like to play sports sometimes? I'm sure he does.'

There was another volley of Japanese, followed by English.

'Japanese boys do not do bad things. Japanese boys always have respect. English boy very proud. Same like all English mens. And English womens. Very bad thing.'

She waited a moment, then she said, 'Peter's mother was killed by Japanese bombs in Singapore. His father is probably dead too. He has suffered very much. If it were your son, would you wish him to suffer more? I beg of you to allow him to go free.'

She watched Hatsuho's face and knew his answer before the interpreter translated it.

'The boy must stay. Punishment not finished.'

'Then I will stay with him.'

'That is not permitted.'

'Try to stop me.'

She bowed and walked out of the hut to where Peter was standing all alone in the middle of the compound. She put her coolie hat on his head, took him by the hand and stood beside him, the two of them together.

They went on standing there as the sun went down and night fell and instead of being very hot it became very cold. They stood there as the sun came up again, all the next morning and all the next afternoon. At the evening *tenko* Peter was allowed to go, but Susan was taken away to the punishment hut where they had locked up Lady Battersby. It was a very small tin hut, only six feet square, with no window, no furniture, only a bucket in one corner.

She lost count of the days spent sitting on the concrete floor with nothing to read, no one to talk to, nothing to look at and nothing to do. She recited all the old poems to herself, sang all the songs, played an endless alphabet game: all the countries she could think of beginning with A, all the towns, all the rivers, all the birds, all the fish, the flowers, the vegetables, the fruits, the trees ... and then back to the beginning again, moving on to the letter B, then C, then D – all the way through to Z. When she had finished, she started again at the beginning.

To make a change, she went out dining and dancing, or swam at the Tanglin Club, or played tennis, or drove out to the Sea View Hotel for curry tiffin, or went sailing with Denys in *Kittiwake* and walked along the lovely beach with the pure-white sand and the pretty shells and the whispering casuarina trees, as they had done before the nightmare began.

She had long conversations with people, too: her father who told her to keep her chin up because the war would soon be won; her mother who said that if she hadn't been so silly as to get off the boat she would have been safe in Australia; Grandmother Penang who advised her never to show the Japs that she was afraid of them. Nana said, comfortingly, that bad things never lasted for ever and all she had to do was wait for good things to come again.

She had a word with Ray, too – just to see what he might have thought, if he'd still been alive – pointing out that it had all been his fault that she was stuck in a prison camp. He didn't seem to feel in the least guilty – in fact he agreed with her mother.

'You were a bloody fool to get off the ship, Susan. I told you that.'

She said resentfully, 'Spending two and a half years in a place like this isn't much fun, I can tell you. And I don't think I can stand it much more, being shut up on my own. I'll go mad soon.'

'Stop moaning and feeling sorry for yourself. Think of the kids instead. You've got to look after them. You've got to see it through, for their sake.'

When she started sobbing he put his arms round her and held her close, like he'd done before at the hospital.

'You can hang on, Susan. You know you can. You're not the sort to give up. You've got more guts than that. You've proved it already.'

After a while, she felt better.

One night, when she was lying awake, she thought she heard the sound of planes in the distance. Not Jap planes because they made a different sort of noise. This was a deep droning sound: the sort of sound that big bombers with four engines might have made. After a while, there was another and very familiar sound – the crump, crump of exploding bombs.

Fourteen

'The Nips keep saying it's just them practising,' Stella told her when they had finally let her out of the punishment hut after a month. 'But we don't believe them. We all think it's our bombers. The natives think so too. They say the Allies are bombing the oilfields.'

'I wondered if I was imagining it – if I'd gone crazy, or something.'

'Wouldn't blame you for doing that. Doing solitary must be enough to drive anyone round the bend. Peter thinks it was all his fault, by the way. He's been miserable while you were in there.'

Poor Peter. She had a hard time convincing him that he wasn't to blame for her punishment.

'Of course you weren't,' she told him. 'I knew what I was doing, and I chose to do it. And I'd do it again as well.'

But he'd thrown away the packing-case bat and nobody played cricket any more.

Lady Battersby died. She departed with perfect dignity and without fuss. They buried her in her navy-blue crêpe frock, wearing her leghorn straw and with her handbag over her arm – as they thought she would have wished. Miss Tarrant said the prayers and Miss Mumford's camp choir sang 'Abide With Me'.

There were four rows of graves now. Those who hadn't died of malaria, beriberi, dysentery, typhoid or something else unpleasant were growing steadily thinner and thinner, weaker and weaker from malnutrition and constant attacks of dysentery. Red Cross parcels never reached them, the camp kitchen garden couldn't produce enough for all and they were existing on the same old diet of dirty rice and mouldy vegetables, tapioca leaves, dried fish, with the occasional hunk of some rotting, maggoty meat hacked into tiny pieces. Their limbs were sticks, their cheeks hollow, their ribs could be counted – unless beriberi had made them swell up like bloated pigs. Teeth were loose or had fallen out and the coconut hairs which made a good cleaning substitute for toothbrushes and toothpaste were in short supply. There was only one charm left on Susan's bracelet – a little owl – and she exchanged it for a pineapple and three small hen's eggs for Hua and Peter. Next time, it would be the gold bracelet itself. And, finally, the watch.

A sack of letters arrived: the first to reach the camp in three years. Captain Hatsuho had made an announcement at morning *tenko* during a long speech about the wonderful generosity of the Japanese Imperial Army towards prisoners of war. They queued up patiently outside the guardhouse, standing in the burning sun for more than an hour until the letters were finally given out. There was nothing for Susan. No news from her father; none from her mother and grandmother – presumably living in Australia. Nothing for Stella either.

'They think we're dead,' Stella said. 'For all they know we drowned when the ship was sunk.'

'But the Japs are always making lists of our names.'

'Yeah, and they're always making bonfires too.'

Most of the letters turned out to be two and three years old and had obviously been hoarded for a very long time.

Susan said, 'Why bother to give them out now?'

'Maybe they're losing the war and it suits them to be nicer to us.'

The natives kept telling them that the news was good: *kaba baik*, they repeated with nods and smiles. *Kaba baik*. But the Allied bombers had not been heard for a while.

The well ran dry. Water had to be fetched from a stream a mile away and carried back in buckets and tins and pots – water for drinking and cooking and washing for six hundred people, and for the vegetable patch as well. The children helped to carry it, too. Susan watched Peter and Hua walking with their cans, chattering to each other in English. In two months' time Peter would be eleven years old. He had grown quite tall, though he was painfully skinny. His face had changed from a small boy's face and she could see how he might look as a young man. Hua, who was probably getting on for seven, had grown too, and her black hair was long and worn in two plaits which she braided herself at lightning speed. Her spoken English was perfect and, thanks to the camp school, she could read and write it as well. Peter had been learning French and German from the Dutch nuns and Miss Tarrant had given classes in English and History and Geography. Somehow both children had survived the fevers and the dysentery, and somehow they had escaped beriberi – perhaps because of the extra fruit and vegetables. But the gold bracelet and the watch had gone the way of the charms and the pearls and now there was nothing left to barter with.

Soon after Peter's eleventh birthday in May another rumour reached the camp. The war in Europe was finished and the Americans were defeating the Japanese in the Pacific. Nobody knew where the stories had come from or whether they were true. *Kaba baik,* the natives still kept insisting. *Kaba baik.* Good news.

In July they were moved to a camp on the other side of Sumatra. At morning *tenko* Captain Hatsuho had told them via his interpreter how fortunate they were. They would be taken by train across the island to a place where there was plenty of shade and water and good food and comfortable accommodation.

'You very lucky. Imperial Japanese Army very good to women and children.'

Almost two hundred women and children now lay in their graves outside the camp as silent testimony to the Imperial Army's goodness. The hospital was overflowing with dying and very ill patients and the remaining prisoners were half-starved, weak, worn out.

They left in a downpour, travelling to the train in open lorries, the sick lying on stretchers, faces upturned helplessly to the rain. Instead of proper train carriages there were airless, seatless cattle trucks, and they spent the first night shut up in a siding where Miss Mathews, the teacher who had known all about Jane Austen, died before dawn. She went very quietly, holding Susan's hand, and apologizing for being such a nuisance.

The train journey across Sumatra took two days and they lived on cold rice and water. Several more of the sick had died by the time they arrived at their destination. They were herded out of the cattle trucks by the guards, loaded into more open lorries and driven at top speed along rough tracks to the new prison camp in the middle of an old rubber plantation. The tin-roofed huts were already occupied by bugs and rats, but, for once, Captain Hatsuho had not lied about the shade, or about the water which ran clear in a rocky creek, though he had lied about the good food. Sweet potatoes, carrots, long beans, turnips, chokos and bringals were brought and dumped outside the guardhouse but, as usual, they were left to rot for three or four days before permission was given to collect them. Sometimes a lump of meat was delivered too – bullock and deer, stinking horribly but edible when cooked and, at least, they had plenty of wood from the rubber trees for the fires. Their new commandant was a little old sergeant called Yamada, who was usually drunk and fell off his soap box at *tenko*. It would have been funny if they had not been past laughter.

A month later, the bombers came over again – close enough and low enough for the Royal Australian Air Force markings to be seen – and the prisoners went out into the compound to watch them and cheer. The guards suddenly became nicer. They no longer prodded with their bayonets, no longer yelled and scowled. Instead, they smiled and offered American Red Cross cigarettes. Permission was given to collect the rations as soon as they were left outside the gate, and the men delivering them said good morning politely instead of calling them foul names. At evening *tenko* Yamada was sober enough to make a very short speech. 'War is finished. We are now friends.' He didn't say who had won the war.

The next morning he and all the guards had disappeared. At midday an army vehicle drew up outside the guardhouse with a squeal of brakes and the driver got out. A white man – the first they had set eyes on for more than three years. Well over six foot tall, broad-shouldered, sun-bronzed, dressed in khaki shorts, shirt, and an Australian army bush hat with the brim turned up on one side.

Nobody in the compound spoke and nobody moved. The digger walked slowly over to the gate and kicked it open with his booted foot.

He stood, fists on hips, staring around at the crowd of women and children watching him in silence. He stared at their ragged clothes, their bare feet, their skeletal frames, their sun-blackened skins, their hollow eyes and sunken cheeks, their matted verminous hair, their sores and their scars.

'Holy cow!' he said softly. 'Oh, my word! Oh, my bloody word!'

Part Three

LIBERTY

Fifteen

The Dakota came in low over the sea to land on Singapore Island at dusk on an evening in September. The aeroplane touched down gently and rolled to a halt. After a while the passengers began to disembark, moving slowly like old people, though many of them were young. The crowd of photographers and reporters waiting on the tarmac pressed forward to record their arrival.

The passengers stood on the aircraft steps, blinking in the popping glare of the camera flashbulbs – still stunned by their liberation.

A reporter, notebook and pencil in hand, barred Susan's way at the foot of the steps.

'Can you tell us how you feel, miss? What's it like to be a free woman again?'

He was young and he looked so clean and smart. His hair was smooth, his suit pressed, his shoes polished. She was carrying her coolie hat, wearing her ragged old blue cotton frock and a pair of muddy Japanese army boots that felt like lead weights on her feet.

She said, 'It's very nice.'

'A bit more than that, surely?' he coaxed. 'How long were you a prisoner?'

'Three and a half years.'

'That's a very long time. What was it like?'

'Pretty awful.'

'How did the Japs treat you?'

'They weren't very pleasant.'

He scribbled in his notebook. 'Can you give me some details? People will want to know how you women managed to survive.'

'A lot of us didn't.'

He paused, but only for a second. 'Do you have any idea how many died?'

'I'm not sure exactly.'

About half, in fact, but she didn't want to talk about it.

'What about these children with you?' he persisted. Hua was clinging to her hand, Peter close behind her. 'What's the story there?'

'They were in the camps, too.'

'Would you mind telling me a bit about them? Their names, and so on. What it was like for them.'

She looked at him, wondering how it would ever be possible to tell somebody anything about a Japanese prisoner-of-war camp who had never been in one.

'I'm sorry, you'll have to excuse me. I can't talk about it now.'

She walked on with Hua and Peter. Behind her, she could hear him accosting old Mrs Brook.

'How does it feel to be free at last, madam?'

It had been an effort to answer him at all. Others had wept copiously since they had been released but she had been unable to cry. The euphoria had evaporated and now she felt like a very old woman must feel. Everything was an effort: to speak, to walk, to eat, to drink and luckily, perhaps, to think.

More Australian soldiers had arrived at the prison camp after that first digger in the jeep and there had been a lot of crying and laughing and hugging. It had been extraordinary and very wonderful to see and talk to white men again.

The Aussies had been shocked by their appearance, though they had tried not to show it. She had seen them shaking their heads, heard them muttering and swearing to each other. They had taken complete charge. The hated white flag with its red circle had been hauled down and ceremoniously burned. They had chopped down trees and cut up firewood and mended leaking roofs. They had distributed cakes of soap and packets of cigarettes and provided food – tins of Australian butter and beef, bacon, milk, white sugar, salt, eggs. They had brought in freshly killed meat – chicken, pork, a whole bullock which they had skinned and cooked over a huge fire – and they had picked fresh fruit in the jungle: papayas, bananas, mangosteens, rambutans.

Best of all, they had brought good manners and kindness. To be treated like a human being and a woman again after years of being treated like the lowest scum was extra-ordinary. No more slaps and blows and kicks. No more bayonet jabs, or screaming abuse. No more having to bow and scrape to evil little men, no more standing in the roasting sun for hours at their sadistic pleasure. Instead, there were smiles and jokes and gentle words and strong helping hands. A cache of Red Cross boxes had been discovered, hidden by the Japs. The boxes had contained medicines, medical supplies, blankets, pillows, mosquito nets: things that would have saved lives and made life more bearable. And there had been tins of food – salmon, meat, powdered milk, jam – and sacks of letters, kept back from the prisoners.

They'd bombarded the Aussies with questions and discovered that Mr Roosevelt had died and a Mr Truman was President of the United States; that the Americans had dropped huge bombs on Japan, destroying whole cities and ending the war in the Pacific; that the King and Queen and Princess Elizabeth and Princess Margaret were all right, and so was Mr Churchill. There was still an England.

They had stayed on at the camp for another month, waiting to be transported back to Singapore. Supplies were dropped by bombers – fruit juice, Nescafé, cocoa, cigarettes, matches, chocolate, sweets and fresh bread which they had not tasted for so long.

Susan had asked one of the diggers, while he chopped firewood, if he knew what had been happening in Singapore. He had leaned on his axe, tipped his hat back, wiped his brow.

'Nothing good. Not from what we've heard. The Japs locked up all the civilians in Changi clink – thousands of them. Men and women. Sounds like they had a tough time there.'

'How tough?'

'Lousy conditions, lousy food, lousy treatment – like you women here. And the

Kempeitai were real bastards.'

'The Kempeitai?'

'The Nips' secret police. Like the Nazi Gestapo. They interrogated prisoners. You don't want to know about them.'

She said, 'My father was in Singapore when the island fell. I still don't know what happened to him.'

He shook his head. 'My word ... sorry to hear that. But I dare say you'll be able to find out as soon as you get back there. He's probably OK. You don't want to think the worst. No sense in that.'

He was a nice young man and she knew he was trying hard to say the right thing. It was a big change to have a man speak kindly instead of yelling and screaming foul abuse. She couldn't imagine how she had ever thought Australian speech so awful. It sounded wonderful to her now. Gentle, drawling, soft.

She said, 'We heard that the Japs massacred hundreds of patients and doctors and nurses at the Alexandra Hospital when they took Singapore. Is that really true?'

He had nodded. 'Yeah, we heard about that too. I reckon it's true all right. The Nips have been doing all sorts of nasty things. Still, they won't be doing them any more, that's for sure.

They had been transported in lorries out of the prison camp and then by train to an aerodrome a hundred miles away, where they had waited patiently for many hours before Dakotas had swooped down from the skies to fetch them. The planes had been used for carrying paratroopers and had hard metal benches down each side instead of proper seats. They had bumped and roared down the runway and climbed up into the skies above Sumatra. The long imprisonment was finally over. She had felt too tired to care.

At the aerodrome in Singapore they were given tea served in cups and saucers with milk and sugar, spoons to stir it, sweet biscuits to eat and cigarettes to smoke. And they sat on real chairs, at real tables. The Red Cross workers wore crisp uniforms; they had pale, soft complexions and shiny hair. The contrast to their own woeful appearance was depressing; even more so, the mirror in the ladies' cloakroom which showed them how truly terrible they looked.

They were driven in ambulances to an Australian military hospital. There they were deloused, took baths in tiled bath-rooms with hot water and scented soap, washed their hair with shampoo, cleaned their teeth with toothbrushes and tooth-paste, used porcelain lavatories and lavatory paper. They were given pyjamas, dressing gowns, brushes and combs, and slept in beds with clean white sheets and two soft pillows. It was all far too comfortable.

'I don't know about you,' Stella said from the bed beside Susan. 'But I'm going to sleep on the floor.'

The next day the Red Cross provided clothes. Undies, frocks, blouses, skirts, stockings, shoes to put on their splayed and leathery feet, as well as face creams, powder and lipstick and nail files. They were given civilized meals on civilized china plates that they ate with civilized knives and forks and spoons.

There were other internees in the hospital, too – women and men survivors from other camps and some from Changi prison in Singapore. A lot of them were very ill and likely to die or to take many months to recover. Susan talked to one man who was well enough to walk around. He had been a solicitor working in Singapore and he described what had happened after the city fell.

'People couldn't believe it – not even then.

It was like a nightmare. The Japs made all European civilians assemble on the Cricket Club *Padang*. Thousands of men, women and children. We were there for hours during the hottest part of the day while they told us exactly what they thought of us whites. No shade, no water, no mercy. Later they made the men march the twelve miles to Changi prison. The women and children had to walk, too. We were already there when they arrived at Changi and as they came marching through the gates we heard them singing at the tops of their voices, "There'll Always be an England". We thought that was pretty splendid, I can tell you. We cheered them like anything.'

She said, 'Did you happen to come across my father, Thomas Roper? I think he must have been in Changi.'

'Tom Roper? Good Lord, yes. He was in the same cell as me for over a year.'

'Do you have any idea where he is now? Nobody seems to know.'

'Oh dear, haven't you been informed? He died a long while ago. It would have been back in December 1942, I think. Or around that time. My memory's not too good, I'm afraid. I'm so sorry. Didn't you know?'

She said quietly, 'No, I didn't know. What

did he die of?'

'Hard to say exactly ... people died of all kinds of things, sometimes there were several causes. You were in a Jap camp yourself, weren't you?'

'Yes.'

'Then you know how it was.'

Yes, she knew.

'Did he suffer very much?'

'We all suffered. Some more than others. I shouldn't dwell on that, if I were you. Much better not.'

'The Kempeitai,' she said. 'Did they question him?'

'They questioned anyone they suspected of any kind of disobedience or conspiracy. Any man who stood out as a natural leader, like your father. It didn't matter that there was no shred of evidence and nothing to justify it.'

'Did they torture him?'

'He was a very courageous man. An example to us all. That's all I can tell you.'

She went on doggedly. 'Did he die because of being tortured?'

'As I said, it was hard to know what a man died of. There was never any shortage of causes. Some died, some survived. That's all one can say. I was one of the lucky ones. I don't know why. I did absolutely nothing to deserve it.'

She felt the same guilt, too: guilt at surviving when so many others had died, and now the agonizing grief that one of them had been her father.

Officials from an organization called the Repatriation of Allied Prisoners of War and Internees came to the hospital. A plump, middle-aged woman in uniform interviewed Susan with Peter and Hua. The plumpness looked strange – so much flesh on bones, among so little.

'I'm very sorry about your father, my dear.'

'Are you quite sure he's dead?'

'His name is here on the list, I'm afraid. He died on the tenth of December 1942 and was buried in the prison cemetery. The Japanese seem to have been meticulous about the Changi lists. I'm sure you'll want to visit the grave and it can be arranged for you, when you're feeling up to it.'

'Yes, I'd like to do that, please.'

The RAPWI woman was being very kind, like the Aussies at the camp, but she kept staring at her. It wasn't the first time that Susan had noticed how people seemed fascinated by internees – they stared as though they were freaks.

'We'll try and trace the children's families but it may take a while. At least we have some helpful details for Peter but it's going to be very difficult so far as Hua is concerned. Her mother is dead, her father missing and all we seem to know about her is roughly where she lived and that she had an aunt called Su. It's not very much to go on but, of course, we'll do our best.'

Susan said, 'I could go to the place myself and see if I can find out anything. I remember exactly where the Chinese settlement was.'

'Do you think you're fit enough to go anywhere yet?'

She had weighed just over five stone on arrival but after one week she weighed nearly six, and her physical strength was beginning to come back.

'Yes, I'm quite all right.'

The woman said, 'We'll find out about your mother and grandmother. That shouldn't be too difficult. As soon as I have any news I'll let you know.'

She waited a moment while more notes were made in neat handwriting.

'Do you happen to know anything about

the massacre at the Alexandra Hospital?'

The woman looked up. 'I heard about it. It was shocking. A terrible thing.'

'I knew some of the doctors and nurses there. I'd like to find out if any of them survived.'

'Anyone in particular?'

'Captain Ray Harvey. He was a doctor in the Australian army.'

'From what I've heard, it could be a bit of a problem too. I gather they were all buried by the Japanese in a mass grave. But I'll certainly try.'

'Thank you.'

'It's all a bit chaotic at the moment, you see. It will take time to sort everything out. Is there anything else I can do to help?'

'Well, there is one thing. The children are getting very fed up in the hospital. So am I, to be honest. It's awfully depressing. Is there anywhere else we could stay?'

The woman smiled. 'Yes, my dear, as a matter of fact there is.'

The YWCA had commandeered rooms at Raffles Hotel for women and children internees. Susan, Peter and Hua were taken there by ambulance – an Austin K2Y exactly like the one she had driven. She sat in front beside the Red Cross woman driver with Hua on her knee and Peter sitting on a tin toolbox beside her. She had tried to persuade Stella to go with them, but Stella had chosen to stay on and help with the nursing while she waited for a passage home.

'I'll come over and see how you're getting on. You can buy me a drink at that posh bar. What's it called?'

'The Long Bar.'

'That's the one. And I'll have a Singapore Sling. In fact, I'll have two.'

The Red Cross driver was hopeless and crashed through the gears.

Susan shouted to her above the whining and the shrieking. 'I used to drive one of these.'

'Really?' The gears shrieked in protest again. 'They're jolly hard work, aren't they?'

They were going down Orchard Road. The bomb damage was still there – all the shelled and burned-out buildings – but otherwise the city looked almost unchanged. She had expected the Japanese to have torn down buildings, built new ones to glorify their victory over the White Devils, to have left their Imperial mark stamped all over their *Syonan*. Not so. The Rising Sun flags had been hauled down, Union Jacks raised in their place and the hotel, no longer the *Syonan Ryokan,* was called Raffles once more. It was now a transit point for army personnel and internees – as many as possible crammed into the luxurious bedroom suites. Nobody danced to an orchestra in the ballroom or dined in splendour at the restaurant in evening dress. Clothes were whatever people stood up in, food was short and, though the Long Bar was open, alcohol was scarce.

But there were ghosts lurking in the shadows. Ghosts from the past. She could hear the murmur of their voices, the echo of their laughter, the beat of their dance music. And the girl she had once been was among them.

Mr Singh still worked at her father's bank. He welcomed her politely into his office and expressed his condolences.

'Mr Roper was a most valued customer for many years. We were indeed very sorry to hear of his death. The situation regarding his accounts with us is difficult until we are in possession of all official documents, but the bank would be glad to do anything it can to assist you and Mrs Roper. Mrs Roper is not with you?'

She said, 'My mother and my grandmother are believed to be in Australia, but I'm still waiting for news of them.'

'You will join them?'

'I suppose so.'

'It would not be advisable for you to stay in Singapore alone, Miss Roper. Much has changed. And there will be more changes. Have you returned yet to your former home in Cavenagh Road?'

'No.' It was something she dreaded. 'Not yet. But the house belonged to my father's company. I couldn't stay there.'

'In any case, there may be nothing left. The house may be a ruin. Do you have funds?'

'Funds?'

He said gravely, 'Money to live on. For your daily needs. For your passage to Australia – when the time comes.'

'No. None.'

'We must see what can be done. Your late father would wish us to help you as much as is within our power. It will be my pleasure to do so.'

She took a rickshaw to Cavenagh Road. The house was still there but with a desolate, abandoned look. The chicks were rolled down, shutters and windows closed. She paid the rickshaw man and walked slowly up the driveway to the portico. The front door was shut, too, but when she tried the handle it opened.

Inside, the house had been stripped bare. She went from empty room to empty room, downstairs and upstairs. Except for the red carpet on the marble staircase and the black and white chicks at the windows, everything had been taken. Her mother's English antique furniture, the tables, the chairs, the sofas, the pictures, the mirrors, the beds, the chests, the wardrobes ... vanished. And the clothes she had dreamed about in the camp had gone. Saddest of all, the green glass Buddha no longer sat smiling at the foot of the stairs.

She went out on to the west verandah, robbed of its comfy rattan and chintz. The sun was beginning to go down, the sky streaked with crimson above the trees. It would soon be time for Soojal to bring the evening drinks – the *stengahs,* Grandmother's *gin pahit,* the iced lime juice – and to light the lamps. The ghosts were here, too.

She sat at the top of the steps leading down to the lawn where she had always sat to feed the doves and where they had fluttered down to perch on her shoulders and coo softly in her ear. Their dovecote had gone, so had all the birdcages hanging from the eaves; Hector's big brass cage too. The lallang had grown feet high, the garden was reverting to jungle.

The grass parted and a small black shape emerged, miaowing loudly. The cat trotted towards her and jumped on to her lap, purring at full volume.

'Sweep, oh Sweep…'

She buried her face in his fur.

'You come back, *missee*. You come back.'

She turned to see Soojal on the verandah above. Not a ghost out of the past but the real Soojal, staring at her as though he could scarcely believe his eyes. She stood up, cradling Sweep in her arms, wiping the tears from her cheeks. He had changed a great deal: he was shrunken and stooped, dressed in shabby clothes, and his feet were bare.

'It has been a long time, *missee*.'

'Yes, a very long time. How are you, Soojal?'

'I am quite well, thank you, *missee*. How are you?'

He was probably just as shocked by the look of her as she had been by him.

'Not too bad, thanks. I came back to see how things were.'

'I am sorry. Not at all good. I do my best to look after the house but everything has been taken.'

'Yes, I've seen. By the Japs, I suppose.'

'Not only them. At first some steal, but then they stop. Their officers forbid it. But other people come and take what they want and in the end there is nothing left.'

She said, 'The *tuan* is dead, Soojal. Did you know?'

'I hear this. It is very, very sad. He was a very good man. Do you have news of the *mem?*'

'As far as I know she's safe somewhere in Australia with my grandmother. I'm waiting to hear.'

'And you, *missee?* What has happened to you? Where have you been? I find out that you are not in Changi prison with the *tuan.*'

'I got away on a ship but it was sunk by the Japs. I've been in a prison camp on Bangka Island and then in Sumatra – until the Allies came.'

He shook his head. 'Very bad. Very bad. Japanese very cruel people.'

'Yes, they can be pretty unpleasant. I expect you found that out too.' She stroked Sweep. 'I never thought I'd see Sweep again. Has he been here all the time?'

'Yes. He stays here and every day I bring food for him. I promise you to look after him, *missee*. Remember? Like me, he waits for your return. He knows you will come back. He is very sure.'

She swallowed. If she wasn't careful she'd start to cry again. She waited till she could trust her voice.

'How about Ghani? How is he?'

'Ghani tries to look after the Buick for the *tuan* but it is taken by Japanese. They make him drive for them. Treat him very bad. Then he is ill and he dies.'

Poor Ghani with his brown moon-face, creased with so much worry. *Missee go too fast. Not safe. Berenti! Berenti!*

'Li-Ann and the other *amahs?* Cookie?'

'I have no news. The Japs killed many Chinese.'

'Amith? Arjun? Kumar?'

'I do not know. They all disappear. These were very bad times.'

'What about you, Soojal? What happened to you?'

He spread his hands. 'I work, *missee*. In Tanglin Club. The Japanese officers are there.'

She could picture them. Strutting about in their ugly uniforms, screaming orders, lolling around, eating and drinking, swimming in the pool.

'How horrible for you!'

'I work so I can eat and live, not die. But I come here every evening to the house and I always say to myself that one day the Japanese will go and the *tuan* and the *mem* and *missee* will return.'

She said, 'I'm afraid I won't be able to come back to live here, Soojal. Nor will the *mem*. Not now that the *tuan* is gone. The house doesn't belong to us, you see.'

'I understand this, *missee*. And I am very sad. Sad for me, and sad for you. It has been very happy here.'

'Yes, very happy.' She swallowed again. 'Would you go on feeding Sweep for me for a while? I'll come back for him later and take him away with me, if I possibly can.'

'I will do this willingly for you, *missee*.'

'Thank you.' She looked around the overgrown garden. 'The pond's empty, I see.'

'Yes, *missee*. The fish were all taken for food.'

'And the doves have gone too.'

'Yes, *missee*, they fly away. Also the other birds. Except one.'

'Oh? Which one?'

Soojal smiled. 'He stays here in the trees. I

feed him, too, when I come. I bring flower seeds for him and he comes down to eat. He is waiting now.'

She shielded her eyes against the sun. 'Where? I can't see anything.'

Soojal lifted his hands and clapped them together loudly. An answering squawk came from the top of the jacaranda tree.

'God Save the King! God Save the King! God Save the King!'

Soojal had hidden the handbag and suitcase that she had left behind in the hall. He brought them to her

'I bury them in the garden for you, *missee*.'

Her passport and the boat ticket to Australia were still inside the handbag, and when she opened the suitcase she found her memories. The evening gown of white satin and pink silk roses, the photos in the album, her favourite doll and her books. She sat on the steps with them gathered up in her arms and wept.

Sixteen

The RAPWI organization had set up an office in Raffles.

'We have news of a John Travers,' one of the officers told Susan. 'He was taken prisoner in early 1942 and held in Pudu gaol, Kuala Lumpur. According to the Jap records, he was a civil engineer with a British construction company. It sounds as though he's probably Peter's father, though I wouldn't say anything to Peter yet, if I were you. One can't be absolutely certain.'

It was a man this time – younger than the plump RAPWI woman at the hospital and not nearly as sympathetic. He stared at her, too, and harder.

'Where is he?'

'That's the problem. We're not quite sure. The prisoners were moved out as soon as it was possible but there's no actual record of where he was taken. He's bound to turn up soon.'

'Peter's waiting for news. It means an awful lot to him. Can't you hurry things up?'

'We're doing our best, Miss Roper. You must give us time.'

He was immaculately turned out: well-pressed uniform, moustache that looked as though it had been drawn on neatly with a black pencil, plenty of flesh on his bones, no signs of wear and tear. She wondered where he had sprung from. Probably some cushy bolt-hole where the war had conveniently passed him by.

'Have you heard anything about my mother and grandmother yet?'

'I'm still waiting for an answer from our Australian colleagues. You must understand, Miss Roper, that you're not alone in your situation. We have a great many similar cases on our hands.'

'How about Hua?'

'The Chinese girl you are looking after? Well, strictly speaking she's not our responsibility. It seems most unlikely that we shall be able to trace any member of her family. I think it would be far more sensible to approach one of the city orphanages. The nuns have a lot of experience in dealing with such cases.'

'She's not a Roman Catholic. She's been brought up Buddhist.'

He sighed. 'Does it really matter, Miss

Roper? So long as she goes somewhere?'

'Yes,' she said. 'I think it does, rather. And the Singapore Chinese are very much our responsibility. We've already let them down once when we allowed the Japs to take Singapore. I don't intend to abandon Hua.'

He looked at her coldly. 'Very commendable, of course. But all we have to go on is that she has an aunt called Su – a very common Chinese name. Do you have any idea how many Chinese there are in Singapore, Miss Roper?' His tone was sarcastic now.

'Yes, I do, actually. Over four hundred thousand. At least there used to be, before the Japs started murdering them.'

'Quite. Well, it's still a large number, so, as I said, it won't be easy.' He had stopped sounding quite so sarcastic. 'We'll do what we can.'

She said, 'Hua has remembered something else that might help. She thinks her aunt may have worked in a shop. She once gave her a jade bracelet that might have come from there.'

The sarcastic note came back. 'I imagine a great many Chinese shops sell jade, Miss Roper.'

He was quite right, unfortunately.

A few days before this she had taken Hua

to the coconut grove by Tiong Bahri Road, where she had once lived. They had stood beside the ditch that had sheltered Susan from the bombs and looked across at the burned-out remains of the settlement, now smothered by jungle greenery. An old Chinese man had shuffled by and Susan had greeted him politely and asked if he had lived there. He had stared at her blankly, without answering. She had pulled Hua forward. Did he recognize her? She had lived in the settlement with her mother and her name was Hua. Her mother had been killed by the bombs. Had he perhaps known her? It had been hopeless. Hua looked nothing like the former doll-like little girl with the fat cheeks and short black hair She was skinny and her hair was long and she was dressed in Western clothes – navy-blue shorts, a blouse, brown Clarks sandals. The old man had again stared blankly for a moment, and then turned and shuffled away.

She had said to Hua, 'Do you remember anything about living here? Anything that might give us a clue?'

'I remember the coconut palms.'

'Anything else?'

Hua had shaken her head. 'I'm sorry.'

'What about your aunt – the one called Su?'

'She came to visit sometimes. She was very nice. I remember that she used to bring presents.'

'What sort of presents?'

'I remember that she gave me a bracelet for my birthday – made of something smooth and green.'

'Jade?'

'I don't know. But it was a lovely green.' Hua had frowned. 'I think she might have owned a shop or perhaps she worked in one. I'm not sure.'

'You mean a shop that sold jewellery? Like the bracelet?'

'I don't know. Perhaps. Maybe she bought it somewhere else. Anyway, it got lost. And I remember that she wore a green dragon brooch. The dragon had red eyes that shone.'

'That may be a help.'

'If we don't find her,' Hua had said, 'can I stay with you? Can I come to Australia with you, if you go there?'

'Of course you can.'

'Can Peter come too?'

'Peter will probably go back to England with his father, as soon as he's found. He has a grandfather in England, too.'

'I wish we could always stay together.'

'My God! *Susan!* It is you, isn't it? My *God!*'

She had almost collided with the officer in the foyer at Raffles.

'Hallo, Denys. Fancy seeing you here.'

'My God!' he said again. 'I can't believe it. You survived.'

'There's no need to look so shocked, Denys.'

'I'm not shocked, but I'm *very* surprised. And relieved and delighted. How on earth did you manage it?'

'To survive? It wasn't easy. First I was shipwrecked, then I spent the next few years in Jap prison camps. Then some Aussie diggers rescued us in Sumatra and we were brought here. The old place isn't quite what it used to be, is it?'

'No, it's rather gone downhill. But you can still get a decent drink at the bar.' He crooked his arm for her to take. 'Let's go and celebrate our dual survival.'

A man was sitting at the piano in the bar – an American army officer who was playing 'Somewhere Over The Rainbow' rather well. The ghosts were there in the shadows, listening.

'Two Singapore Slings,' Denys said breezily to the bartender. 'Nothing less will do.'

'Certainly, sir.'

She was impressed. 'There's supposed to be a terrible shortage.'

'Oh, I know this chap. He was here in the good old days.'

'When you were on the scrounge?'

'Absolutely. Thanks to Raffles I never went totally without. Cigarette?'

When he had lit it for her, she said, 'Don't ask me about the camps, if you don't mind. I'd sooner not talk about them.'

'Wouldn't dream of it.'

He wasn't staring like the others exactly, but he was taking careful stock of her.

'I look pretty awful, don't I?'

He put his head on one side. 'Well, the clothes are certainly different, sweetie. Not really your style.'

'We were given them by the Red Cross.'

'That explains it. You must get some others as soon as you can. And you're much, *much* too thin – but that won't last, fortunately. You'll soon fatten up. Apart from that, I rather like the New You. Very grown-up.'

'You mean old and haggard?'

'No. I mean grown-up. Ah, here come our drinks.'

They clinked glasses.

'I haven't had one of these for years,

Denys. It's delicious.'

'Nor have I, actually.'

'So, what have *you* been doing? You don't look as though you've been languishing in Changi, or some other similar place.'

'I haven't.'

'How did you manage to avoid it? Did you hide in a cupboard, or something?'

'I took myself off. It seemed a good idea.'

'Took yourself off?'

'Off the island.'

'Where did you go?'

'Across to the peninsula.'

'But it was overrun by the Japs.'

'You could avoid bumping into them, if you knew the drill. There were quite a few of us chaps, actually. And a whole lot of Chinese who didn't like the Nips at all. They were rather rough types. You wouldn't have cared for them. No manners.'

She stared at him. 'You mean you became a guerrilla?'

'They're monkeys, aren't they?'

'Don't be tiresome, Denys. You know very well what I mean.' She'd heard about the guerrilla bands operating in the jungle against the Japs. Cut-throats, brigands, thugs. Looking at Denys leaning languidly against the bar, Singapore Sling in one

370

hand, cigarette drooping from the fingers of the other, ginger toothbrush moustache, innocent blue eyes ... it was impossible to imagine him as some sort of Malayan Scarlet Pimpernel.

'You're making it up, Denys.'

He pretended to be hurt. 'How could you doubt me?'

'Easily. You always made things up. Tell me more and I might believe you.'

'Sorry. My lips are sealed.'

'Then I don't believe you.'

'OK. Let's talk about you instead.'

'Not the camps, please.'

'Not them,' he agreed. 'How about your family? Tell me how they are.'

She told him about her father dying in Changi and about her mother and grandmother.

'The RAPWI people have finally managed to track them down in Perth. I'm supposed to be going to join them, as soon as I can get on a boat.'

'You don't seem exactly thrilled about it, sweetie. Why don't you stay here in Malaya?'

She said, 'Once upon a time nothing would have dragged me away, but I feel differently now.'

'How so?'

'Everything's changed, Denys. And there are too many ghosts. Don't you feel that?'

'I don't believe in ghosts.'

The American piano player had switched to 'I Only Have Eyes For You.' She had danced to it so many times. 'They're everywhere – specially here in the hotel. Ghosts from the past. Can't you feel them?'

'No, I can't say I can.'

He was taking stock of her again. Probably thinking she'd gone completely barmy. Maybe she had.

'Anyway, what are you going to do, Denys? Go back home to England, as you always planned to do?'

He downed some more from his glass. 'I've rather changed my mind about things, like you. I fancy the Old Country could seem a bit tame now. I think I'll stick around Malaya for a bit longer. See how things go.'

'In the Straits Police?'

'Might as well. It's not a bad career. Why don't you stay on with me?'

'You asked me that once before.'

'Actually, I asked you to go back to England with me. Now I'm asking you to stay on in Malaya.'

'The answer's the same. I told you, Denys ... I just don't want to stay here any more.'

'You'll think differently when you get to Australia. You'll hate living upside down.'

'Probably.'

'They eat their peas with their knives, you know.'

'It won't worry me. I ate with my fingers for three and a half years.'

'Good Lord, did you really? Fancy that.'

She smiled at him. 'Do you remember when you took me to the Governor's bedchamber, Denys?'

'How could I forget? You were sick over the verandah.'

'Because you gave me all that filthy drink. It wasn't very gentlemanly of you.'

'But I wasn't a gentleman, sweetie. I was a cad from Cads' Alley. Remember?'

'You were good fun, though.'

'I hope I still am.' He beckoned to the bartender. 'I think that calls for another drink.'

A letter arrived from her mother and she took it into a corner of the hotel gardens. She sat on a bench in the shade of a palm tree, staring at the envelope and the familiar writing before she opened it and began to read.

The news about poor Daddy was the most terrible blow. Your grandmother and I had

373

prayed that you and he had somehow survived in Singapore, even though we had received no news of either of you. We had almost given up hope. Thank God that you, at least, survived.

Whatever possessed you to get off the ship, Susan? You could have been safe here in Australia with us. You caused us such anxiety and grief. The authorities say that a passage will be arranged for you as soon as possible so that you can join us in Perth. There's no point in our returning to England until things have improved. I hear that everything is still rationed there.

It has been very hard adjusting to life in Australia. We have had to exist on very little money and the climate here is even worse than in Malaya. It is extremely hot in summer and very dusty and the flies drive us mad. There are no servants and the Australians don't approve at all of Grandmother having Zhu and say so. Of course, she takes no notice. She has every intention of returning to Penang as soon as possible and none at all of coming to England.

You will be very sad about Daddy. I know how much you adored him and, of course, he adored you. He could so easily have come to Australia with us but, as you know, he would never have deserted his beloved Malaya. I shall never really understand why.

374

'Miss Roper?'

She looked up. The man must have approached very quietly because he was standing only a few feet away. A tall, fair-haired man – very thin and dressed in the ill-fitting, mismatched garments of a liberated prisoner.

She folded the letter and put it away in her pocket.

'Yes, I'm Susan Roper.'

'I'm awfully sorry to disturb you, but they told me at the desk that I might find you in the gardens. We've never met. You don't know me at all, I'm afraid.'

'Yes, I do,' she said. 'You're Peter's father.'

'How on earth did you guess?'

'Because you look so much like him. Or he looks so much like you.'

He smiled, with Peter's quiet smile. 'So people have always said. How is he?'

'He's fine. You'll find he's grown a lot. He's quite the young man now.'

He said, 'I'm not sure yet how it happened but I understand that you looked after Peter in a Jap internment camp, after my wife died in a bombing raid on Singapore. I can never ever thank you enough.'

'It's a long story. Peter will tell you all about it himself one day, I expect.'

'I gather he's here, at the hotel. Could I possibly see him?'

'Of course. He's playing cricket with some of the other boys. I'll show you where.'

Peter was standing at the crease preparing to bat, but when she called his name he turned round. She watched from a tactful distance as John Travers walked on alone across the lallang grass towards his son.

Seventeen

It was a different bartender and no Denys was present to work his magic with the Singapore Slings. He had mysteriously disappeared. Taken himself off, as he would doubtless have put it.

'Sorry about that, Stella.'

'No worries, Susie. I'll settle for barley water.' Stella looked around the bar. 'This is the first time I've ever set foot in here. It must have been quite something.'

'It was.'

They lit cigarettes. Stella said, 'Any news of them getting you a passage?'

'Not yet.'

'Nothing doing at the hospital either. We're getting pretty fed up over there, I can tell you. It's the middle of October, for heaven's sake. The Yanks have all gone home weeks ago, but we're still waiting. The men are all saying that RAPWI stands for Retain All Prisoners of War Indefinitely. Anyway, it's wonderful news about Peter's father turning up.'

'Yes, wonderful.'

'I'll bet you'll miss Peter, though.'

'Very much.'

She had almost cried saying goodbye, but you didn't make a blubbing spectacle of yourself with English boys of eleven years old and embarrass them. You kept a stiff upper lip and pinned a smile firmly on your face, even though saying goodbye was breaking your heart.

'Goodbye, Peter,' she'd said brightly. 'Good luck at the school in England.'

'Thanks.'

'If I send you my new address, will you write sometimes?'

'Rather!'

He'd forget her, of course he would, once he started his new life. With any luck, he'd forget most of the war. The camps would become just a hazy memory.

'Well, bon voyage.'

He'd said quietly, 'Thanks awfully for everything.'

She'd smiled at him. 'We had some adventures, didn't we? But we survived. We made it in the end.'

'Yes, we jolly well did.'

As he'd walked away with his father, he'd looked back once over his shoulder, smiled and waved again. She'd kept on waving and smiling, too, until he was out of sight.

Stella said, 'What about Hua? Any progress there?'

'Not a thing. I've promised to take her with me to Perth if we don't find her family.'

'Maybe that would be best for her. Give her a brand-new start.'

'Maybe.'

Most people would probably agree with Stella, but would they be right? Hua was Chinese. Would she be welcomed in Australia? Would the Australians even let her in? Would she be happy there if they did? Didn't she belong with her own people?

Stella said, 'I went to see some big shot in the army the other day. Told him all about what happened to the other nurses – the way the Japs murdered them in cold blood.

He asked me if I'd mind giving evidence at a War Crimes Tribunal. *Mind!* What a joke! It's the one thing that kept me alive in those bloody camps – thinking about those bastards paying for what they did.'

Susan thought, I'm not really like Stella. I don't feel her hatred or thirst for revenge. I don't feel anything much at the moment, and I'm not sure that I ever will again. She sat staring blankly at the spiral of smoke rising from her cigarette, while Stella went on talking. She was saying something about one of the ex-POWs whom she'd been helping to nurse at the hospital.

'He'd been in a camp in Borneo and spiked his leg on bamboo doing forced labour. It turned into one of those huge tropical ulcers – I remember a Dutchwoman having one like it in our camp. The flesh rots away right down to the bone and the whole system gets poisoned. She died in the end, and this bloke thought he'd had it but one of the camp doctors saved his leg and his life. The same doc had saved a whole lot of other lives, too – worked wonders with all sorts of made-up instruments, invented clever ways to treat things. Of course, they hadn't any medicines or proper equipment – same as us. He said the doc's name was Harvey and that he was an Aussie. So I said, you mean *Ray* Harvey, and he said, yes, that was the one: Captain Ray Harvey. So Ray couldn't have died at the hospital, like we always thought.'

She stared at Stella. 'Do you think it's really true?'

'I asked him, was he a tall bloke with brown hair and greenish eyes? He said yes, though he couldn't remember the eyes. They were in this camp at Sandakan in Borneo where they were building an airfield for the Japs. Forced labour – like us, only much, much worse, by the sound of it. They died like flies. All the usual diseases. Beatings, starvation, torture, executions, worked to death...' Stella shuddered. 'I couldn't believe some of the terrible things he told me and he said he hadn't told me the half of it and none of the worst – not by a long chalk. He said Ray used to stick his neck out for them – defending them and trying to put a stop to the bad treatment and get things improved. He said the Japs punished him for it. They gave him a really bad time.'

'God ... how horrible.'

'Yeah, it all sounded pretty grim. Then, at the beginning of the year, the Japs suddenly decided to march them off into the interior. Nobody knew what for – they just kept them marching west for days and days, over the mountains, and if somebody couldn't keep up with the rest, the Japs shot him. This chap only survived because when he collapsed he pretended to be dead. Luckily for him some natives found him and took care of him. He said there were nearly three thousand prisoners on that march – Australian and British – and he'd heard from some other bloke that, in the end, only a few Aussies survived.'

'Was Ray one of them?'

'I asked that but he didn't know.' Stella eyed her 'You want him to be, don't you?'

'Well, of course I do.'

'A bit more than "of course", I'd say. You want him to be quite a lot.'

Chinatown had come back to life, now that the Japs were gone. The shop-house shutters had been opened, the doors unbarred, the brightly coloured paper lanterns hung up, wares set out.

Hua held Susan's hand as they walked up and down the streets – Temple Street, Trengganu Street, Smith Street, Sago Street, Banda Street, Pagoda Street. Past the medicine shops stocked with dried frogs and lizards, antlers and horns, trays of mushrooms, baskets of dried sea horses, octopus, sharks' fins, ginseng and healing herbs. The food shops offered their dried fish and crocodile, their black sea slugs, their white chrysanthemum tea. The clothing shops displayed their embroidered *cheongsams* their dainty slippers, their bolts of sumptuous silks. There was fine porcelain – bowls and spoons and ornaments – pairs of Fu Temple Dogs in bronze and brass, wooden mah-jong sets, chess sets carved out of ivory. And there were jewellery shops – from those selling the cheapest trinkets of brass and glass to those set with the finest precious stones to be found in the East.

'This is Hua,' Susan said in Cantonese to each jewellery-shop proprietor. 'Her mother was killed by a Japanese bomb that fell on Singapore in 1942, and we are looking for her aunt whose name is Su and may live in Chinatown. Can you help us?'

They shook their heads. In one shop there was a woman called Su but she had no niece.

'I had a son,' she told them. 'But the Japanese took him away. They dragged him out of this house and executed him. He was seventeen years old and he had done nothing wrong.'

Susan said, 'I'm so sorry.'

The woman looked at her with hatred. 'The British are to blame. They are to blame for everything. Because of them many thousands of Chinese died in Singapore. Because of them my son is dead.'

'I'm very sorry.'

'That will not bring him back to me.'

They left the shop and walked away, shaken. Susan thought, who could blame her for feeling so bitter? What she had said was partly true.

'We'll keep trying,' she said to Hua. 'There are still some more shops.'

They went into three more.

'This is Hua.'

Heads were shaken again, and so it went on. They turned into Banda Street and found a shop selling nothing but jade jewellery and carved animals – dragons, horses, pigs, frogs. Inside, Susan admired a cream-coloured lion streaked with bright green.

'Can I help you?'

The man who had appeared from the back of the shop was Chinese and dressed in Chinese clothes, but he had spoken in good English.

She said, 'Are you the proprietor?'

He bowed, palms pressed together. 'I am

at your service. Are you interested in the lion? It's a very fine piece. We call it mutton-fat jade. Jade can be many different colours, you understand. Even black.'

'We're not here to buy, I'm afraid.' She put her hand on Hua's shoulder. 'We are looking for this girl's aunt. Her mother was killed in Singapore when she was about four years old and her father is probably dead too. Hua can't remember her family name but she had an aunt called Su who may have worked in a shop selling jade. We are trying to find her.'

He frowned. 'My wife's name is Su. She had a niece, Hua – her sister's child – but she died in 1942 when the Japanese bombed the city.'

'Where did they live?'

'By Tiong Bahri Road.'

'I was there in Tiong Bahri Road when the bombs fell. Hua didn't die. Her mother was killed by the bombs, but Hua survived. They dug her out of the ruins and gave her to me. I took her to Alexandra Hospital and after-wards I took care of her for the rest of the war.'

He studied them for a moment without speaking. Then he went away and returned with a Chinese woman.

384

'This is my wife, Su. She says that she was told that her niece had died.'

'Did she see her body?'

'No. The burial had already taken place. Many in one grave.'

Susan said to the woman, 'I believe that this is your niece. She was rescued from the ruins after the bombs fell and given to me to look after.'

The woman moved closer to Hua, searching her face. 'She does not look the same as my sister's child.'

'She changed a great deal while she was in the camps.'

'The camps?'

'Japanese internment camps for women and children – on Bangka Island and in Sumatra. I took Hua out of Singapore on a ship, but it was sunk by the Japanese. When we reached the shore they put us in a prison camp. Australian soldiers brought us back to Singapore after the war was over.'

'Does she remember me?'

'She remembers that her Aunt Su visited her home and that she once gave her a little green bangle – of jade perhaps.'

'It's true. I did.' The woman took a pale-green bangle from a case and held it up. 'I gave Hua one like this one, only smaller –

made for a child. It was for her third birth-day.'

Susan said, 'Was it like that, Hua?'

'I think so.'

The husband spoke. 'There are many such bangles in Singapore. Many girls called Hua. How can we be certain?'

'Hua also remembers that her aunt wore a green brooch – a dragon with red eyes that shone.'

'Wait, please.'

The woman went into the back of the house. After several minutes she came back with a brooch – a green dragon with shining red eyes.

'This is what she remembers. The dragon is jade and the eyes are rubies. And here is a photograph of my sister Lina, holding Hua when she was three years old. I took it my-self on her birthday. Her husband, Tan Soo, Hua's father, died of a sickness soon after she was born. They were very poor.'

Susan looked closely at the photograph. The young Chinese woman was holding a little girl: a chubby little girl with short black hair and a fringe, wearing a bangle on her wrist.

'This is Hua. She looked exactly like that when she was given to me.'

The aunt smiled at Hua and took hold of her hands. 'I believe you are truly my niece. We have no children of our own and we welcome you with our hearts. From now on, this is your home, if you wish it to be.'

The Changi grave was marked with a simple wooden cross – not unlike the crosses outside the camps on Bangka and Sumatra, but better made and with the names clearly carved, not pencilled or burned in.

The nice RAPWI woman said, 'I'll wait for you over there, my dear. Take as much time as you like.'

She had brought a wreath of flowers and laid it down carefully. There had been so many graves, so many crosses. And this one was the hardest to bear of them all.

It was a bad connection and Stella was shouting down the telephone.

'Susie, do you want a lift to Sydney? I ran into an old friend of mine who's a pilot in the RAAF. He's flying some stretcher cases down there tomorrow in a Dakota. He says he'll take me because I can help with the nursing and there'll be room for you, too – if you don't mind sitting on the floor.'

'But Sydney's miles from Perth, isn't it?'

'Around two thousand. But you could come and stay with us and we'll arrange to get you there. I know Mum would love to have you. So would I. Can you be ready first thing in the morning?'

She said, 'Would there be room for one more?'

'I doubt it. Bob's doing us a big favour as it is. Do you mean for Hua?'

'No, we found her aunt. She's gone to live with her and she's very happy about it.'

'Great news. You'll miss her, though – same as Peter.'

First Peter, now Hua. The little girl who had clung to her so tightly and so trustingly. Both of them gone.

'They're with their own families. It's better for them.'

'Yeah ... you're right there. Well, who's this other person you want to bring along?'

'It's not a person,' she said. 'It's a cat.'

Eighteen

So that was Australia down there. The ends of the world, spread out thousands of feet below. The land discovered by Captain Cook and settled by thieves deported from England for stealing loaves of bread and orchard apples and suchlike. All Susan could see through the plane window was bare red earth, what looked like a river and absolutely no sign of human habitation. She sat down on the floor again and leaned against the bulkhead. The Dakota droned on, rising and sinking gently.

Stella's friend, the pilot, came out of the cockpit. Tall, tanned, broad-shouldered – rather like the digger who had turned up at the camp gates. It must be all the steaks they ate.

'You OK down there?' He was shouting at her to make himself heard above the din of the engines. 'Sorry it's such a lousy ride for you.'

She shouted back. 'I'm fine, thanks.'

He smiled, showing strong white teeth: all

the better for tearing at the steaks. Her own teeth seemed to have lost the power to chew at all after the years of mushy rice.

'First time in Australia, Susie?'

'Yes.'

'Well, I hope you like it. It's a beaut country. Staying long?'

'I don't know yet.'

'The natives are pretty friendly, you'll find.'

'Even to Poms?'

The teeth gleamed. 'So long as you don't whinge.'

'I'll try not to. Does this plane know how to fly itself?'

Another gleam. 'Don't worry, the co-pilot's up front. How's the cat getting on?'

She peered into the wicker basket containing Sweep. 'He seems to be sound asleep at the moment.'

'That's good. When we arrive, pretend he's luggage. And that you're a nurse, same as Stella, so make sure you mop somebody's brow and look busy. That way there won't be any hold-ups with the officials.'

'Thanks for letting me stow away.'

'Glad to help. We'll be coming down at Darwin soon to refuel. Then we go on to Sydney. It's a long way, but it's worth it for the view when we get there. Wait till you see Sydney Harbour and the Bridge. That's really something.'

The Dakota landed at Darwin, engines bellowing in reverse as it slowed. Out on the tarmac it was steam heat, as hot as Malaya but with none of the Eastern magic. Tin huts, bare earth, a few trees, not much else. Nothing very beaut about Australia, so far.

She slept on the flight down to Sydney and Stella woke her, shaking her excitedly by the arm.

'We're coming down ... we'll be there soon.'

She could remember feeling the same sort of thrill, long ago, when she was returning to Singapore from England by boat and waiting on deck for the first sight of the outer islands and the line of palm trees on the distant horizon.

The Dakota was descending gradually, making a gentle turn. Stella was looking out of the window.

'There are the Heads. And there's the Harbour. And there's the *Bridge*. Oh, my God!' Tears were streaming down her cheeks. 'Christ, there were times when I thought I'd never see any of it again. Just take a look at *that!*'

Susan got up and looked. She saw below the deep blue and glittering Pacific Ocean dividing the heart of a city, and a gigantic bridge that spanned it in a single arch from shore to shore.

Stella was mopping her eyes. 'What did I tell you? Isn't it bloody marvellous?'

'I asked Mum and Dad about Ray,' Stella said. 'They'd heard on the bush telegraph that he'd been taken prisoner by the Japs at Singapore, but that's all. Apparently his mother died two years ago. Very sad. His sister, Verity, still lives in Sydney, Mum says. She works as a secretary on Macquarie Street. I could find out her home address and we could go and see her this evening.'

They were sitting in the garden of Stella's parents house under the shade of a coolibah tree, like the jolly swagman, and watching Sweep who was watching something else intently – an Australian insect of some kind.

'She might mind.'

'No, she won't. And you want to find out about Ray, don't you?'

'It would be rather nice to know if he's OK.'

Stella said a touch sarcastically, 'Yes, it would rather, wouldn't it?'

Verity Harvey lived in an apartment on the other side of the Bridge. She was small and slight with brown curly hair. There was no resemblance to her brother that Susan could see, except in the colour of her eyes.

After the introducing and the small talk which included admiring the view of the Harbour from the window, Stella came straight to the point.

'We both saw quite a bit of Ray in Singapore before the Japs took it, Verity. I was nursing at the Alexandra Hospital and Susan was driving ambulances.'

The sister smiled at her. 'I know about you, Susan. Ray mentioned you in the letters he wrote to me from Singapore.'

She was very surprised. 'Did he?'

'Yes, several times.'

Stella said bluntly, 'We don't know what happened to him, Verity. That's the thing. We don't know if he's dead or alive.'

'Well, he's alive. God knows how. Did you know he was in a Jap POW camp in Borneo?'

'Yes, we found that out. And about the Sandakan march. We heard all about that, too.'

'Then you know it's a miracle that he survived. He was in a hospital in Borneo for a while, but the air force flew him home last week. I went down to Rose Bay when the flying boat came in. It was quite a moment, I can tell you, watching it land on the water. You see, I'd thought for a long time that he must have died. The last time I'd heard anything was in '43, about eighteen months after he was taken prisoner. I got a card from him. Not a proper letter, just one of those printed POW cards the Japs gave them: *my health is excellent, I am working for pay* – that sort of thing. They ticked some things and crossed others out and it told you nothing. He'd signed it at the bottom but the date was eight months earlier. Then I didn't hear a thing after that except how badly the Japanese had been treating POWs.'

'Susan and I were interned for three and a half years. We know what bastards they can be.'

'How dreadful for you both. I'm sorry. I'd no idea. We had it pretty easy here in Australia. There was a bit of a scare after the Japs landed in New Guinea. We thought that they might try to invade us from there, but of course they never managed it. We've been very lucky.'

Stella said, 'Is Ray here in Sydney?'

'Not at the moment. They wouldn't let

him go back to work yet, so he went off to our grandparents' place out at Warranga. I'm driving there myself at the weekend, would you both like to come with me?'

'Not me, thanks, Verity. Mum and Dad are just getting used to having me home. But Susan would. Wouldn't you, Susie?'

'I really don't think—'

'Oh, do come,' Verity said. 'We could surprise him. Give him quite a shock, as a matter of fact.' She smiled. 'You see, he thinks you're dead.'

Silvery gum trees dotted green hills and beyond them lay more hills – purple smudges against a blue sky. The narrow road ran straight for miles and miles, the Holden churning up a long wake of red dust.

'Warranga's about a hundred and fifty miles from Sydney,' Verity said. 'Our grand-parents bought the house and land years ago to retire to. My grandfather says it reminds him a little bit of Devon without the hedge-rows, but he left there when he was sixteen so he's probably forgotten what it's really like. Have you ever been to Devon?'

She shook her head. 'I've only been to England a few times. I've always lived in Malaya.'

'Yes, Ray told me that. In fact, he told me quite a lot about you when he came home. He's never talked about the Jap camp and I haven't asked – but he talked about *you*.'

'I can't think why.'

'Can't you? You were on his conscience, for one thing. He'd found out that the ship you were on had been sunk and he thought you must have drowned – you and two children. An English boy and a little Chinese girl, he said. There was no record of any of you. He said he'd pretty much ordered you to take the children out of Singapore with the hospital nurses, and it was all his fault. He'd wanted you to get to safety and instead you'd died. He felt very bad.'

She was pleased to hear it.

'Well, it *was* his fault, but I don't hold it against him – not any more.'

'How well do you know Ray, Susan?'

'We've only met a few times. None of them very satisfactory. We always seemed to argue.'

'Yes, he told me that too. It didn't seem to make any difference.'

'Difference?'

'To how he felt about you. He fell for you the first time he ever saw you. At some party, he said. You were busy being a snooty

Pom being gracious to rough Aussies.'

She remembered, with shame, how condescending she'd been. How patronizing. *How long have you been in Singapore? Where do you come from in Australia? How nice. How long will you be staying here?*

'I'm afraid that's true.'

Verity smiled. 'As I said, it didn't make any difference.'

'How is he?'

'He was pretty bad when he got back – but he's getting a lot better. God knows what the Japs did to him – he's got the most terrible scars but he won't talk about it. Not a word.'

She thought of the silent ex-POWs at the Singapore hospital and their haunted eyes. 'They seldom do,' she said.

The house at Warranga stood at the end of a mile-long driveway. It was a large one-storeyed wooden building with a corrugated-iron roof, and shaded from the sun by wide verandahs, window blinds and giant pots of greenery. Not unlike many houses in Malaya. Some horses were grazing in a grassy paddock under a group of trees beside a stream. She could see why it might have made the grandfather think of Devon without the hedgerows.

'It's beautiful,' she said. 'I didn't know Australia could look anything like this.'

The grandparents were another surprise, not old and bent, as she had pictured, but sprightly and youthful.

The grandmother took her arm. 'Ray went off with one of the horses and he won't be back for an hour or so. Verity asked me not to tell him you were coming.'

Ceiling fans creaked inside the house, reminding her again of Malaya. The floors were dark polished wood, the furniture Victorian, the lamps old-fashioned with glass shades. A grey-haired, bony woman in a print apron brought tea and cake served on English china.

'This is Jessie,' the grandmother said. 'She came from Scotland years ago. We couldn't manage without her.'

Afterwards, the grandmother showed her the rose garden that she had made beside the house.

'I had all the plants sent out by ship from England,' she said, as they moved slowly from bush to bush. 'I picked them out from a catalogue. A few of them died but the rest have flourished. So long as you keep them well watered, they don't mind the heat. I've never been home but I'd like to go one day and see some of the beautiful English gardens. Get a few new ideas, and some new plants.'

She referred to England as home, just as the English had always done in Singapore. But those people had been talking about the country where they had been born, whereas this woman had never even seen it.

They were admiring the perfect form and creamy petals of Elizabeth Harkness when the grandmother looked up.

'Ray's back, I see.'

He was standing on the verandah, leaning on the balustrade, watching them. Susan wondered how long he had been there. She thought in horror, God, he looks as though he's been through hell. And then, as he didn't move or speak, she thought, in panic, he doesn't recognize me. He's wondering who on earth I am. The Sydney hair-do and the new frock haven't made any difference. I still look like a camp scarecrow.

The grandmother broke the long silence. 'I believe you two have already met.'

He nodded. 'Too right, we have. Hallo, Susan.'

After supper they sat out on the verandah

with the oil lamps lit and the insects fluttering and flitting around, which reminded her yet again of Malaya. No Soojal to bear *stengahs* or iced lime juice, though. Instead the grandfather brought out cold Australian beers and uncorked a bottle of Australian wine made from grapes that they'd grown at Warranga. It tasted good.

Ray had asked about Peter and Hua and she had told him about her father, and about her mother and grandmother, and about Stella. No details – just the bare facts and no sentiment. The rest would keep. She knew better than to ask anything about the deep and livid scars around his wrists. *Ray used to stick out his neck for them ... the Japs punished him for it ... they gave him a really bad time.* Her heart ached with pity for what he must have suffered and she felt like weeping. But he wouldn't want pity. Or tears.

She sat silent now, listening to them discussing the Australian wine and the grapes and the grandfather talking about the plans he had to enlarge the vineyard. The night air was warm, almost as warm as it had been in Singapore, and she could smell the sweet scent of the English roses in the garden below the verandah. She watched Ray from her dark corner and sometimes he glanced her way.

'You two will have plenty to talk about, I should think,' the grandmother said later and the three of them went off to bed, leaving her alone with Ray.

'Actually, I'm rather tired too,' she said. 'There's no need for us to talk about anything, is there?'

'I think there is. If you don't mind.'

She sat down again.

'Smoke?' he asked.

'No, thanks.' Her hand might shake. She'd never felt shy before in her life; not until now.

He fired up the match with his thumbnail and held it to his cigarette and the flame illuminated the terrible scars. He leaned against the verandah post, smoking the cigarette.

'I owe you an apology, Susan, for what you've been through.'

'You do, rather.'

'It was my fault.'

'Yes, it was.'

'I thought you'd drowned on that ship – you and those two kids.'

'We nearly did.'

'How the hell did you manage to survive?'

'I'll tell you about it one day.'

He nodded. 'Fair enough. You're alive, that's the main thing.'

'So are you. That's another main thing.'

He smiled. 'I reckon we must both be born survivors.'

She said, 'Actually, to be fair, it could have been just as bad if I'd stayed in Singapore. I gather Changi was pretty grim.'

'I wasn't there. We were sent to Borneo.'

'Yes, I heard.'

There was silence for a moment, except for the frantic beating of a moth's wings.

'Well, now you're finally Down Under, what do you think of it?'

'I haven't seen anything much. Mostly Sydney.'

'How do you like it?'

'Not bad.'

'That's praise, coming from you.'

'Stella drove me around. I've seen Paddington, King's Cross, Circular Quay, Bondi Beach, the Botanic Gardens...' She ticked them off on her fingers. 'And I've been on the ferry across to Lunar Park – that was fun – and she took me to Taronga Zoo. That was amazing. They had kangaroos and wallabies and koala bears and a duck-billed platypus. I'd never seen any of those before. You have some really weird animals. And all those horrible poisonous spiders and snakes – far worse than in Malaya. It's a wonder any of you survive.'

'We're used to them. What do you think of our Bridge?'

'You can see it from all over the city, can't you? Everywhere you go. Round every corner. It's quite a sight.'

'Did Stella take you up the coast? Did she show you Whale Beach, Palm Beach, Pitt-water?'

'There hasn't been time.'

'That's a pity,' he said. 'When do you go on to Perth?'

'Wednesday next week. I'm flying Qantas. It's all booked.'

'How long will you stay there?'

She shrugged. 'My mother wants to go back to England as soon as possible. My grandmother wants to go back to Penang.'

'How about you? Where do you want to go?'

'I expect I'll end up going to England.'

'It's a long way away.'

'Yes, it is.'

'I thought you didn't like it over there.'

'I don't, but there's not a lot of choice. I don't want to go back to Singapore now.

Too many ghosts.'

'I know what you mean. But you must see a bit more of Australia before you go. Can you ride a horse?'

'I used to have my own pony.'

'Good. I'll take you out tomorrow, if you want. Show you round Warranga. It's a wonderful place.'

She said politely, 'I'd like that. Thank you.'

There were flashes of lightning out in the darkness – an electrical storm going on in the far distance, the faint grumbling rumble of thunder. Another reminder of Malaya. She thought of the dance a hundred years ago at the naval base when she and the sub lieutenant – the one who had been such a good dancer – had watched a night storm out on the mainland. *What if the Japs didn't come from the sea? Supposing they come from the peninsula instead? Oh, they'd never try that. The jungle's virtually impassable. A snake couldn't get through.*

She said, 'Stella and I heard about what the Japs did at the Alexandra. We were afraid they'd killed you. We thought you must be dead.'

'I was one of the lucky ones.'

'And Geoff?'

'He wasn't so lucky.'

'I'm very sorry,' she said. 'Milly will be too.'

'What happened to her?'

'She got away on one of the liners, but I haven't been able to find out yet if she's safe. Everything's still in such chaos in Singapore. It's going to take ages to sort out.'

She got up from her chair and went over to the verandah. She looked up at the night sky and the stars.

'That's the Southern Cross up there, isn't it? Those five stars.'

'Yeah. Same as on our Aussie flag.'

'I didn't know that.'

'Don't tell me you've never noticed them?'

'Sorry, I can't say that I have. I mean, I knew there were some stars on your flag but not what they were. But I know all about swagmen and billabongs and jumbucks. Stella taught the children to sing "Waltzing Matilda" in the camps. We did a lot of singing.' She went on stargazing. 'And I used to spend a lot of time watching the stars at night. They were a big comfort. I'm not quite sure why.'

'Maybe because they were still there. Something to hang on to.'

'Yes. It was the worst thing about being in solitary – not being able to see them.'

He said quietly, 'The Japs put you in solitary?'

'For a bit. But I wasn't alone. I talked to everyone I could think of while I was there. I had long conversations with them. Even with you.'

'Even me?' He sounded surprised and amused. 'My word. Fancy that.'

'Even you. Only you weren't feeling at all guilty about what had happened. You agreed with my mother that it was my fault for getting off the other boat in the first place. In fact, you were rather beastly about everything. You said I'd got to put up with things and keep going, for the children's sake.'

'I was right, wasn't I?'

'Yes, you were absolutely right. And you were nicer later.'

'How nice?'

'As nice as you were in the Alexandra when I made all that stupid fuss. But you've probably forgotten about that.'

'No,' he said. 'I haven't forgotten.'

She craned her neck to see more stars.

'When I couldn't sleep at night in the camps, I used to pretend other things, too. Make them up. We all did. Mostly to do with food because we were always so hungry.

We'd lie there, making up menus and choosing our favourite dishes. Other times some of us would dress up in our best clothes, curl our hair, put on powder and lipstick and go out to dinner. I went out with you, one night.'

'You don't say! Where did I take you?'

'Back to that Hawaiian place up on the hill with the band and no food. I ate all the fruit in the cocktail and I was still starving.'

'Sorry about that. How was the rest of the evening?'

'Not a big success. We argued and you were very rude about my shoes, as usual.' She stuck out her foot. 'What do you think of these? I bought them in Sydney.'

'You'll break your ankle one of these days.'

'That's what you keep telling me. How about this frock? I bought it in Sydney, too.'

'You look beautiful in it.'

'I didn't look very beautiful in the camps.'

'Nobody did.'

'That's true. I don't think I'll ever look like I did before.'

'None of us will.'

'And we'll never get back the three and a half years we lost.'

'They weren't totally wasted.'

She understood him. 'I suppose not.'

After a moment, he said, 'I used to take you out at night, too. Lots of times.'

'Oh?' It was her turn to be surprised. 'Where did we go?'

'Different places. All with good food.'

'You were lucky. What did we eat?'

'All kinds of stuff. Indian, Chinese, French. Sometimes we went where there was a band so we could dance. We got on like a house on fire. You'd be amazed.'

'Yes, I would. Very. Are you sure we did?'

'Dinky-die, as we ex-convicts are so fond of saying.'

'It wasn't like that in my version.'

'Well, you got it wrong.'

She said, speaking to the stars, not to him, 'I've always been wrong about you, Ray. I want you to know that. And wrong about Australians. And about Australia. As a matter of fact, I like all three of you quite a lot.'

'Enough to stay?'

'I'm not sure. I don't know what to do. Do you think I should?'

He stubbed out the cigarette. Came over to the verandah rail where she was still staring at the stars; turned her towards him.

'You know bloody well what I think, Susan. Verity told me she'd spilled the beans.'

'I didn't believe her.'

'Why not?'

She looked up at him. 'How could I, Ray? We've always squabbled, you and I. You've always seemed to disapprove of me – you said I was spoiled, remember? And I've been pretty foul to you. How could I possibly believe it?'

He smiled slowly. 'My word,' he said. 'We'll have to do something about that.'

They stopped the horses at the top of the hill. The land stretched away for miles and miles under the hot sun and the blue Australian sky decorated with puffy white clouds – red earth, green grass, yellow wattle, silvery gum trees, the smudged purple distance.

'Well, what do you think of it all, Miss Roper?'

'It's pretty amazing, Captain Harvey.'

'Worth staying for?'

'On balance, I think so. Yes.'

'Dinky-die, as we say?'

'Dinky-die.'

'Spoken like a true Aussie,' he said. 'You know, I always reckoned you'd come round to us, in the end.'

Epilogue

Ray and I were married in Sydney by the end of that year. He had already returned to work at St Vincent's Hospital, where he later became a consultant surgeon. We moved, with Sweep, into a house at Mosman on the northern side of the Harbour and our children grew up there.

My mother went back to England and eventually married a rich and charming widower. Grandmother returned to her home in Penang with Zhu and stayed there until she died. Hector went back there too, recaptured by Soojal and shipped off to Penang, protesting loudly all the way. He outlived Grandmother and, in spite of his unsociable ways, we gave him a home with us in Sydney. The children taught him to sing snatches from 'Waltzing Matilda.'

Peter has written to me regularly over the years and I went to see him once during a visit to my mother in England. He'd grown into the fine young man I'd always expected him to be. He went up to Oxford and then into the Foreign Office and, as I'd predicted, he ended up as Sir Peter Travers. Hua still writes to me, too. She grew up to become an English teacher in a school in Singapore and sends me photos of herself with her Chinese husband and her beautiful children. Stella married a doctor and went off to live happily ever after in Brisbane. I found out, eventually, that Milly had reached South Africa where she spent the rest of the war before returning to England. We wrote to each other regularly for a while until the correspondence dwindled to Christmas cards. She married a solicitor and lives in Yorkshire. I expect that, in time, she forgot all about Geoff.

Many years after the war, I happened to see a photograph of Denys in the *Sydney Morning Herald*. He had become something very high up and important in the police and was on an official visit to Australia. He still had the same toothbrush moustache but he was looking very solemn and serious – quite unlike the Denys from Cads' Alley that I knew. I wonder if he still remembers.

Even now, the camps return. Nightmares about them wake me in a sweating panic and sometimes they pop up unexpectedly by day, and in the oddest places. A woman in front of me at the supermarket checkout queue puts a bag of rice down on the counter. There is a hole in the corner and a small handful trickles out – about a day's ration. I stare at the innocent little pile of grains and I'm back in the camps again. I don't suppose they will ever go away.

I have been back to Singapore to visit my father's grave and to see the war memorial to the civilians who died during the Japanese occupation, but I shan't go back again.

The house in Cavenagh Road has been pulled down and replaced by a block of apartments. House, gardens, tennis court, aviary, goldfish pond and the pet cemetery have been erased, so has the surrounding jungle. The bullfrogs and the cicadas croak and chorus there no more.

Singapore has become an ultra-modern Asian city. Where there was green growth there is grey concrete and where there were historic colonial homes there are glass sky-scrapers, luxury hotels, shopping malls and international restaurants, all hermetically sealed in air conditioning. Land has been reclaimed from the waterfront for more building and the old labyrinthine streets have widened into ordered highways. The hawkers' stalls have vanished, the pavements are spotless, the native markets sell foreign tat to tourists.

It's a very impressive city but it's not my *Singapura*. My Lion City was creaking fans, tiled floors, rattan chicks, verandahs wide open on to lallang lawns, the lushest greenery, the sweetest scents and the brightest flowers. It was a swarming, clamouring jumble of life, smelling fragrantly of curry and spice and all things nice, and of things not so nice. Chinks, Stinks and Drinks, as the old saying went. Nobody would say that now.

I loved it passionately and it's gone. And the *tuans* and the *memsahibs* are gone, too. So is their way of life, crumbled to dust along with the mighty British Empire.

The British deserved to lose Singapore to the Japanese – there's not much dispute about that – and they paid a terrible price in suffering and lives. Where exactly the blame lies for the defeat isn't so clear. There may be some truth in the theory that the Battle of Malaya was lost in the ballrooms and bars of Raffles and Tanglin. But the stories of arrogance, complacency and incompetence are more than matched by the tales of immense courage, heroism and self-sacrifice.

Whatever her faults, there'll always be an England. And she's free.

The publishers hope that this book has given you enjoyable reading. Large Print Books are especially designed to be as easy to see and hold as possible. If you wish a complete list of our books please ask at your local library or write directly to:

Magna Large Print Books
Magna House, Long Preston,
Skipton, North Yorkshire.
BD23 4ND

This Large Print Book, for people
who cannot read normal print,
is published under the auspices of

THE ULVERSCROFT FOUNDATION